JULIP

BOOKS BY
JIM HARRISON

FICTION

Wolf

A Good Day to Die

Farmer

Legends of the Fall

Warlock

Sundog

Dalva

The Woman Lit by Fireflies

Julip

POETRY

Plain Song

Locations

Outlyer

Letters to Yesenin

Returning to Earth

Selected and New Poems

The Theory and Practice of
Rivers and Other Poems

NONFICTION

Just Before Dark

JULIP

JIM HARRISON

Houghton Mifflin / Seymour Lawrence
BOSTON NEW YORK

Library of Congress Cataloging-in-Publication Data
Harrison, Jim, date.
Julip / Jim Harrison.
p. cm.
"First appeared in *Esquire* in slightly different form" — T.p. verso.
ISBN 0-395-48885-0
I. Title.
PS3558.A67J84 1994
813'.54 — dc20 93-43961
CIP

Printed in the United States of America
BP 10 9 8 7 6 5 4 3

Book design by Melodie Wertelet

"Julip" first appeared in *Esquire* in slightly different form.

TO SAM LAWRENCE

When the wine is bitter,

become the wine.

RILKE

CONTENTS

Julip

JULIP GOT HER NAME, a mixture of a flower and a drink, by her parents' design in the first flower of a somewhat alcoholic marriage. Her father bred, raised, and trained bird dogs of various breeds. Her mother was from one of the leading families of Ashland, Wisconsin. Lest anyone mock the fact, every community owns its leading families, which exist mostly as a result of hard work (if only in the distant past), at least modest prosperity, and being either Congregationalist or Episcopalian. It was, and is still, considered to have been a bad marriage for Julip's mother, Margaret, whose father, a dry-goods merchant, had sent her off to Lawrence College (a Germanic suckhole) at no moderate expense in hopes that she would marry well. It was a sad day for her father when Margaret threw over her porkish fiancé from Milwaukee in favor of a quick romance with a young man of few prospects from Duluth, with no possessions other than an old Ford convertible full of English setters. Margaret's father gave them a used car for their wedding because the convertible had no top.

It was a little startling to the dry-goods merchant to see his family business dissolve in the face of the usual shopping mall onslaught, while his daughter and her dog-trainer husband had their photos in society pages of Chicago and Milwaukee papers. It is a cultural oddity that dog trainers, golf and tennis pros, horse trainers, fishing guides, much like writers and artists, are socially acceptable in a way that wealthy parvenus never are. The tycoons of the Midwest who continue their boyhood passion for bird hunting can scarcely train their own dogs for reasons of time and specific skills. These men develop an unbalanced affection for dog trainers for the simple reason that the outdoorsmen appear to be less abstract and venal (untrue), and are leading a more manly life than can be led in a law office or brokerage house.

So Julip's father and mother had a foreshortened heyday until her birth and her dad's drinking reached levels of true impropriety. The year was divided between South and North. From November and the beginning of quail season to its end in March, they lived in various locations of Alabama, southern Georgia, northern Florida, settling by the time she was ten at a large plantation near Moncrief owned by Philadelphia people. By the end of March they headed back to the Ashland area, to a small farm of a hundred acres surrounded by cedar swamp, then broken again by fallow fields dense with dogwood and aspen, ideal cover for grouse and woodcock and the training of dogs.

They lived well enough, especially after her mother began cooking for rich folks, which doubled a modest income. Margaret was totally without talent or instinct for motherhood due to a panoply of neuroses that would never be unraveled, but was a genius in the kitchen. There were never less than a dozen dinner guests at the quail plantation and she was preoccupied with cooking to the point that she neglected her children, Julip and Bobby, and her husband, which made them feel lucky. It's an old word but Margaret was a virago, and even her silences were tortuous.

Julip liked to say she was raised in a trailer, but the quarters offered the dog trainer were a pleasant bungalow. She and Bobby had fled in her fourteenth year to a nearby trailer on the estate to escape their mother. Dad would frequently come over with a bottle of whiskey and they'd play a tearful game of gin rummy. Often he'd fall asleep on the trailer couch, waking at daylight to look after the dogs which at this estate numbered forty-eight English pointers and a few retrievers.

It was a schizophrenic upbringing, and if it were not for an interested teacher in each place she would not have been saved. She was not unlike the legion of dislocated armed-services brats to whom a true home has been, and will always be, an attractive fiction. But to the degree Julip was saved Bobby was shattered, both by the reality of their situation and by an imagination so errant it boggled the clinical psychologist after the shooting.

*

"Remember when," she said to Bobby, who was behind a pane of glass almost permanently, the glass soiled by breath, tears, fingers — the longing between prisoner and imprisoned. "Remember when we cut the hole in the trailer floor?"

His face was dissected by what appeared to be fine chicken wire embedded in the glass. She had lost him. His Adam's apple bobbed and his bad eye framed by the wire drifted off, ignoring her question.

"I like it here. I have a black friend named Ralph. I'm teaching him how to read and write because he doesn't know how. Ralph's gay."

"Is that what you have in mind for yourself?" she asked, trying to prolong his attention.

"No. You know that I'm nothing. Mom and you and Marcia saw to that. At least that's what they told me."

"So it's our fault," Julip said. "I don't doubt that. Everybody on earth fucks up everybody else. That's not exactly new, is it?" She only added the question to keep him going. Until now he had refused to see her, nor had he answered any of her letters the past three months.

"I doubt that. I believe in free will, not predestination. I told them what I did so I could stay in the Forensic Center. Another prisoner told me: Keep bullshitting, it's a lot better here than Raiford. There was a pond and birds out the window. So I said everything I could think of to keep them interested and stay there longer."

She glanced over at the clock and then behind her at a guard, who seemed to be studying her fanny on the chair with an intensity she had grown accustomed to over the years. She turned back to her brother with the whisper of an ache beneath her breastbone.

"I saw a new lawyer," she said. "He told me you would've got off if you admitted you were crazy. You would have spent a couple of years in the nut hatch, then got out. You still might be supposing that I can get your victims, judge, and prosecutor to agree to a change of plea on your part."

"No way. I'm not crazy. I shot those fuckheads out of free will and that's that. I admit that Dad told me it was okay."

"Bobby, you know Dad is dead." Tears flowed upward into her throat and his features blurred.

"Maybe he's dead to you, but not to me. He told me to go right ahead and shoot those who defiled my sister." Bobby became rigid for a moment at her tears which she hastily wiped away.

"I never once heard him use the word 'defile,' but maybe you did." She added the last to humor him. "How come you agreed to see me after all this time?"

"I need my little bait box. You know, under the old trailer floor where we cut the hole. I need my arrowheads, stones, and marbles. Jim Crabb lives there now but he'll let you in. The key's under the doormat if he's gone."

Now he stood and stretched with the awkward muscularity of one who burns up his rage by pumping iron in the prison weight room. He affected, she thought, the wry smile of the doomed, but maybe that's how he felt, doomed, but having done what he set out to do. Her voice became thin, plaintive.

"I pray no one hurts you in here." She broke down again at the thought of how her life had twisted his own.

"They don't fuck with a crazy who shot three men. I love you, Julip."

"I love you, Bobby."

"I'll tell Dad I saw you."

He waved before she could respond, turning and walking out the door where a guard waited. In her throat a sob married a scream and became nothing.

*

At the motel the maid had refused to pick up the condom that the lawyer had dropped, unused, beside the night table. Julip reflected that men put on condoms as if they were dressing a simple-minded doll, and often, as in this case, a doll with a broken neck. The maid had also turned off the air conditioner, and Julip felt she could smell distinctly the odor of everyone who had stayed there in order to visit husbands, brothers, fathers, and friends at Raiford: the sharp, cheesy odors of grief and loneliness. She shook some cologne into the air conditioner, turning it to HI COOL, took off her clothes, and showered without drying off, th
better to imitate a breeze off a northern lake. She disl
Florida or anywhere south in early summer, except f
West when she visited the Boys and there alway
breeze. Inland the wet heat was frightening

through invisible blood, the air the same temperature as your body. She took out her dog album and diary from the bottom of her suitcase, both singularly intimate, leafing through the photos as sacramental reminders that glued the world together: every dog she had owned and also those she had trained for others, like her father had done. She had given the animals a sense of purpose and they had loved her for it — Labradors, springers, setters, Brittanies, English pointers. Under "Florida, Bide-A-Rest Motel, May 23rd," she wrote:

> Saw a pug in a car. What for? Don't know. Irish setter near road, clipped short for heat, dancing around dead toad. Not too smart. I stopped. Eager to show me toad. I said "go home." He did. Bench-bred nitwit. Lawyer, so-called friend of Dad's. Paid with sex as he is an expensive lawyer to help Bobby who is nuts period. Got to get the wounded Boys to accept change of plea. All three to forget the holes shot in them. We had dinner of good seafood. I ate like a Lab as lawyer drank five manhattans and bottle of wine. About fifty I guess. Normal fee three thousand to start. Would settle for "friendliness," or so he said, if in fact he does anything for Bobby who has never been the same person for even one day. My Emily Dickinson is out in the car dammit. Call Frank to see if Rose is in heat. Ship her to J.D. in N.D. Dragged recently hit raccoon off road into weeds so he would not keep getting run over. Lawyer cried then left.

*

the time she started the car she was frankly pissed at
y. She stepped outside to let the air conditioner kick
dering just how he had come up with the word
whether it was from TV or perhaps something he

had read. One year younger than her own twenty-one, Bobby had always owned a relentless gift for self-drama. Perhaps, like Dad, he simply had too many emotions. Dad would have a single drink, admittedly a big one, and tears would well up, leaving others present to wonder if the weeping that day was due to sadness, anger, incomprehension, or nothing in particular.

She decided the car was cool enough now so that her ass wouldn't stick to the seat. The new Subaru station wagon with dog screen had been a winter gift from one of the three wounded, Charles. It had been dealer-delivered on a blustery day in Ashland, Wisconsin, the air thick with snow carried by what was known locally as an Alberta clipper. There was a red ribbon on the steering wheel and a note card reading, "To my darling, Julip. Con Amore, Charles." The dealer, who had known her parents, wondered what "con amore" meant. When she told him, he said, looking at the new car, "That's quite a bit of love." Now she was embarrassed as she backed out of the parking space, glancing over at a coal-black woman she had seen earlier at the prison trying to start an old Dodge. Julip called out, "Can I help?" But then the Dodge turned over and the woman smiled and waved. This fragile bit of contact lifted Julip's spirits and she set off for Moncrief, north of Tallahassee up on the Georgia-Florida border, perhaps two hours distant, to retrieve Bobby's bait box, hidden under the linoleum where they had tried to conceal the wild piglet.

*

Jim Crabb stood in the hot yard in the de rigueur white-trash camo outfit, leaning against a blue pickup as battered as the trailer that had once been her home. Julip had called from the gas station back down the country road, and she supposed that this was the pose, of all others, he had decided on: careless, bored, needing the support of the truck as if his legs could not quite bear up under the weight of his balls. Jim Crabb was the definitive ex-Marine, a category as pronounced, specific, and hallowed as the ex-Princetonian. She had known him since childhood, and if anything the sense of general dreariness he filled her with had increased. He was, simply enough, the lamest dickhead she had ever met. As she drew closer she noted that he had doused himself with a cologne reminiscent of car deodorant, which warned her of a pass.

"Nice-looking dog." She drew near the stout pen that contained a Catahoula wild-hog dog, an animal so baleful and maudlin in its pen as to appear comic, though less so when it was tearing apart a wild pig.

"You might say that." Crabb drew closer during his favorite expression. Along with the deodorant he smelled, as always, of peanuts, which he was wont to describe as "nature's perfect food."

Crabb was known widely around the countryside as a man who had wrecked three pickups while shelling peanuts and drinking beer at top speed. He was also a deviate with freak hots for little girls. Her own memory of his sickness was more funny than traumatic. They had been about eleven, she and her cousin Marcia from Virginia, and it must have been right after church on Sunday because they were in dresses. At the far end of the plantation's quail pen Julip had a setter pup on a tether and the pup was pointing the penned quail. Jim Crabb, who was about sixteen at the time and was cleaning the pen, called the girls "little bitches," at which point Marcia mooned him.

As Julip only realized that moment in the trailer yard, Marcia's moon waved a red flag. Jim Crabb came out of the pen and walked them over behind a huge live oak where he offered Marcia a dollar to do it again, only close up this time. Marcia didn't need a dollar, her parents were well off, but she reenacted her moon, only jumping away when Crabb touched her bare bottom. Julip was teaching the pup to sit and heel and hadn't been particularly interested until Crabb offered to show them how a man "did it to himself." She wasn't sure she would have laughed at the sight if Marcia hadn't set the pace. Poor Jim Crabb lay on the ground with his eyes squeezed shut, pulling at himself mightily. Marcia told him to hurry up because they didn't have all day. The puppy licked his face which broke his concentration and his reddish noodle began to shrink. Marcia taunted him about his disappearing "dickybird" and he offered another dollar for Marcia to stand over his head. Julip noted this brought him to instant life again, but as he was shooting his stuff all over the place Bobby showed up, took in the scene, then ran off yelling for Dad, which turned it into a real bad day for Jim Crabb. Dad came running from the house and out past the trailer, where he cornered Crabb, slapped him silly, and wedged him into a Sky Kennel, of all places, for a trip to the sheriff.

Only now in the trailer yard did the whole matter sadden her a bit, and that was because of her mother's reaction, which was both sententious and oblique. "Love is a beautiful thing for when you are eighteen the body is sacred I pray this doesn't scar you this insane boy should be locked up forever," she droned on, an open recipe book before her, glancing at the book during her blather. Julip and Marcia giggled and Julip got slapped. Now as she headed for the trailer steps she wished she was religious so she could ask God who was more pathetic, her mother or Jim Crabb.

Crabb, in fact, was breathing down her neck as she opened the door. "Back off, you fucking pervert," she yelled, and he tripped off the stoop in surprise.

"I'm changed," he said, picking himself up quickly.

"I'm a normal human. I got a diploma from Social Services in Tallahassee."

She listened to him with moderate interest in the kitchen of the trailer as she drank a glass of funky water. His diplomas were from courses in "anger management" and a two-year-long effort by psychologists to reeducate his sexual tastes. She continued to listen as she entered the trailer bedroom to lift up the linoleum and find Bobby's bait box. But when she opened the door the wind left her and she drew her breath in sharply. The entire room, both walls and ceiling, had been papered solid with photos from *Hustler* and other sex magazines: photos of gynecological intensity, countless ladies you could see well inside of, an abattoir assembly line of organs.

"Not much mystery hereabouts." She laughed, gathering herself and stooping to the sheet of florid linoleum that covered the opening to the secret compartment she and Bobby had devised to hide the wild piglet.

"What do you mean by 'mystery'?" Crabb asked, kneeling to watch her fetch the bait box out of the hole. The piglet's food and water dishes were still there from over seven years ago. Her eyes began to mist at the memory that this precious animal had been taken from her because her mother thought pigs smelled like tooth decay.

*

Anticipating the Tallahassee rush-hour traffic, Julip decided against driving the two hours back to Raiford and opted for the idea of getting up early to make the morning visiting hours. She pulled off near a boat launch on Lake Jackson and took her diary and volume of Emily Dickinson out on the dock, slipping off her sandals to trail her feet in the water, staring at the bass minnows darting through the peppergrass.

She intended to jot down a plan of action in her diary but the choices were limited and obvious: see Bobby's forensic psychologist, go to Key West and get the victims to agree, get the lawyer to reopen the case, get Bobby to admit he was crazy. The prosecutor might be easy because he had thought Bobby nuts for refusing to accept the fact that he was nuts in the first place. The judge in Key West (there was no jury) had several times referred to Bobby as "Galahad," spelling it out for the puzzled court reporter before doling out seven to ten years, the minimum under the conditions which involved premeditation. The not so subtle and inadmissible factor was that if you really intended to kill someone, you didn't shoot them repeatedly below the crotch with .22 shorts — a caliber, however, that can sometimes be fatal elsewhere on the body, especially the head. The languid court-appointed attorney had frequently pointed out that if Bobby had meant to kill the three men he would have used his .270 Weatherby, his Remington 30.06, or even his 12-gauge semiautomatic duck-hunting shotgun. There was a lackadaisical attempt among the defense lawyer, prosecutor, and judge to get out of the impasse but it was made impossible by Bobby, who said he would shoot the men again if they didn't behave. The judge had no choice but to mete out the sentence and head for the golf course, where on the seventh tee he would slice his shot while meditating on the berserk hormones of the young. At Duke Law School, he thought, there should have been a course called Love, Death, and Greed 101 which would include the dope, alcohol, and loneliness that fed the implacable machinery.

Sitting on the dock, Julip saw it all as "old business," the kind of thing her student council a few years back would file away with the crepe paper expenses for the school dance. The point now was to be as firm and methodical as you were when you started a pup on live quail or pigeons.

She looked down at her feet in the water to check for possible waterborne monsters, pulling up her skirt to sun her thighs. She opened her dog-eared Emily Dickinson, actually chewed on by a pup, to a poem she loved but didn't really understand — not to say that anyone did.

Wild Nights — Wild Nights!
Were I with thee
Wild Nights should be
Our luxury!

Futile — the Winds —
To a Heart in port —
Done with the Compass —
Done with the Chart!

Rowing in Eden —
Ah, the Sea!
Might I but moor — Tonight —
In Thee!

Far out in the lake a bass boat approached and she began to think of Johnny, the first love of her life, whom she now admitted to herself had been a terminal nitwit. She turned as a mid-sized blacksnake wiggled through the cattails. In the fall and spring of her junior year of high school she and Johnny were inseparable, and when she went south with her family for the late fall and winter they wrote daily, though his letters were mostly about milk prices, weather, and basketball. He lived with a brother, Kurt, and his parents on a large dairy farm a few miles down the gravel road from their kennels.

Now the bass boat was coming in fast, in the manner of that peculiar breed, the bass fisherman, who her father felt was way down there on the hunting and fishing food chain with deer hunters, who in the north dressed in brilliant orange on the simple expedient of not shooting each other. While the guide backed the trailer to the boat launch, the client came out on the dock to greet Julip, who had neglected to lower her skirt. She did not know that she had been glassed thoroughly from out on the lake with the expensive binoculars guides use to keep track of one another. It is a profession full of spite and secrecy.

"Helluva day," the client said, standing beside and a little behind her. She glanced up as she pushed down her skirt, noting that his sporting clothes were new, and his chinos were wildly wrinkled around a small paunch that was destined to grow and grow despite the surge of hormones occasioned by a day's fishing. She could tell, however, by his face that he wasn't a bad sort, just that his mere presence in her problematical day bored the shit out of her.

"I want my mother," she said blankly in answer to his weather report.

"Of course," he said, startled and withdrawing back down the dock forever.

Though it wasn't polite, "I want my mother" always got rid of them fast, along with "Are you my real dad?" — both of them suggested by her cousin Marcia, who had carried waywardness to an astounding level. Marcia had stopped through Ashland on April Fool's Day, appropriately enough, with a Latin boyfriend, driving from Georgetown to Aspen in a Porsche for the late skiing, powered by cocaine and pills. They had gone into town for lunch, and when Marcia took off her sweater she revealed a T-shirt that said, "I Fucked a Republican and It Was Real Ugly." Not the sort of thing one wore for lunch in Ashland, Wisconsin. And when Julip told her about the shooting incident and Bobby's imprisonment — Marcia had been in Europe until recently — Marcia sobbed loudly, went into the bathroom, and vomited.

Back on the dock Julip figured she'd better call Bobby's forensic psychologist to see what further hurdles might come from that quarter. She had met him briefly just before and during the trial and thought him kind and pleasant, though he hadn't explained "deeply delusional" to her satisfaction. His name was Wiseman and he was evidently Jewish, though she had no clear idea what that meant, there not being any Jews on quail plantations and few in northern Wisconsin. But Wiseman had given her his home phone number in case she became overly distraught and needed to talk to him.

She lifted her feet to let them sun dry, catching sight again of the blacksnake in the reeds. Last night's lawyer had a tongue as dry as a snake's skin. Perhaps, she thought, she wasn't repelled by either snakes or lawyers with dry tongues because they were just what they were, and she had always saved her energy for the main chance. Even Johnny, who had betrayed her, had been stored in a cool dark place. There had been a splendid summer and fall but after she left he had impregnated a girl she hated at a beer party. He was married in a snap of the fingers, in the fashion of the local German Catholics. It was all as sudden as the death of her father on a Minnesota roadside a year later, an apparent suicide according to her mother, whom Julip often thought of murdering. "He did himself in," Margaret had said. His ashes were in a small oak box the kennel hand, Frank, had made lovingly for that purpose.

*

Julip checked into a motel in Tallahassee beyond her budget, avoiding the blushed smirk of a young desk clerk so fungoid she bet he was still cherry.

"The hot place to go is Dojo's," he said.

"What's that supposed to mean? What's a hot place?" She had decided on mild punishment.

"You know what I mean. Swinging. A good band." His voice trailed off, the remnant of his presumption disappearing with the coldness of her stare.

"I'm a Christian, not a weirdo street slut, and I resent your bad manners. Perhaps I should talk to the manager." She began tapping the room key hard against the counter as the blood filled his face.

"Please. I only had this job a few months." All he wanted was to be a regular guy and he had gotten it wrong again.

"Relax. Just try not thinking about your pecker for a whole day. It'll do wonders for your skin. Promise?"

"I promise." Now she had shoved him into a higher zone of anxiety than he'd ever known, further confused by the wink she gave him as she walked away.

The trifle with the desk clerk, however, did nothing for her. Life's struggles are not helped by flip victories, her teacher in the North had repeatedly told her, a prim young woman so upright that students loved rather than derided her. She was not as lovable, though, as the teacher in the South who was always trembling on the lip of nervous collapse and told Julip in a Wal-Mart parking lot that to ninety-nine out of one hundred men she would always be simply a piece of ass. The challenge for a girl was to find number one hundred. Sad to say, this beloved teacher had flown the coop to live with some New Agers out in Arizona. It was a little startling, on a warm March evening, also in the Wal-Mart parking lot, the night before Julip left with her family for the North, to have this teacher announce, "We are others." When Julip questioned this notion in earnest, the teacher asked who the other inside her was that questioned herself. That added up to at least two. The teacher could count five more others for herself before she began weeping at the beauty of the cosmos above her in the early spring night. There was evidently a place in Arizona where this cosmos could be seen more clearly than in Georgia, so off the teacher went, abandoning her bookkeeper husband and her fourteen-year-old computer-junkie son, who barely noticed his mother's absence.

The spring of Julip's senior year had been truly dreadful — her season in hell, in fact. She took to drinking despite her father's sodden example, smoked pot on the way to school, at lunch hour, and in the evening. She assumed a fresh and vulgar way of speaking. Her lost love Johnny became a "fucking dummy" and his child bride, who appeared to be constructed of Play-Doh and resembled Miss Piggy, became a "fucking pig."

Julip's teacher of the North took her aside several times to tell her that gender was not the central fact of life, and that she should subdue the Iago in her, a character Julip rather appreciated in Shakespeare class. The teacher had also advised her to search for her higher self in Emily Dickinson, Julip's favorite writer. Sometimes she even did her hair like Emily, in those Empire curls at the temples. At times there is nothing quite so consoling as being misunderstood, and Emily Dickinson was the best possible example of this condition.

On the motel bed her problems dissolved in a piece of particularly shitty institutional art, a raised-brush-stroke rendition of a landscape in an uninvented country, including a big-eyed donkey staring out from a row of Lombardy poplars.

To Julip art was something you disappeared into, if only for a moment. When she was a child a wealthy man had given her father Audubon's grouse and woodcock prints and she forever strained after the hanging grapes with the ruffed grouse, or merely sat in the shadowed stillness with the woodcock. Naive as it was, there is no response to art so genuine as the desire, the often heart-rending pull, to be within the work. Off the kitchen in a hall of the plantation house when she had been summoned, usually for punishment, by her mother, there had been two Edward Curtis prints that had troubled, mystified, attracted her: Two Whistles, his face powdered and a crow perched on his head, and Bear's Belly, the Arikara medicine man cloaked in the skin of a bear. After being chided or spanked she wanted to hide within the bearskin robe of Bear's Belly, having been drawn to the eyes of the man who promised an earth without the small-time bullshit of punishment. It was strange, she thought, that in Wisconsin Indians were subjected to abuse that far exceeded that of blacks in the South. Somehow, though, the message inherent in the memory of these two men was that it was important not to approach life with the attitude of a hurt child. It got you nowhere in life, she had decided, and it certainly was the way to ruin a potentially good bird dog during training. Life and bird dogs required a firm hand.

So she called Dr. Wiseman, who without hesitation invited her over to his home. On the way she uttered a pointless prayer against a repeat of her experience with the lawyer, then smiled when she thought of her first meeting with Charles, soon after her father's passing. Charles had brought back a headstrong male setter her father had sold him two years before. They went for a walk in the back forty in a piece of cover she knew held both woodcock and grouse. The setter's name was Jack and he lazily worked an alder and dogwood thicket, pissing on five stumps in a row, then chasing a snowshoe rabbit, yelping in broadening circles, oblivious of Julip and Charles, who fairly bleated, "Come Jack, come to Daddy please, right now Jack." When the dog ignored him, Charles began howling, "Jack, you motherfucker, I'm going to kick your ass," which Jack disregarded in his pursuit of another rabbit.

Julip had sent Charles off to sit on a stump two hundred yards in the distance, then she knelt down in the path of the berserk dog, whose tongue had begun to loll as he caromed through the ferns and dense thickets. Finally Jack took notice of her low whistle and wandered over, flopping down in breathless exhaustion. She pinched his ear lightly to remind him of his bad behavior, then soothed him, rubbing his tummy until he regained his breath, at which point she drew a grouse and a woodcock wing from her coat pocket, passing them under his nose. Jack sniffed the wings and stood, his training and genetic destiny gradually occurring to him as a child at play looks up with delight to see the father's car driving into the yard. She pointed out a thicket in the direction of Charles and whispered, "Where are the birds?" knowing that in the covert of dogwood and alder a grouse brood made its home. Jack pointed a young grouse which Julip flushed, then she sent him a quarter mile farther where he skidded to a stop near a swale. This time it was a woodcock, and she waved Charles over and they let the dog hold the point for a long time, rigid, elegant, his tail upraised, his head low with neck twisted to the strong scent of the bird, a nearly heraldic image.

Within a few days she thought she was in love with Charles, though in discomfiting moments he struck her as a more complicated version of her father, perhaps a long-lost uncle who had entered her life for the purpose of making it both interesting and unnerving. She guessed that he had a ready supply of money because he didn't speak of having a job and had driven all the way from Georgia to have his dog's bad habits corrected. When she asked him how old he was, he became confused and checked his wallet, discovering that he was forty-five. His only apparent interests were the natural world, hunting, and fishing, though he bore no resemblance to the hundred sportsmen she had met. Outside of sex he seemed to deal with life with a detached melancholy. Julip imagined that he had a wife and family stored somewhere but she had not considered it her business. Still, her instincts told her to stop the brief affair as soon as he left, but there were daily phone calls. When plane tickets had arrived for Key West the weather in Wisconsin had been cold and rainy, she was lonely, and she said in the bathroom mirror to her eventual regret, "What the fuck, why not?"

*

She passed Dr. Wiseman's house within the subdivision speed limit, glancing at the neat bungalow that looked like it belonged somewhere in the North rather than in Florida. The doctor was there on the lawn with a woman his own age, both of them staring up a tree with a plump yellow Labrador sitting beside them, also staring up the tree. Julip became faint-hearted, but then she thought, Fuck it, and turned around. For some reason she remembered her precise thought when she boarded the plane in Duluth to go south to visit Charles: I'll never be the same, but then I never have been.

*

Five hours later, on the way back to the motel, Julip suspected she had used a whole box of Kleenex and the question had become whether her brother was worth saving.

It had started awkwardly with Dr. Wiseman's wife, Mildred, acting rather cool and cynical as if a young girl couldn't have any real problems. Later she told Julip that it was only that everyone's neuroses tended to devour their life — she was in the same line of work as her husband but in private practice. She made all the ardent college-age feminists Julip had met look like Mary Poppins.

The object in the tree turned out to be someone's pet guinea fowl. It glanced down at them, then away in goofy displacement, releasing a scattering poop which the dog sniffed, then lapped.

"Yoong!" Mildred yelled, or so Julip thought, though the dog's name was Jung. Julip pointed out that Eskimo dogs eat human poop, then was embarrassed. Wiseman and Mildred stared at her, digesting the information with amusement, then delight. "Astounding," Mildred shrieked. Then Wiseman paraphrased Yeats by saying that Love had pitched her palace unreasonably close to the place of excrement.

"Potty mouth," Mildred said, pinching his ass. "Time for soup. Come, Yoong!" But Jung wouldn't come, so Julip made the whistley hiss of a red-tailed hawk and the guinea fowl flushed from the tree in alarm, shooting through the hedge toward the wild thicket of a vacant lot. Wiseman sprang to catch Jung's tail and wrestled the dog into submission.

"That dog could use some work," Julip offered.

"No shit," the Wisemans said in unison.

*

Supper turned out to be chicken soup with a whole chicken in it, which was new to Julip. Wiseman opened a bottle of Pommard that she recognized as one of Charles's favorites. While Wiseman carved the chicken, Mildred touched Julip's arm and jaw line. "The bastards must be on your case day and night. You'll never know the pain of being homely and intelligent."

"Mildred, may I remind you I have a professional relationship with her?" Wiseman said. "You have no right to infer that Julip is not intelligent." He looked up from ladling broth over the carved pieces.

"I'm talking about myself, asshole. Homely and intelligent." This made them laugh and Julip glanced around nervously at the strangeness of the house. They were eating in the kitchen, she supposed, because the rest of the house was stuffed with books and art, mostly abstract. "I was *summa* and he was only *magna*," Mildred stated to Julip, who was beginning to wonder if there was going to be a proper time for her questions. She looked down at Jung, who was resting his chin on her knee under the glass-topped table. Charles had asked her in Key West to sit in the nude on a glass-topped table with him peering up from underneath. He referred to this activity as "fighting boredom." She hadn't minded at the time because she was engrossed in a mystery novel. Besides, Marcia had told her that older men do strange things to get their peckers up.

*

After dinner Mildred lit a cigar and Dr. Wiseman did the dishes. Julip began to feel at home with them, especially when Mildred quizzed her on how to train the dog. Julip pointed out that you had to be consistent with four commands — sit, stay, come, and heel — and you couldn't do much with an animal until these commands were ingrained. Mildred showed her the dog's quarters, a spare bedroom, and it was there that Julip perceived the nature of the problem: the room was an elaborate mockery of a child's nursery, with toys and cushions, even dog posters on the wall. "Very nice," Julip said, having run into the syndrome with dog owners before — a dog is not genetically designed to be a surrogate child but to fulfill its nature as a dog.

Back in the kitchen it was suddenly all business. Dr.

Wiseman sat at the table with a notepad, coffeepot, and cups. He asked Julip if she minded if Mildred joined them, as her point of view might aid the proceedings. Julip felt her scalp itch and a lump arising beneath her breastbone as she nodded in agreement. She had already told Dr. Wiseman on the phone that her intent was to spring Bobby, and he began by saying that he agreed and would do all that was possible to facilitate Bobby's release. However — and this was a long footnote — a number of questions came to mind, and it was difficult to know where to begin.

"Marcia?" suggested Mildred. She peered at Julip closely over the top of her glasses. "Naturally, as old married fucks we discuss each other's cases. My advanced graduate work dealt with the relationships of fantasy and psychosis. I need to know if the bear, the pig, and Marcia are actual entities."

"I don't know about any bear," Julip said in the slightest of whispers, though somewhere in her brain she began to hear a noise. A bear noise. Also her mother screaming.

"But the others. The pig and Marcia?" Dr. Wiseman asked, doodling on his notepad in what appeared to be concentric circles, beginning on the outside and swirling to the center. "Sometimes your brother tended to be playfully delusional and it was difficult to separate fact from invention."

"The pig was a pet wild piglet. Its mother got shot and Bobby and me tried to raise it but my mother found out and had my father get rid of it. He carried it out to a swamp but he was drinking so he didn't go very far. By this time the piglet was tame so it followed Dad home and a male Labrador killed it and ate it right in front of us. Bobby said then that Mother must be sacrificed by pushing her off a cliff."

"Where did he get that idea?" Mildred bore down.

"He liked to read books about ancient times from the school library." Julip had begun to cry and wanted them to say that it was horrible what happened to her piglet, but then she supposed that wasn't part of the procedure. Charles's friend Ted, who also had become her lover, had been having his mind analyzed for twenty years and told her about it. Ted was always having what he called "breakthroughs" and she rather hoped she might have one herself.

"Bobby said that right after the pig died he became officially married to someone named Marcia. His first cousin, in fact. Is this true? I don't recall how old he was at the time." Wiseman's face was knotted in puzzlement.

"He was eleven, and me and Marcia were twelve. I was the vested virgin preacher. That's what he called me, anyhow. It was really Marcia's idea, but we were always up to no good when we were together."

"Was the marriage consummated?" Mildred asked.

"Pardon?" Julip was thinking about the white dress she wore when she married them. The ceremony took place on a dock on the duck pond. A curious alligator had drifted by, which Bobby announced as a good omen straight from the gods.

"Did they make love at that age?" Mildred repeated the question.

"All the time. Quite a lot. It's always been Marcia's favorite thing."

"I'm afraid I didn't get a clear picture from Bobby of the men, your lovers, that he shot — other than that they were older rich men who took advantage of you." Wiseman raised a hand to cut off a question from Mildred.

"That's where he's wrong." Julip was a little pissed, not knowing where to start. "We didn't have much money when I was growing up. Even when I got to visit Marcia her family paid for the tickets and they always sent me her leftover clothes which were real beautiful. When I was a girl I had this list of all the places I wanted to go, like tropical islands, New York, and San Francisco. So when I helped Charles with his dog and we fell in love he sent me tickets to visit him in Key West which is a tropical island. One down, I thought. Charles takes pictures everywhere in the world for magazines. He makes an honest living but his wife is rich — and it isn't his fault. He gave me the car sitting out front. Arthur has been married quite a bit and you might say he's kinky but so what's new? Sometimes he gets fifty thousand dollars for a painting that only takes him two weeks. He sent me first-class tickets to San Francisco and it was fun to sit up in front where everyone is polite. Ted writes novels and stuff for Hollywood. He has mental problems but I was used to being around mental problems in my family. He's always saying that his heart is an interminable artichoke. That type of crazy thing. He gets in these moods where he can see underground to the roots of trees and deep in the ocean. When I met him in New York he told me he was going to become a creek. You must know about that kind of nuttiness? So I made love to them."

"All together?" Mildred was insistent.

"No. They didn't know about each other until after the trial. I mean they're close friends but I saw Ted and Arthur in other places. I didn't know Bobby was spying on us."

Suddenly Julip remembered the bear and began weeping in earnest. It was when she was four. The bear hung around their farm in Wisconsin and her dad used to catch fish and put them out on a stump for the bear to eat. They would watch from the porch of the farmhouse except for her mother. The bear stopped by every evening just before dark for a snack, whether it was a fish or a lesser meal. Her dad said the bear was young, maybe a year and a half old, and probably only recently had left the company of its mother. Julip's mother was sensibly angry about a bear so close to the house, and her father said this summer was it, and they wouldn't feed the bear the next year when it would be too big anyway. Her dad said it now was about sixty pounds, the size of a fourth grader in school.

The best thing was when the bear came out of the alder swale and flounced around the stump as if it were dancing. Then one July evening it was still very hot and Bobby was on the couch because he had a fever. Her dad was supposedly off looking for a lost setter but probably was at the tavern, her mother said, and there was nothing on the stump for the bear. The twilights are long that far north and it was after ten-thirty when Julip heard a rifle shot out near the mailbox on the gravel road. She went to the open window where she had dead June bugs lined up in a row in hopes they'd fly off again. There were two more shots and she saw car lights and a spotlight out on the road, then the car took off in a shatter of gravel. There was just enough light for her to see the bear dragging itself down the driveway, dragging itself quickly by the main strength of its forelegs and making a howling sound, which trailed off in gurgles before the howling would begin again. Julip ran downstairs and Bobby was screaming, too, with their mother restraining him on the couch. She yelled, "Don't you dare," but Julip grabbed the flashlight and went out on the porch, shining the light on the bear's face. The light made the bear's eyes as red as the blood coming out of its mouth. In the kennels in back the dogs were all howling like wolves. The bear crawled under the porch and Julip rushed down the porch steps and knelt shining the light on the bear, who had crawled to the far corner, the dirt matting on its bloody hide.

Now her mother was at the door yelling for her so she went up the steps and tried to calm Bobby down so her mother could call on the phone. Her mother couldn't find her dad at three different bars so she called the game warden, then she turned on the radio real loud so they wouldn't hear the bear but they could still hear it over the symphony on the public radio station. Then the bear stopped squalling and her mother turned down the volume, and then the game warden came and dragged the bear out, and Julip didn't get to watch that part though she saw him lift it into the back of his pickup. He came into the house and washed up in the kitchen and she heard him say to her mother, "Poor little girl," meaning the bear. Julip somehow thought the bear was a boy. At dawn she looked out the window and her dad was asleep in the car.

"They must have been very cruel to you. Is that what you're thinking about?"

Mildred was patting her on the shoulder and Julip came back to consciousness of the room with difficulty. The nasty aftermath was that she, Bobby, and her mother drove off that morning for a week with her grandparents, abandoning her dad to the farm. When he came to get them, she heard him say to her mother that he had joined AA though it didn't stick.

"If they were physically abusive it's still possible to prosecute." Wiseman, fueled by Julip's tears, had become angry and began pacing the room. "Occasionally I'm ashamed I'm a man," he added.

"You should be," Mildred chimed in, then gave Julip a hug, offering her more Kleenex.

"It's not that . . . ," Julip began, her face in a wad of tissues, begging time while she thought of something to say. She didn't want to talk about the bear that had reappeared from so long ago. If this was what Ted called a breakthrough he was welcome to it. "They were mostly kind, harmless. I like them, mostly." She stared into the darkness of the wet tissues. There was the image of her dad asleep in the car with flies on his face, then waking, stumbling out of the car to kiss her goodbye, the whiskey coming out of his skin. She had whispered, "Can I stay with you?" But he either didn't hear or pretended not to. She now said, "It's been nearly two years, and every day I think about my dad committing suicide."

"What do you mean?"

She pulled the Kleenex away and Wiseman was sitting next to her with a fresh dose of concern on his face.

"I mean my dad killed himself. Up in Minnesota."

"Who told you that?"

"My mother. What do you mean?" Julip had begun to think she was dealing with the Mad Hatter.

"How did she say it?" Wiseman was insistent.

"She said, 'He did himself in.' Over the phone. We never had a funeral."

"That's not true. Your father was in a sleeping bag in a picnic area up near Fergus Falls in Minnesota. Some drunk teenagers ran over him in their car. I want to know why your mother would say such a thing."

"I'm not sure — she always just rattles on," Julip said. "But probably because she feels guilty. Bobby probably told you she went off to Virginia with the man she cooked for . . ." Julip's voice trailed off with the enormity of it all. She felt a lightness bordering on the dizzy, and tried to focus sharply on Wiseman's face. She turned to Mildred, whose own face was contorted.

"How utterly horrible. That inhuman bitch!" Mildred hissed.

"This all should make you feel better," Wiseman said, sighing, actually an exhalation meant, unconsciously, to expel the evils of the world. "What I mean is, it's very difficult for a young woman to get over a father's suicide. And it's very important for you to give up any idea that you could have saved him. Do you understand?"

"Was he drunk?" Julip sensed the relief of her father asleep, being run over rather than shooting himself or whatever.

"A little. A point-oh-five if I remember. I secured and tried to show your brother the autopsy report to erase his notions that your father is alive."

"I don't understand why Bobby didn't tell me it wasn't suicide." There was the tonic of a rising anger against her brother.

"I suspect it was a misunderstanding. And you hadn't been in contact to speak of. Your mother only told him your father had been run over by a car after he escaped the alcohol rehab clinic."

Jung had begun digging at the living room rug for private reasons. "Yoong, no!" Julip said sharply, and the dog rolled over, quivering as if poleaxed.

*

On the way back to the motel Julip screamed "Motherfucker!" a dozen times, which at least was different from her ordinary sadness over her family. She tried the radio but some asshole was singing that his girlfriend had always been the wind beneath his wings, and Julip cocked a foot, kicking the volume dial off the radio face. This pleased her beyond reason.

Before she left, she had taken a walk with Mildred and Jung. Wiseman had begged off due to fatigue over human folly. Julip walked Jung on a leash over which he struggled mightily, though he was no match for the trainer. If anyone had been out walking in the neighborhood that warm summer night in Tallahassee, the assumption would have been mother and daughter, with the mother keeping up with the girl and unruly dog only with effort. They managed to talk once the dog was schooled into compliance. Mildred asked if she had enough money for the mission to Key West, and Julip said she had a credit card, though she wondered privately how much juice was left in it. She asked Mildred why older men were so fascinated with younger women. The question came out of her diffidently but Mildred made a full stop under a street light where Jung snuffled the dead insects gathered there.

"The information isn't conclusive," Mildred said. "It's like one of those minor diseases, however painful to the victims, that don't seem to merit research money. The *British Psychoanalytical Journal* said the problem — perversion, condition — has existed in two thousand cultures, mostly among alpha-type, aggressive, successful males who have the time, money, and inclination. It doesn't appear connected directly to the Lolita complex which borders on pedophilia. In my own practice I've noted that it pretty much comes down to the unlived life. Last year I treated a prominent banker who ran off with his granddaughter's seventeen-year-old babysitter for a couple of days."

Jung yelped, having managed to get his nose stung by an insect. He growled and clacked his teeth, then rubbed his nose. Julip stooped to comfort, pointed at the bugs, and said "No." Then she turned to Mildred. "My old boyfriends said that they were too busy when they were young and they're making up for lost time."

"Frankly that's lame, self-indulgent. Ask them why they're the minority who feel compelled in that direction. Naturally, we're all pulled toward what excites us, and your friends — an artist, a photographer, and a writer —

are members of a group that are renowned whiners. They think they're historically entitled to misbehave. They're incredible fantasists and they sit around dreaming up what will make their dicks hard. This is just a vague outline. I'd have to talk to them."

"What excites you?" Julip was taken aback by her own boldness and added, "You don't have to tell me."

"Men with high foreheads, big hat sizes. Intelligence. A stupid man is like a garden slug to me. I always loathed the blandness of athletes. Nullities, organs with perfect teeth." Mildred was laughing. "And I like men who wear Mennen Skin Bracer!"

*

Back at the house after they had said goodbye, Mildred pressed several hundred dollars on her. She didn't want Julip to have to ask her "asshole boyfriends" for money. Now in the car, at a stoplight, Julip searched deep in her bag for the needle-nosed pliers she used to attach dog tags to collars. It worked on the radio volume, so no real harm was done.

In truth, she hadn't listened carefully to what Mildred had said — when you like someone you rarely question your motives for liking them. For instance, she did not question the fact that the Boys were heels, slobs, whiners, perverse, or simply "jerk-offs," as Marcia observed when she met them, though there was the troubling notion that they all shared the boozy sentimentality of Julip's dad. At least they weren't mean-minded like so many of her dad's rich clients, one of whom had stuck a finger in her when she was nine, then swore her to secrecy. She hadn't told anyone because her parents were having their own troubles at the time. Beyond all the principles and explanations there was an actual, intensely messy world revolving and she felt her main job was to get Bobby out of prison, whether he deserved it or not.

At the motel the same fungoid room clerk passed her a new volume of Krishnamurti with a flower pressed in it — in apology, he said.

She stared at him with curiosity as the fluorescent lights buzzed in the after-midnight stillness. "Thank you," she said. "I see you're taking the high road."

She quickly walked off before he could ask a question. The high road was Marcia's idea for when men gave you books or flowers, while the low road was lingerie, dope, money, or a direct question. The lack of uniqueness was certainly dreary, she thought, tossing the book on the dresser. She quickly shed her clothes for a shower, her skin prickling with fear when she was sure she heard someone in the bushes outside her window. She affected nonchalance though she was stark naked, turning lazily to the phone and noting the drapes were parted a crack when she had left them tightly closed. She dialed the desk to confirm her suspicion that no one would be there, let it ring a half-dozen times, hung up, then strolled toward the crack in the drapes, pausing to look at her left tit as if it possessed the mystery of life. She was buying time to prepare a line, but settled for screaming, "Get out of here, you dumb cocksucker," then opened the drapes to see the desk clerk stumble backward and sprint toward the office. She waited a couple of minutes, noting that Krishnamurti looked a lot like the drawing of Kahlil Gibran on a book a junior-college instructor had given her. Ted had given her Rilke's *Sonnets to Orpheus,* which was even more mysterious though less likable than Emily Dickinson. She dialed the desk again.

"Village Inn. May I help you?" He was still breathless.

"I called the cops."

"Oh, please . . ."

"I didn't call the cops. Just kidding. But my brother's getting out of Raiford prison next week and he's going to cut off your nuts for starters. Good night."

With that accomplished, she turned to her pre-bedtime poem:

> *It's such a little thing to weep —*
> *So short a thing to sigh —*
> *And yet — by Trades — the size of* these
> *We men and women die!*

Quite a puzzle, she thought, deciding that it meant if you can't weep, you're so much dead meat, plain and simple.

There was an urge to enter Jung in her dog notebook and diary but the day's events would have taken a whole night of writing. She dozed off, waking at three A.M. to the slightest of noises. She had neglected to turn out the lights and the room looked garishly stupid and there was a note under the door. She read:

> Please forgive me, I guess it was just love at first sight. I won't bother you again. I hope you don't tell your brother anything as consider me vanished.
>
> Fred (desk clerk)

*

It was a strange, wakeful night, her imagination seemingly electrified by the details of her life, and a fresh anger emerging from the fact that her father had simply been killed rather than committing suicide. Within her vertiginous state it was the only clear principle: it wasn't that her dad didn't want to see her again, he just got run over, a traffic fatality. He was drinking and so were the teenagers. The real torment now was what to do about Bobby and whether he was sufficiently sane for life on the outside. And would the prosecutor, the judge, and the Boys, as they were known in Key West, agree to psychiatric treatment rather than prison. She couldn't very well ask the victims for Bobby's treatment money, which left a single option. She turned on the light, looked up a number, and dialed, though it was only five A.M. The achingly familiar voice was sleepy.

"Hello?"

"Is this my onliest mom in the world?"

"Julip, I tried to call you yesterday."

"Prove it."

"That's easy. Your kennel man said you went to Florida to try to get Bobby out of prison. Is that smart?"

"What do you care?"

"If you only called to insult me, I can hang up."

"Sorry. Why did you call me yesterday?"

"My employer wants to send you to college."

"Why call him your employer when you've been fucking him for years?"

"I forbid you to use the *f* word."

"Beg your pardon, ma'am. Would he mind using that college money to send Bobby to a nice place for the brain damaged? He's what they call delusional."

"He always was. I could ask about the money."

"Please do. Another small item is why did you tell me Dad committed suicide when he got run over by some drunk teenagers?"

"I didn't tell you he committed suicide."

"You said he did himself in."

"I don't recall that."

"Bullshit. Why did you wait until I was away at Marcia's to send him to the clinic, with your boyfriend paying the bill?"

"Mr. Stearne loved your father. You might remember that your father worked for him for ten years."

"That doesn't get you off the hook."

"Your father became impotent from his drinking. I hadn't had any affection in a long time."

"You haven't answered my question."

"Mr. Stearne couldn't keep him on unless he dried out. He pitched over on the dinner table in front of the governor. It was easier on you not to be there."

"Oh, bullshit."

"Julip, I'm just a human being." Her mother's voice was now quavery. "You'll be in my prayers. Good night."

"Hold on a minute. I don't want to be in your prayers. I want you guys to pony up some money for Bobby's treatment."

"I'll do what I can. Anything for my family. And Julip, don't ruin your life being pissed at me."

"I never heard you swear. Actually that's a good thought. Thank you. Meanwhile, I'll call you in a few days from Key West. And I want you to promise me one single thing."

"Yes, dear."

"Next time my dad dies, can we have a funeral? Don't just send a lacquered box full of ashes."

"That's not funny, Julip."

"No shit," she said, slamming down the phone, damp, exhausted, but relieved.

She slept then, a deep, unbelievably sweet sleep, until the phone woke her four hours later. It was Mildred, who said she'd thought Julip might sleep in, and wanted to offer to come down and help if things got too difficult in Key West. Julip thanked her, agreeing with Mildred's notion that Julip had been through a nightmare for two years. "No shit," Julip said again, and they both laughed, hanging up in unison. With the click of the receiver she remembered a lovely dream she had been having. Her piglet the Labrador had eaten had become half piglet and half the bear that died under the porch, wonderfully alive in a blueberry marsh in Wisconsin. When she looked at the animal closely its eyes were her father's. What good luck, she thought.

*

Meanwhile, a full day's drive to the south, in Key West, the Boys were getting a late start on the day's fishing. After ten days of their annual tarpon outing they were collectively in a fit of deep lassitude. Arthur, the painter, said it was no fun anymore and maybe it never was. Charles said of course it was fun, maybe they were just getting too old to carry on the kind of misbehavior that had become, after fifteen previous trips, traditional. Ted, a circuitous brooder, offered an even half-dozen reasons why they were not having as much fun, including the prevalence of AIDS but excluding the obvious one that Julip wasn't there, as she had been the past two years, at least nominally with Charles. Nothing could follow up the sheer excitement, the nightmare, of being shot the year before and then talking about it, but that soon passed at their favorite bars — Key West has always been a town of Cuban and white-trash passion, and the wounds the Boys bore from the .22 shots were minuscule indeed.

They were, in fact, "mostly nice," as Julip described them to the Wisemans, though mostly harmful to themselves. In their mid- to late forties, they felt the malaise of that period no deeper than other men but were considerably more dramatic about it than all but a few. Some on the outside thought it was a testament to the depth of their friendship when it was revealed that all of them had been seeing Julip rather than simply Charles, who had met her first and brought her down to Florida. After Bobby's trial, at which their appearances were perfunctory, they had gone trout fishing in the Wind River area of Wyoming and worked it all out, though they remained far from having a good laugh. More out of fatigue than wisdom they had, in any event, decided to banish the shooting from everyday consciousness.

But on that particular morning things hadn't gone well. The previous evening they had eaten massively, and drunk the same, in pursuit of three secretaries from Cleveland, one of whom had called Ted "Gramps" in jest, which had sent him home in a snit where he did two medicinal lines of coke and drank a half bottle of whiskey watching the late movie. Arthur and Charles came home in exhaustion at four A.M., maintaining that they had "sort of" gotten laid but were too bleary to sort out the details.

A scant three hours later Charles had woken them for fishing. It was unthinkable to miss the big spring tide that was arriving mid-morning, the kind of tide that brought fresh schools of tarpon out of the Gulf Stream. But when they picked up their sandwiches at Herman's they ran into an old gay friend with a Kaposi's sarcoma lesion on his neck, and back in the car Arthur began to weep. Ted made a misdirected attempt to comfort him by saying the free lunch was over for everyone. Arthur, though a vastly successful painter, was not the least bit interested in reality, and Ted's comment made him densely maudlin. Soon after, on their way out of Garrison Bight in the skiff, Charles decided to break the oppressive ice by stalling the boat and letting the last of the outgoing tide carry them under the bridge, at which point he yelled "Bang!" the shout echoing up against the bridge framework.

Ted and Arthur shuddered, then screamed in anger at Charles. It was here that Bobby had ambushed them with his .22 semiautomatic exactly one year before. Charles had taken one shot in the thigh before he had the immediate sense to dive overboard and hide behind the boat's transom. Ted and Arthur had scurried around trying to hide behind each other and the skiff's small console, taking two shots apiece, with only Ted's knee requiring any relatively serious medical attention. Now, depending on his mood, Ted walked with either a slight or a pronounced limp. Way back in college he sometimes limped for no reason, and now he had one. Charles's little joke, however, brought hung-over outrage from Arthur and Ted.

"It's the anniversary of our near-death experience," Charles said. "I thought we should lighten up." He opened a small cooler, revealing a bottle of Cristal and an eight-ounce tin of beluga. "A snack for later," he added, and Arthur and Ted perked up a bit.

*

In truth, Julip wasn't particularly pretty or classically handsome, certainly not overwhelmingly so, but she was alive. This isn't a solipsism, because most people aren't alive, other than in a technical sense. The recurrent theme of androidism is so ubiquitous because it has a basis in fact. Julip was vivid, immediate, and almost involuntarily filled out her life to its limits, moment by moment, with a rare amount of emotional energy. Ted had told her she was one of the very few blood banks in a world of hemophiliacs, which she had thought over carefully to determine if it was vaguely romantic or another one of his asshole comments. If Ted didn't have a few drinks, a Quaalude, or three hits of a joint in his system, he was an encyclopedia on the subject of melancholy. Once in New York Julip asked why, since he was so apparently successful, he didn't act successful, rather than moping around unshaven in old clothes. His eyes brimmed with tears and he rushed to the mini-bar of their hotel suite.

Before she left the motel in Tallahassee, she called Frank back home to make sure the setter bitch had arrived out in Bismarck. He said yes, also that her mother had called, and Marcia had left a number in Palm Beach, which Julip wrote down. She knew Marcia wanted to go see Bobby but didn't think this meeting of nut cases was a good idea at present.

In her car she checked the road atlas and swore when she saw that Raiford was a detour, but she had promised Bobby his childhood bait box. While the car cooled off she stood against a fender, checking the contents of the box: marbles, tiny arrowheads, the marriage license they had concocted for him and Marcia, a neatly folded treasure map of Ecuador ordered from *Argosy*, a small photo of Bobby and Marcia they had taken of themselves in one of those machines, with Marcia's bare tits and tongue sticking out. Marcia's mother was Julip's father's sister, dead since Marcia was ten, from an alcohol-related car accident in Georgetown where, Marcia pointed out, it was hard to get up that much speed. They had decided early on that a dead mother and Julip's were pretty much the same thing.

On the way to Raiford, near Starke, Julip would have been amused to see Charles's skiff staked off Ballast Key and the Boys sharing a single plastic spoon for the beluga and toasting the good life with champagne. This time it was Ted who broke into tears while Charles and Arthur stared off at the pearlescent horizon, dense with heat and humidity so that they were all wet with sweat without even moving.

*

It went rather gracefully with Bobby after an awkward moment with a very old guard who looked up while inspecting Bobby's bait box and said, "These guys are all kids."

"What do you mean?" Julip asked out of curiosity.

"Look at these marbles. And a treasure map. They all got their box of stuff and dirty pictures. That's all I mean. Criminals are just kids. They didn't want to grow up and be responsible prison guards." He laughed at this, and passed Julip through the door, wishing he could give her a goose in the butt. In addition to her being vivid, all the years of working bird dogs with her father and on her own had given Julip an improbably shapely body. While tuning up dogs in the last month before the grouse season opens, it was nothing for her to walk a dozen miles a day over rough landscape.

Bobby was delighted with his treasures, sorting through them, studying the treasure map as Julip explained her plans. He nodded with a smile. "So I got to admit I'm nuts. That's the bottom line?"

"Yes. What's so bad about admitting you're nuts?"

"Nothing. After you left the other day, Dad told me to admit I'm nuts if it'll get me out of this place."

"May I ask how he talks to you?"

"Not in a human voice. He talks in the voice of an animal."

This answer made her nervous, after her dream in the motel. "Marcia's in Florida. She wants to know if you'll see her if she comes to visit."

"My so-called wife. Tell her she can visit if she brings a

nude picture. A wife's obligated to do that. She's probably cheating on me."

"I'm sure you remember the divorce. You had Marcia sit in the pup tent and you circled the tent three times saying, 'I divorce you.'"

"We're still married in the eyes of God. Remember Methodist Sunday school? That's what they said. If she doesn't bring a nude photo, tell her to forget it. I'm horny as a goat. Remember old Martha's goat that used to blow itself?"

She remembered. Old Martha was an Anishinabe woman who lived in a shack a mile down the road from their farm in Wisconsin. Julip would bring her small baby food jars of her father's whiskey and Martha would make blueberry pancakes using wild rice she ground up for flour. They were the most delicious pancakes in the world with Martha's homemade maple syrup. Bobby was her favorite, and when she died when he was eight he brought violets to her grave in the Indian cemetery until, as usual, his mother forbade him to do so. It was Martha who gave him the arrowheads.

"What did you do with the rest of that stuff Martha gave you?"

"Hid it on our farm."

"It's not our farm. It's Mother's."

"Nope. She wrote and told me she gave it to us. Half yours. Half mine. It's not worth much anyhow. If you get me in a nut house, I'm going to escape and go to Ecuador. You got to pay me half what the farm's worth for a grubstake."

"She never told us the same thing."

"You're right there. I was remembering when Marcia and you did all those sex experiments on me. I could use some of that now. It would be kind if you'd sneak me a peek of tit."

"Bobby, I'm your sister!" Julip hissed, flushing with blood and anger.

"It didn't matter then, why does it now? And if you don't want to, don't do it. I've been meaning to ask you. Why did you fuck those old guys?"

"I liked them. They were more interesting than young guys I knew. I got to go places."

"That's a good answer. Maybe they didn't defile you after all. You got your own free will. Tell them I promise not to shoot them again. I'll swear it on my Modern Library Giant edition of Friedrich Nietzsche. My problem is that I'm a rope dancer."

The Nietzsche was a new one to Julip. Bobby's capacity to find fresh bibles to live by had been going on a long time. If pushed, she thought, she could remember a dozen or so figures, including Ayn Rand, Hesse, Hemingway, the New Testament (a brief phase), and a Tibetan by the name of Trungpa. Bobby's schoolteachers all thought that if he'd had an ounce of good sense he could have gone far, wherever that might be. At least, she thought while getting up to leave, he didn't drink. Bobby considered alcohol to be the "water of weakness," a notion that probably came from the same place as her "defilement."

"I love you, Bobby. I'll do what I can."

"If you loved me, you'd show me a tit," he crowed, leaping straight into the air from his chair in a single fluid motion.

She blew him a kiss and fled.

*

There was a long delay getting on the turnpike near Wildwood. She stopped at a Burger King — it was nearly three and she had forgotten breakfast and lunch. Two ambulances raced toward the turnpike on the road's shoulder and she took out her diary to catch up during the delay, then dripped a glob of mayo from the Whopper onto the diary. "Motherfucker!" she shrieked.

"Did you call me?" said a boy in the next car.

"No. I made a mess. Excuse my French." Julip noted he was good looking but too young. She backed her car over to the corner of the parking lot for privacy.

> I'm in the thick of things. Homesick for Wisconsin already. Too fast like the Boys and my clients who always want a biddable dog. Tick-tocks I call them. Tick left, tock right. Like the thing on a piano, metronome? That's because everyone's in a rush and the dogs can't stretch out and find birds. A dog following its nose can't be a machine. So they want shock collars and I say fuck you and your shock collars. Bobby was pretty nice today though a tad nuts. He did not get any training at all when younger! I didn't get much either but I don't have mental problems (that I know of). My heart goes out to the insane, like that brain-damaged setter I couldn't heal. Vet said a brain parasite. I could fix Wiseman's dog in a day or two though I doubt they'd be consistent. I should have answered the Boys' letters this year but I was sick of the whole thing including them. They all said they were sorry when they were the ones who were shot. That must be the victim stuff you read about in the Modern Living page of the newspaper. No one grows up, they just get tired. Or few indeed. No stopping for dead animals on the turnpike. Too dangerous.

*

By the time she reached the Palm Beach exit it was evening and she was soothed though exhausted. The beautiful country between St. Cloud and Fort Pierce had been a comfort, and she guessed that was the way Florida looked years before — palms, savannahs, swamps, palmettos, sawgrass, clouds of birds, a gorgeous, deep green, funky smell. She was down to only four tapes she liked and alternated between Jim Pepper, Neil Young, an old Grateful Dead called *The Wake of the Flood,* and her single classical tape, a gift from Arthur, Mozart's *Jupiter* Symphony. Other than being absorbed in the music and the landscape, she had been half singing, half chanting the names of the favorite dogs in her life, nearly seventy in number. It was at least five more hours to Key West and she was tempted to go for it but there didn't seem much advantage in arriving wrecked. But then she remembered she was supposed to call Marcia, so she checked into a Best Western, pleased that the air conditioner was already on, also relieved that the desk clerk had been a senior citizen reading a Bible. Just to be on his good side she asked him to remember her in his prayers, which delighted him. Methodists were always doing that, and she hoped the gesture would help her credit card clear. It did.

When she called Marcia she got a succession of three voices, one female and two male, with Spanish accents, before Marcia's throaty drawl came on.

"Jewel baby, where are you?"

"Hee-Haw Junction."

"It's Yeehaw Junction and you're not there. Don't fib."

"I'm here. At a motel. Bobby says he'll see you but there's a small catch. He wants nude photos. You ought to have a drawerful."

"Not on me. Can I go up there tomorrow?"

"Suit yourself." Julip was too tired to run on at the mouth and steadfastly refused Marcia's invite to go to a party for Argentinean polo players, which was scarcely what she needed that night. Marcia, however, insisted she stop by to say hello, so Julip gave her the address off a matchbook. She drew her warm bottle of white wine from the suitcase, was too lazy to go for ice, and flipped Dickinson open at random, for counsel:

Witchcraft has not a Pedigree
T'is early as our Breath
And mourners meet it going out
The moment of our death —

Too scary to be of use, she thought, stripping for a shower and sipping the wine. A joint was better after a long day's drive but she didn't want to get caught on the road and add to her difficulties.

In the shower she sang her dog names, almost merrily, but her throat stopped at Zeke, who followed Blossom, Kate, Jessie, Jack, Punch, and Mack. Her father had sold Zeke, a high-powered English pointer, to a Japanese for use as a foundation stud for twelve thousand dollars. Julip was thirteen at the time and Zeke was her favorite to take on long walks up in Wisconsin. She had been bitterly angry at her father, who had used the money to buy a fancy step-side pickup rather than to pay debts, paint the house, take her mother on a promised vacation to New York. It was, in fact, the single occasion she could remember when she had been sympathetic with her mother. Julip mourned poor Zeke's flying off to Japan, then one evening stole the new pickup, taking three setters in the cab with her and three cans of Franco-American spaghetti as a special treat for the dogs. Early the next morning she was found a scant dozen miles away, mired to the axles on a swamp road, by the same game warden who came out after the bear was shot. Her father apologized for selling Zeke which, she noted, did nothing to get her beloved dog back.

She was toweling off when she heard Marcia at the door. Marcia threw a package on a chair and busied herself opening a bottle of Meursault she had swiped from her host's fridge. Julip remembered a summer evening in New York when Ted drank three bottles of the wine with dinner, then had fallen out of bed on his face.

"You got any Valium?" Marcia was edgy, strung out as if she had been doing coke.

"I never have any Valium."

They went through this every time they met. Once when Marcia visited Key West, she had stolen Charles's pills, which pissed him off, though he forgave her when she slept with Arthur so athletically that Arthur missed a day of fishing, out of exhaustion. Ted had moped when Marcia shrieked at him, "Who needs your fucking mind games."

"Get a load of this one." Marcia pulled out one of her special five-paper bombers, lit it, and dragged deeply. "Jamaican primo." She coughed, letting out a billow of smoke and passing it to Julip. "Maybe I'll just stay here, and leave to see Bobby early in the morning. Is that okay?"

"Sure. I guess so. I mean, I'm tired so you can't jabber all night." The joint and cool wine were beginning to make Julip feel dreamy. She observed that Marcia wasn't looking all that good beneath her tan. "What you doing down here, anyway?"

"Fucking off. Remember Enrique? A long time ago?"

"The worst asshole I ever met. A real whiner."

"You bit him." Marcia shrieked with laughter.

Julip thought of it as her ugliest sexual experience. She was only thirteen and her mother had sent her off to Washington to visit Marcia in hopes she would "meet a better class of people." Marcia's stepmother was a rail-thin society woman who had sent them off to a junior dance at a South American embassy where their young host was Enrique. Even among a group so young there was a lot of drinking.

Enrique had taken her and Marcia on a tour of the house which, to Julip, was a palace. They ended up in the cold back seat of Enrique's father's bullet-proof limousine with a bottle of brandy. Enrique took out his very large penis and Marcia began playing with it, then sucking on it. Enrique begged Julip to try it and she thought why not, since the brandy made her feel sophisticated, but then Enrique held her head too far down so she gave him a good nip, whereupon he screamed and began crying. "It's not even bleeding, you little chickenshit," Marcia said, and then they fled after Enrique said he was getting his father's bodyguards. Marcia's stepmother was upset when they returned home so early, so Marcia said Enrique had tried to rape Julip. "Boys will be boys," said her stepmother. "I trust it didn't come to anyone's attention."

Julip recovered from this unpleasant reverie by swallowing a full glass of wine and taking another hit on the joint, this time a big one. She dropped the towel she was still wrapped in and put on a summer robe.

"You don't deserve better tits than me," Marcia said, unwrapping the package she had thrown on the chair. It was the cheapest model Polaroid camera and Marcia studied the instructions, laughing. "We got to get Bobby's pictures before we're too fucked up." She handed it to Julip, who had taken hundreds of dog photos but never anything else. Marcia shed her cotton dress and stood braless before the mirror on the bathroom door. "This is too funny to feel sexy," she said, fiddling with the TV clicker. She rejected MTV in favor of an Oral Roberts sermon, for "contrast."

"I think Bobby likes tits," Julip said, looking through the viewfinder. The camera jiggled because she was laughing at the sheer daffiness of it all. There were apparently normal girls — and a very few in Marcia's category. Julip thought she herself was kind of in the middle.

Marcia was vigorously rubbing her breasts in front of the mirror. "I could use a bicycle pump."

"They're fine, dear. Not your best point but good enough."

"Fuck you." Marcia took off her panties and sprawled on the bed, trying to move sensuously to a hymn on the television. She caressed herself. "Start shooting, I haven't had an orgasm in years except by myself."

"You're bullshitting again." Julip shot away, deciding to come closer to fill the frame.

"Last time was with your brother when we were seventeen. That's four fucking years. Maybe I'm a lesbian."

"You're just sort of single-minded," Julip said, finishing the film and looking at the stack as their clarity emerged. "Then how come you sleep with so many men?"

"Because I'm stupid and aimless. I must have fucked a hundred morons, with no luck except Bobby. How about you?"

"I always have a great time, but then I've only had six. Johnny in high school. Frank, my kennel hand, when he broke his foot — to make him feel better, you know. The county agent in March . . ."

"A drug agent?" Marcia put her panties back on in general despair.

"No, a county agent. He advises farmers on agricultural problems. I planted some buckwheat to draw in Canada geese but it didn't grow. I seduced him. And then the Boys." She reflected that the rubbery lawyer didn't really count.

"What about Bobby?" Marcia said with a trace of cattiness.

"That doesn't count. We were only thirteen and you

made me do it. And how's anyone supposed to know what's wrong if no one tells you?"

Now Marcia was sniffling. She relit the joint and downed another glass of wine. "I think I'm going to shoot myself if Bobby rejects me. I want to marry him when he gets out." She began to sob and Julip sat beside her on the bed, giving her a hug.

"You can't get married to your first cousin. It's illegal. That's what I heard, anyhow."

"I already checked it out. You can do it in Arkansas and Mississippi. Or in Mexico where we won't tell anyone. If he won't marry me I'm going to shoot myself." Now she was shaking with sobs and Julip held her in her arms.

Besides being a little stoned and drunk, Julip poignantly felt the duty of getting Bobby out of prison or her dearest friend on earth would shoot herself. "Even if I get him out he won't be free. He'll have to go someplace where they can work on his mind. You know, a hospital."

"We'll get married and I'll live close by." Marcia's sobs subsided. "I will never get over my first love. I'd rather die." She blew her nose on the corner of the sheet and it began bleeding. "That fucking cocaine is killing me."

Julip got her some tissues, then turned out the lights after drinking two glasses of water. Ted had told her: lots of water before bedtime and you were bound to feel better in the morning. The down side was that you had to get up in the night and pee. Ted traveled with a dozen jars of vitamins, washing them down with whiskey if need be. And what's more, he knew the reason for every one of them. Marcia asked her to leave the bathroom light on — she hated waking up and not knowing where she was.

They snuggled together on the queen-size bed with Julip reciting, at Marcia's insistence, both the Lord's Prayer and Now I Lay Me Down to Sleep. This had been going on since they were children. Marcia couldn't manage to memorize anything — even her own phone number presented difficulties.

"Mother, may I?" Marcia whispered.

"I wish you wouldn't. Why don't you grow up?"

"Triple please? Just for a minute. One single minute."

Julip presented a breast and Marcia nursed on it, an act that had begun when they were twelve and Julip's nascent breasts started before Marcia's.

"Time's up," Julip said, watching the course of the second hand on her travel clock. They slept with Julip having to push her away only once during the night. Usually it was more.

*

Julip was startled when Marcia woke her to say goodbye just after daylight. There had been a dream of Zeke, the pointer, on a throne in a Japanese robe. So at least he was being well taken care of, though when Marcia whispered "Goodbye, I love you," it occurred to her that Zeke must be dead by now. In the dream Zeke's eyes looked slanted, as if he had begun to look like his owners, just like owners gradually look like their dogs. Marcia was out the door, but then came back with a cup of coffee and a receipt from the motel office. She had paid the bill, a unique act of consideration for her. She put the cup of coffee down on the nightstand next to Julip's head.

"The pictures really suck but I feel good about myself for going up there. That's how people talk nowadays, you know, feeling good about themselves. How the fuck do they manage?"

Julip opened her eyes a crack, then affected sleep. She didn't feel up to a dawn mudbath. Marcia kissed her forehead and left. The birds were pleasantly loud and Julip was relieved to hear a car start. Marcia had had a theory she reinterpreted from her shrink, that older men liked her and Julip because they were waifs and could readily be taken advantage of by anyone. When she explained this to Julip on the phone, there had been a long silence, and then Julip had said, "Bullshit. I'm a dog trainer, not a waif," and hung up.

She bit the bullet, sipped the coffee, and reached for the telephone. She called Charles, who said he was up anyway for an early tide. It had been nearly a year since they had talked, though she had heard all of their voices several times on her answering machine. There was politely nervous small talk at the beginning. Charles said Arthur and Ted were in a state of mutiny and wanted to leave town. It was extremely hot and humid, the fishing was good, but they weren't having much fun. Arthur had taken to spontaneous crying jags in the boat, and Ted was drinking too much whiskey and talking about the world AIDS problem. How was she? "Wonderful," she said for no reason, then explained she wanted to see him at three on the pier, near Martello Towers, then Arthur at four, Ted at five, then Charles again at six for a wrap-up. Charles was polite enough not to ask why, readily agreed, and closed by saying "I love you," which caused tremors in her stomach, already weakened by last night's dope and wine.

*

When she stood next to her car trying to ready herself for the last leg of her trip, she had what she thought later was an out-of-body experience, her first, though it was one of Bobby's specialties. It was still only a half hour after daylight and the marsh behind the motel was loud with water birds. Overhead, just sprung from their night roost, a grand flock of crows flew westward. She shivered, swept away to

Wisconsin where on cool summer mornings before the heat gathered in the woods she'd run a dozen bird dogs at once with whistle, quirt, and pistol to honor a point and flush. Now she was up there beside another marsh, hearing the whippoorwill's last cry and the morning call of the loon from the pond back in the woods, hearing the wingbeats of the ravens that often followed her, the bells on the dog collars tinkling in the greenery, and her pants wet with dew to her knees, the dogs becoming wet and sleek with the same dew in the waist-high ferns, until she came to rest a few minutes near a partially uprooted huge white pine, and the disused bear den under the roots, perhaps the home of her bear, the "poor little girl."

Quite suddenly she was back in the car, deciding that her home and dogs were enough to fill a life. If something else good came along, that was well and fine. If not, not. The weight of her father, brother, mother, seemed to have gone westward with the crows. Also the weight of the Boys waiting in Key West, no doubt now in a dither about her arrival.

She didn't know how much they had come to depend on her, more in spirit than in presence. The fact was that more than her supposed attractiveness, her vividness, she was so ordinary that she reminded them of the value of life aside or beyond work and exhaustion. She was totally without their distortions and had grown tired of drawing them out of the hundreds of little funks that success is heir to. It did not occur to them to feel any particular responsibility to her, mistaking her ordinariness for a free spirit, and by and large in their world one felt no responsibility beyond one's family and the work at hand. In short, outside of their work they didn't quite know what they were doing. When camera, paintbrush, and pen were put aside, they were right out there in la-la land with the Bloomingdale's teenyboppers wired on speed. Only their sporting life held them on earth, and its seams frequently burst. The arrival of Julip would put a top back on the world. They didn't want her to be like them, and she wasn't. They scarcely understood that with sufficient exposure she would be doomed to falter, to hand over her life to tracking ghosts like they did — the long, dead wait for something that could lift them out of the average messes they had made.

She started the car with the sure and certain strength that she knew when to bail out of the burning plane, which was, of course, after she bailed her brother out first. If he wanted to escape to Mexico or wherever with his childhood wife, they would be well out of the way. She smiled when she imagined the Boys trying to figure out the reason she was coming, and which of them she might prefer, or why she insisted on talking to them separately.

*

She reached Key West in time to cool her heels in the judge's outer office, hanging on the wan hope that the sympathetic smile he had given her after the trial meant something, also his quiet advice that she return to Wisconsin and "steer clear of those playboys." Her heart sunk, though, when the judge bustled out of his office at one-thirty with two men in summer suits bent on lunch. He waved away his receptionist, glanced at Julip, not stopping until he reached the door and looked at her again, then came over, his face a mask of abrupt pleasantness.

"Why hello, Miss . . ."

"Julip Durham, sir."

"Of course. Sam Hinckley called from up in Starke. A fine lawyer. He said your family wished to reopen the case of your unfortunate brother. I'm certainly agreeable and I suspect the prosecutor will be agreeable as long as the young man is confined to a mental facility and receives proper care. I assume Sam told you that under Florida's victim law there can be no change in status without due consultation with the victims. While they certainly don't have the final word on your brother's release to another facility, their feelings on the matter must be considered."

"Of course, sir." She was enchanted by his resonant baritone and wouldn't have minded sitting on his lap and talking about the weather. The other two men had drawn closer and were looking at her appraisingly with a predator's fake grin. The judge made the slightest of bows and they were gone. She heard them chortling out in the hall but simply didn't give a shit because things were finally going well. She couldn't believe the luck involved in the drunken lawyer with the limp noodle actually doing what he said he would do.

She checked into a cheapish motel up near Dennis Pharmacy, where she had her favorite Key West lunch of black beans and rice, safe from discovery by the Boys since none of them would conceive of eating in a drugstore. She spoke in pidgin Spanish to the plump Cuban waitress who seemed glad to see her again, then bent her head low as one of Charles's previous girlfriends passed by. Or was it Arthur's, or Ted's? It was hard to figure out, but the same girl had congratulated Julip in the Full Moon Saloon, on her first trip two years before, for being that year's "lust slave." The girl was sincere, if a bit daffy, though the Boys were uneager to answer any questions on the matter.

Back in her motel Julip dressed in a sleeveless blouse, white shorts tight across her bottom, and sandals, putting a dab of lavender scent on her neck. The outfit and scent tended to send all of them into a hormonal trance. She called Mildred as promised, chatted briefly, with Mildred closing on a poignant note of advice: "Go for their nuts." Julip said she'd do her best, though at the moment she was anxious to see them, in the same way one checks a watch and looks out the window waiting for an old friend. She certainly didn't know that over the past twenty years three of the house fräuleins, or lust slaves, had eventually died, though that may not be an odd statistic for the girls that yearly stream into Key West for the sun and other possibilities.

On the walk to Martello Towers and the pier, she was struck again by the dazzling sun and heat, the flowering shrubs, the sheer number of mangy guard dogs within fenced yards, the dank quiver the un-picked-up garbage full of rotten shrimp shells caused in the pit of her stomach. It was a town where until evening it looked like everyone had just got up. She wondered again, while she stared at a rottweiler with a scarred face, how Bobby had managed to follow them around for a week without being noticed by her. When she asked him in jail before the trial, he whispered that he was "the hero with a thousand faces," another of his favorite books. He had waited to commit his crime until after Charles took her to the early morning plane. Now the rottweiler got up and wiggled toward the fence but she continued on, having read they had been misbred into unreliability like pit bulls. A client had stooped to a friend's springer and bared his teeth in a smile and had got the tip of his nose bit off. Strangely, she thought, the asshole still thought he knew everything about bird dogs except how to keep from getting his nose bit off.

*

Only a few blocks away from the strolling Julip, Charles stood at the edge of the pool, looking down at the big bodies of Ted and Arthur circling in a dog paddle.

"You guys look like manatees," Charles said. "We're

trying to save the manatee and I guess we're succeeding."

It had been a tough day since Charles had wakened them with the news of Julip's imminent arrival. They had gone fishing for a half day anyway, staking on the Lavinia Bank off Cottrell Key, with the early visibility grotesque, the light flat, sweltering, and gray so that it was difficult to tell sky from water on the horizon. They saw several schools of tarpon, perceivable only by the wake through the water, a stray caudal fin, but blew the casts because the lead fish were generally deeper and completely invisible, the whole school surging off the flat when the fly and fly line hit the water. Around mid-morning there was a slight breeze from the southwest and the rippling effect on the water's surface made the fish more visible. Charles hooked and jumped out a smallish tarpon around fifty pounds, breaking the leader, as always, after a few minutes so the fish wouldn't become exhausted and susceptible to sharks. Over the years they had caught hundreds of tarpon and never killed one, believing that to mount a fish was a vulgar display.

By eleven the temperature was over ninety and they had finished their single gallon of water and split the only bottle of pop in the cooler, experiencing a horrible thirst caused by an involved Oriental meal they had made for two schoolteachers from Atlanta the evening before: dry-fried beef, a hot-and-sour crispy fish, shrimp with ginger and jalapeños, a Thai chicken-and-noodle salad which was far too hot for the schoolteachers, and "Taipan," a poached fresh ham with spinach. The teachers got very drunk, and they all went nude swimming after a few lines of their postdinner wake-up powder, cocaine. But then one of the teachers, who had a bad sunburn, kept shrieking "You guys are wild!" and puked in the bushes. Her friend took her home. The friend promised Arthur she would return but hadn't done so.

By late morning the thirst had become unbearable, which led them to the unbearable topic of Julip. "Maybe she's going to shoot us, one by one, in broad daylight," suggested Ted, never one to hold back an errant thought. "I'm not going to be surprised if I'm dead before dinner." He hopped up on the bow and brayed out across the water, "Today is a good day to die."

The ugly fact, discovered when thirst drove them in early, was that their hippy-dippy maid hadn't arrived and there was the crushing chore of unmade beds and filthy dishes covered with pissants and flies. Arthur busied himself counting exactly thirty-seven dirty glasses and kept yelling "Thirty-seven" as a litany until Charles drowned him out with old Carla Thomas–Otis Redding duets on the stereo. They felt virtuous, like sturdy peasants, cleaning up the mess until Ted discovered the maid had been there just long enough to find their Ziploc of cocaine, hidden inexpertly in the freezer under a pile of ginger and Chinese sausages. Ted, of a deeply paranoid nature, was the only one to mention the year before that some weirdo in a number of disguises had been following them, the weirdo turning out to be Bobby up there on the bridge, bapping away with his .22-caliber semiautomatic.

Back at the pool, Charles was ready to go meet Julip, then decided to fix drinks first. When he came back outside Ted was singing "We're heading for the last roundup," which irritated Arthur, who disliked beginnings and endings. They anxiously accepted their vodkas at the pool's edge.

"You know what deer are like in the summer?" Ted began to ruminate. "Maybe they'd kill themselves if they knew what was going to happen in the fall when they start getting shot. After that comes the winter when they die by the hundreds of thousands from starvation and disease. Just in case you guys don't know it, at our age we're living in November. It's all over but the bad part."

This spiel might have impressed Charles and Arthur had they not heard something similar several times a day. Ted looked at them and screamed, "I love her! I'm going to drown myself!" and he let out his air, sinking to the pool's bottom in a stream of bubbles. Arthur's eyes got misty as Charles made his way to the gate. Arthur called out, "Tell her I'll marry her," to which Charles responded, "Tell her yourself. You're next."

In previous times more slack would have been cut for this threesome, but this is an age when not much slack is cut for anyone. However otherwise accomplished, they were rounders, and we have always had rounders with us — probably every country club on the continent had a half-dozen members who behaved worse. "They all know we're assholes," said a writer friend of Ted's, meaning women. And it was the rock-bottom puzzlement of life and time: there is an ideal woman who will return to you the kind of sexual life you could have had at nineteen but didn't. That this was not meant to be for man on Earth did not stop millions of fools from looking. It was puzzlement, pure and simple. A thousand dollars in the wallet wasn't proportionately more pleasurable than a ten-spot. Honors were dreary, the mail and phone calls were to be avoided. The horizon was as invisible as it was when they were nineteen, but now its nature was deeply sensed. An actual surprise would have astounded them now that their time was sliced so precise and thin. They were unquestionably kind and generous men, polite in mixed company, loaning money in bulk to less fortunate friends, still flipping books of poems open at random, hoping for secrets. And they all knew that in a traditional culture they would be busy by now learning how to be Elders. But this was America and you weren't supposed to stop the generalized churning until you announced retirement or, more simply, the lights were turned out.

*

Out on the pier Julip was immersed in a delicious breeze that had picked up when the afternoon wind shifted westerly. She was on the lee side of the island and the water was a clear sandy beige near shore, deepening to bright then darker turquoise out farther where the water picked up the wind, and beyond that, the mauve penumbra of the Gulf Stream moving north.

She wondered at the idea that she could be so sunk in her problems that she had forgotten the beauty of the ocean. The first year she came down, Ted and Arthur hadn't arrived yet so Charles took her fishing for three days, mostly in the backcountry, a wilderness of tidal cuts, mangrove islets abutting the Gulf where she had been transfixed by the cormorants, frigate birds, pelicans, ospreys, skimmers, three rare roseate spoonbills, and the multifoliate sea life that passed under the boat when they were staked for tarpon. One hot afternoon she and Charles had smoked a joint and rubbed each other with mango slices and made love on the rough deck of the skiff, with Charles on the bottom to save her skin. The only bad thing that day, running home from the Gulf side, was the smell of an enormous beached sperm whale. And worse than that, men were cutting the valuable teeth from the whale's mouth with chain saws, the great domed forehead of the whale making the men look puny.

When she saw Charles way back on the beach coming toward her, she remembered Bobby had told her that she had free will and she became instantly pissed. The only class she'd cared for at junior college had been an introduction to anthropology where a very old English feminist taught them that in nearly all cultures in the history of humankind men had worked to deprive women of their free will. The girls in the class who weren't dumb as posts seethed with resentment. Several times the teacher had Julip and a couple of other girls over for tea and cookies, and they were all awed at the number and beauty of the artifacts their teacher had collected in a lifetime of fieldwork around the world. She had taught at the University of Chicago and had been on the staff of the Field Museum before coming north for retirement and teaching part time. She allowed that she had even slept with Cree men during a long winter on Hudson's Bay in the early fifties. Julip felt if she hadn't been destined as a dog trainer she would have emulated this woman, whom the boys in the class called Old Turnip.

The reverie slipped away as Charles neared in his peculiar rolling gait. He was shy enough to avert his glance as if fascinated with the water he'd spent half his life on. He offered his hand and she took it, then he tried to hold on and she withdrew hers.

"You're looking good," he said. "Did you wear that outfit to torment me?"

"Of course not. Have you been sick?" He had aged far more than a year and there was a mottled pallor beneath the tan.

"Caught amebic dysentery in Africa. I was following this tribe called the Tuaregs around. It's complicated shitting yourself to death when there aren't any toilets."

"I bet," she said. "You always read cookbooks on the toilet. You said it all went together." He blushed and they laughed.

"What can I do for you? I can't think of anything I wouldn't do for you." He turned away with the curious shyness that affected him when nervous.

She breathed in deeply and spoke in a rush. "If you and the others agree, the judge can order that Bobby be released from prison into a mental place, you know, where they can cure his delusions."

"Of course. Don't be silly. Fine by me."

Her eyes began to tear and she turned away. He put a hand on her shoulder and she shrugged it off. "What do you think the others will say?"

"Arthur will agree. I don't know about Ted. He's been hitting it hard. Also, he's a paranoid."

"How come when we first fell in love and came down here . . ." Her voice trailed off because she hadn't expected to ask the question. "What I'm asking is why didn't you want me to be faithful?"

"I told you. Because I was married and it didn't seem fair to you." It was Charles's turn again to avoid a glance.

"It's not normal. I loved you and I didn't want to be handed away."

"I had no idea you'd seen them until after the shooting, really not until the trial."

"I don't mean just them. To anyone. I felt like a throw-away, you know. A real expensive toy. You paid for the tickets. That's a lot in some places. And the car, which is a lot more. I got the feeling you didn't want any responsibility for me. Is that it?"

Charles turned abruptly and walked out to the end of the pier, another fifty yards. Even at that distance she could see he was becoming very angry. One evening on the deck of the Pier House they had had a bad meal and Charles threw the whole table into the ocean.

"Then why did you fucking come back the next year?" he bellowed.

"I thought I'd try again," she screamed. "You were nice to me! You bought me presents!" She closed the distance, arms across her chest. They'd also had a fine time in the summer when he came up to work his bird dogs, ignorant of the fact that she'd just visited Ted, his closest friend, in New York. Now he stared at her, his anger vanishing.

"Let's run away," he said, simply enough.

"To Wisconsin. You can help with the dogs, you mean? I guess we wore out the chance to run away."

"We could get married if you like."

"You're already married. And I'm too young for you."

"I'd get divorced. When I got too old you could farm me out and grab someone younger."

"I don't want to get married or run away. I want my free will. I just want to love someone and not get fucked over."

There was a long silence while a jet landed at the airport a mile away, wobbling in the increasing wind. She looked away when he wiped his tears on his shirttails. "I guess it's Arthur's turn. I'll do all I can to spring your brother." He walked past her, back down the pier.

"You coming back at six?" she said, in barely more than a whisper. She wasn't letting him off with being noble.

"Why not?" He turned with a resolute smile. "I'll bring a joint. You'll probably need it after Ted."

She watched him all the way back to the beach where Arthur was lurking under a palm tree with a paper sack in his hand. She felt tremendously queasy about Charles, wondering how you could love someone that much, then have it all dissipate like it had with her high school sweetheart, Johnny. There was the pathetic, anguished feeling of living within a pop tune sung by any of a hundred singers she loathed. She still had genuine emotions and it was difficult to endure the fake. She remembered when she was ten, visiting Marcia just before Marcia's mother died. Her mother was drunk in their house in Georgetown and playing Janis Joplin's *Pearl* at top volume. Julip ran out into the backyard, trying to distance herself a little from the pain in the voice. She couldn't imagine how such a person managed to stay alive.

*

After Charles, Arthur was a tonic. He lumbered toward her with a big grin, carrying a good deal more weight this year than last. He was the kindest man she had ever known, though definitely certifiable in some respects. The year before, he had hired two call girls for an evening and one of them had told Julip she had counted every one of his thirty-two drinks, several grams of cocaine, plus the night-long wrestling. Yet he had wakened puzzled that he wasn't feeling well. "You must have a bug," the call girl told him and he had been pleased with the diagnosis. "There must be a bug going around this fucking town," he had muttered at breakfast.

Now as he neared he paused to look around with that peculiar expression painters have when they frame their surroundings.

"Boy, what an outfit. I'd give a king's ransom to stick my face in your ass, but fat chance for that. Once again I've been victimized by my love."

"You always were a bottom feeder. What was that fish you said you were like?" Marcia had accurately told her that older men spent a lot of time going down on girls because it restored their energies. Older guys kept their eyes open, she had said, while younger ones closed theirs, as if unsure they wanted to know what they were doing.

"The flounder," he said, dropping the notion that he was a victim of love, opening the sack in his hand. "One of the noblest fish. You got a choice between a Pepsi or a fresh lemonade with Stoli. Also I brought you a sandwich. You're looking too thin. Eat or die, that's what Ted says."

"Pepsi. I can't have any booze in my system if I have to deal with him. What did Charles tell you back on shore?"

"Nothing. The prick wouldn't tell me anything. He said I liked surprises. I also made you a sandwich. The best imported *foie gras* on Cuban bread." Arthur liked surprises and confusion, and nothing thrilled him like a real mess that was resolved happily and immediately.

She bit into the sandwich wondering how to begin. Why did the Boys eat food so rich it made your cheekbones tickle? "It's real simple. Bobby can get out of this terrible prison, Raiford, if you agree to him being sent to a nut house."

"Of course. Why not? Maybe he'll shoot us again. It was by far the most interesting thing that happened to me last year. I'm sending you a painting and the name of a dealer in Chicago, so if you go broke on the dogs, the dealer will take it off your hands."

"I can't believe that," she teased. He had a legendary tendency to offer paintings to ladies.

"Let's go to the fucking phone pronto. I'll call the gallery. I'm also offering this genius hand in marriage." He put out his right hand, his eyes brimming with tears.

"Oh, for God's sake. You're on your fourth marriage."

"I don't disagree. But it's waning."

"I can't marry you. When I'm thirty, you'll be almost sixty."

"But you told me in San Francisco I was twelve. I didn't think you'd accept but I wanted to ask anyhow. Also I was wondering if you could get me a photo. I know Charles took these sexy pictures of you but he won't let me see them or give me one."

"Of course." Julip blushed. At the Mark Hopkins in San Francisco she had looked at a dog-eared magazine in Arthur's open suitcase and had been appalled at the stop-action pictures of jism flying through the air toward the waiting faces of women. When he came out of the shower she was hiding in the closet, having left a note on the open magazine on his pillow: "I'm leaving until you throw this sick piece of shit out the window." He looked around the room wildly, then flipped through the magazine, saying goodbye, went to the open window, and watched the magazine flutter to the street far below, whereupon she jumped out of the closet screaming with laughter.

"I thought you were gone." He was unnerved.

"Did you think I was down on the street waiting for the smut? How could you throw it out when some poor kid might find it and become a lifelong pervert." It was the kind of confusion that needed an immediate resolution. Later, when she asked him why he had the magazine in the first place, he'd only say, "I'm real visual."

Back at the pier, he asked for a goodbye kiss during which he was surprisingly polite. "Sure I can't fix you dinner? You're going to need some garlic after you see Ted."

"I don't know. It depends on what happens. Is he really that bad?"

"Yup, ready for the farm. Now just remember you can count on me to take care of you if your life goes haywire."

She bowed and off he walked down the pier, looking straight up in the air, fixed on cloud shapes. She craned to see if Ted was back there in the palm trees. She knew that every year or two Ted had to be sent away to dry out, either voluntarily or fueled by threats by his doctor, publisher, agent, and family. She turned, hearing a shout out at sea. It was Ted on a beach-rental Sunfish heading toward the end of the pier, screaming, "I can't control this fucking thing!" She ran out toward the point of impact and looked over the rail where he was swimming toward a ladder. He cut his hands on the coral-encrusted rungs, and when she helped him over the rail he said with stark simplicity, "The wounds of Christ."

"Why did you come this way? What about the boat?"

"Fuck the boat! The element of surprise. I see you're wearing those shorts to torture me."

Julip wandered over to the other side of the pier to collect herself. She was terrified when she looked back at him slumped dramatically to his haunches. If he were running at a field trial, his owner would have shot him as a mad dog. Maybe the judge would take two out of three and she should run for it herself.

"I talked to Charles," Ted began slowly, his voice so low she approached closely to hear. "I wasn't about to come out here without knowing what you wanted. You're asking me to die. Your brother is a psychopath and he'll strike again, so you're asking me to die. I'm the one that noticed him all that week. That fuck's a killer if there ever was one. But then I suppose I should die for you, you know, die for love. It would be a pure death. You would be killing me. Like in nature where the bugs eat each other."

Now he began to weep, a sodden middle-aged heap, leaning against the railing in a squat position, the dried salt water on his face now streaked with tears. For Julip there was the awful memory of her father during the last summer in Wisconsin when she was eighteen. He had come home terribly drunk from the tavern on a hot Saturday and her mother slapped him and he walked stumbling off into the woods. Julip took their best bitch, Rose, to track him down when it began to get dark, fearing that blackflies and mosquitoes would bite him to death. She packed water, matches, mosquito dope, and a flashlight in a daypack, and kept Rose on a tether so she wouldn't think they were looking for birds, and waved her dad's cap before Rose's face so she'd know what they were looking for. It was dark before she found him, sleeping against a white pine in his underpants, his body filthy with algae from taking a dip in a swamp pond where he'd taught her to hunt frogs. She rubbed his scrawny body with mosquito dope, started a fire, then looked for his clothes. When he woke up and gulped the water, he had that same look that Ted did now, nose pressed to an invisible wall he couldn't see beyond. Ted couldn't stop weeping so she knelt beside him and hugged him as she had her father.

"I'd be better off dead than the way I am now. I was thinking on that sailboat that if you would marry me, your brother wouldn't shoot me." He glanced sideways at her, suddenly bright-eyed with the idea.

"But you're already married."

At the hotel in New York he had talked to his wife on the telephone, mostly whining to her, as Julip read on the couch beside him. He had hired a car and driver to take her around the city while he made dozens of phone calls, but she had sent the driver back to the hotel and had taken the Circle Line boat tour around Manhattan. What an incredible and gorgeous city, Julip had thought, and if she weren't a dog trainer she might live there for a while. On the boat she sat between two dorky servicemen from Kansas because an old man up on the bow had scared her by whispering obscenities. Back at the hotel Ted was on the phone again with his wife, whining about the afternoon spent on the phone.

"I know I'm married but your brother probably doesn't. That's what counts." He rose to his feet with a manic smile. "All you have to do is send him a copy of our marriage license, for Christ's sake, don't you get it? Then he wouldn't shoot me."

"I don't see how you're going to get an actual filled-out marriage license." She suspected he hadn't been taking his lithium, which he always said dried up his creative juices.

"How do you think I got my private detective's license?" He looked into his thick wet wallet, drawing out a full inch of bent-over hundred-dollar bills. He gave her five of them as an afterthought. "Buy yourself a pretty dress," he said, and began to walk away. She followed, trying to give back the money, but he waved her off. "I love you so much I could die, but I'm not going to. The fact is I'm too fucking smart to die for the time being."

By the time they walked off the pier, Ted was merrily telling her a Hollywood joke. She had always thought it odd that as a writer he couldn't tell a joke or story worth a shit. He'd jump from the beginning to the end, then back to the middle, get lost in a recipe, a new bird he'd possibly discovered, an ignored book from 1937, or why his left boot was wearing out faster than his right. He gave her a chaste kiss just as Charles stepped out from behind a palm tree with his binoculars around his neck. Ted gave him the thumbs-up and rushed off. Charles sighed and took out the promised joint.

"Why were you spying on us? He's harmless." Julip was well past tired of protective attitudes that ended up with someone wagging his dick in your face, the easy step from altruism to desire.

"He mentioned drowning himself," Charles said, passing her the lit joint. She refused it, wanting to feel normal for a while. "I didn't want you trying to save a two hundred pounder. I called his wife and said he's ready for his retreat. She said he has been for months."

They walked hard for a solid hour in silence after she briefly explained Ted's marriage license plan.

"What are you going to do for your wedding night?" Charles joked. "I thought if anyone, it should be me. I discovered you."

"I'm sleeping with Emily Dickinson." She let her "discovery" pass as they walked, thinking of the bumper sticker she'd seen in Kentucky on the way down: "Wherever you go, that's where you are." It was disturbingly direct, and that was the wonderful thing about Charles — he knew when there wasn't anything to say and you could walk a whole hour in peace. You could be where you are without being totally addled. The only time Ted had come up to Wisconsin, he had arrived with closely cropped hair and two zafus, cushions for Zen sitting, declaring somewhat like Bobby that he was becoming a Zen monk. She and Ted walked off into the woods and sat on the cushions for an hour during which he did a great deal of fidgeting. She did not tell him this was essentially the same thing she did every dawn after the long run with the dogs. She would make them all sit down for nearly an hour for discipline in utterly alert stillness, their ears perking, noses wiggling, eyes rolling toward her as they sat under the white pine her father wandered to when he was terminally drunk. Ted and Zen seemed the same mix as her dad and AA.

*

They stopped at her motel room where Charles dozed on the bed with a baseball game on TV while she made several calls, first to Sam Hinckley, the lawyer up in Starke. He congratulated her on the progress, but given the "volatility of the situation" he asked her to get the Boys to sign a simple statement that they agreed to Bobby's transferral. She thanked him and tore out a back page from her dog diary, composed the statement, then called her mother, who said that Mr. Stearne's lawyer was looking into places near Washington for Bobby. Julip noted that her mother's voice was acquiring a more refined accent but decided it wasn't the time to mention it. In the background she could hear ricky-ticky music. Mr. Stearne was known to possess one of the world's largest collections of Dixieland records, a music she found insufferable.

"I'd feel better if Bobby were in a place where I could visit. These days a mother's love is underrated. I should add that Marcia called after visiting Bobby. I just pray that you become a fine young lady like Marcia."

"You've been praying a lot lately," Julip quipped, buying time. It would be fun in a sick way to be around when Bobby ran off with Marcia to be married. "But I want to thank you for the help. You've been a real peach."

"I always tried to be a good mother, Julip."

"I know. We're all living proof that nobody's perfect. I'll call when I get home."

Julip put down the phone and selected a skirt and blouse. Despite the heat, the shorts could be stored now that her mission was nearly accomplished. She refused to meet Charles's pleading glance and headed into the shower. It occurred to her she had forgotten the final element, the prosecutor, but then he was the one who tried to work out the asylum compromise Bobby had refused.

Just to be a bitch she came out of the shower in the cheap, skimpy towel the motel offered and made the call and appointment for the next morning. She dried off in front of the air conditioner, just out of Charles's reach, turning slowly in the cool breeze and making a feeble attempt to keep covered with the wet towel. She was pleased to note that his hand tried to cover the hard-on under his khaki shorts.

"Do you love your mother?" she asked. "I'm just curious." She snapped the towel at his hand.

"Why are you doing this?"

"Just answer my question. Do you love your mother? Then you can take it out."

"I love my mother," he said, taking out his erect dick and blushing.

"That's an odd thing to talk about when you're thinking about fucking. Shame on you. Now I want you to close your eyes and count to one backwards from ten. Actually, put the pillow over your face."

"Ten . . . nine . . . eight . . ." came Charles's voice, muffled under the pillow. She arranged herself, hovering over him, aiming his dick with a hand. When he reached one, she thrust down, screaming "Bingo!" and rotating her bottom as if she were working a pepper grinder. She noted by the bedside clock that he lasted a scant twenty-three seconds. He mooed like a pissed-off cow and she rolled off screeching with laughter. It took a full minute before he could laugh, and then rather weakly, more like a cough.

"Quite a joke," he said, putting his hand on his chest as if to still his heart's thumping.

"I just wanted to get the job done," she said, kissing him.

*

You can always tell what kind of boy a man was, because that's what they still are under the veil of physical growth, or so Julip thought as she swam laps in the Boys' backyard pool. Charles was in a post-coital slump that reminded her of Bobby's surly daze that always told her he had probably been in his bedroom or out in his hideout masturbating. Sitting by the pool with a drink, Charles was slack-jawed and remote, trying to give the impression of being lost in thought. She paused in mid-lap to tease him out of his mood, resting her bare breast on the pool's edge.

"May I have a sip of your drink, sir?" she asked, then examined her breasts with a worried look.

"Something wrong?" he asked, stooping and offering her his Scotch.

"Just lately I think one has grown smaller. It keeps me up nights with worry."

"Nonsense. They're the same. Perfectly lovely. You're being a hypochondriac."

"Don't call me that, goddammit. You guys spend hours worrying about your weenies. The left one is definitely smaller."

Charles touched her left breast tentatively, as if he might be splashed or stopped. The life was returning to his eyes. Over his shoulder she noticed Arthur, who was making her favorite dinner, peering out the kitchen window, and she gave him the finger. His head darted back, discovered again. The year before while making love to Charles she had seen Arthur's big nose around the edge of a doorjamb and had thrown a nearly full can of Pepsi which sailed expertly through the door crack, hitting the wall of the hall and splashing the voyeur.

"We could weigh them on the coke scale," Charles suggested with enthusiasm.

"Oh, never mind." She continued swimming laps, listening to the rumbling approach of a thunderstorm and watching the first spatter of raindrops on the pool's surface. She aimed to swim off her nervousness over Ted. The others had signed the paper on the kitchen counter, both with a kindly flourish, but Ted hadn't returned from his wedding license mission. Arthur said he had burst in, showered, shaved, then dressed in a summer suit and tie, and was off, all the time singing "Born Free," which he did to grate Arthur's nerves.

Now the thunderstorm increased in intensity and Charles and Arthur were shouting from the patio door, saying that she'd be electrocuted in the water. She swam on in the deluge, her stomach tingling with the scent of Arthur's manicotti coming out the kitchen window. Never one to small-time it, Arthur usually made three kinds, on this occasion her favorites: fresh lobster, spinach and ricotta, and Italian sausage with basil and ricotta, all with different sauces. The Boys proudly felt they had pioneered ordering multiple entrées in restaurants — they could not bear being disappointed in matters of food, and three entrées were a minimum in their home cooking because, as Ted said, you couldn't stop at two, what with even numbers being unlucky. In phone calls, visits, and letters over the more than two years she had known them, they had announced the collective loss of over a thousand pounds in their dieting.

Now there was a particularly loud and ragged crash of lightning and Charles and Arthur rushed out yelling incoherently at her. Jesus, she thought, but then the thunder was deafening, the sound throbbing the water in the pool. She became a little frightened, moving to the edge of the pool where they each grabbed an arm and plucked her out, running for the patio door.

She stood in the kitchen shivering in her undies as they continued to sputter angrily at her. She hugged herself and said, "Yes, Daddy, I'm sorry, Daddy," trying to make a joke of the whole thing, then immediately wished she could suck the words back like a reversed tape. The lights flickered off and on and the men looked so stricken she thought she could see the skulls beneath their skin. They looked down, up, and away but not at her, with Charles giving off a strangled cough and Arthur gazing up at the ceiling fan.

"God, I'm sorry," she said. "What a stupid thing to say."

*

She sat in Charles's bedroom for about an hour until the rain stopped at twilight, then put on her skirt and blouse, wishing she had a dry pair of underwear. She checked the dresser drawers, putting on a pair of Charles's Jockeys to amuse herself, tucking them up under her skirt waist so they wouldn't fall down, then went out to the dining room where Arthur and Charles were sitting on a sofa morosely listening to Spanish guitar music. She flopped down between them, taking a hand of each.

"I refuse to accept that I fucked up my last night in town," she said, and Arthur patted her head as a father would. They listened to a man and woman yelling down the street but ignored it, as public quarrels are nothing extraordinary in Key West.

"Sticks and stones can break my bones but words can never hurt me," Arthur said without conviction. He got up and put the pans of manicotti in the oven, then said, "Love is no fun." He opened a magnum of wine and poured himself an enormous glass.

Charles gave her a hug and got up to make a salad. Julip went over to help and he pinched her ass. "I'm going to start fucking women my own age. I wonder where they hang out," he said, gulping down Arthur's glass of wine as if it were water.

"I'd call Midnight if Ted wasn't such a geek," Arthur said, then looked through his wallet for the number. Midnight was an enormous Cuban whore whom Ted found threatening but Arthur adored. Julip had seen her at the Winn-Dixie supermarket with her two little boys and they had chatted about school problems.

The kitchen air conditioner was on the blink and both Arthur and Charles were sweating profusely, which gave her the idea for a trick. She pushed them back against the counter and began jumping straight up and down until Charles's underpants slipped down to her ankles. She picked the garment up and wiped the sweat off their faces and shoulders. It was so direct and simple-minded that they were thrilled, but then they heard more yelling, a police siren, and the unmistakable sound of Ted's voice rising above the other noise.

*

At first it was difficult to sort out the mess. Ted was sitting on the sidewalk steps in front of a trim bungalow, holding a clumsily picked bouquet of flowers and a large plastic sack of stone crab claws. He was being guarded by an old woman with a poised walking stick and an old man holding a pistol to his head, plus a minuscule Jack Russell terrier. Julip recognized one of the two cops as Mike, who always winked at her or chatted when she was having lunch at Dennis Pharmacy.

While the other cop was trying to reason with Ted and the old folks, Mike was waving a few curiosity seekers away, including Charles and Arthur, who had reached the scene just before Julip. Mike whispered to her, "This is one of your boyfriends, right? Don't worry, that's a fake pistol, a fucking squirt gun. The guy's a fucking nut case, kiddo." Mike waved his billy club at Ted, whose face was garishly lit by the bubble on the cop car, his jaw clenched in self-righteousness, lucidly drunk as he babbled an explanation to the other cop.

"When I was on a Guggenheim and went to Sweden all flowers, even those on private property, were deemed public property. In short, in civilized countries, including England and France, one can pick a bouquet at random."

"Who gives a fuck about foreigners? You came in my yard and picked our flowers," the old man yelled.

"Arrest this hippie shitheel!" the old lady demanded.

"Hippie? It's strange to call the olive oil king of Florida a hippie. This suit cost me a grand. And I'm keeping the flowers. I've been shot in the head before and it doesn't mean shit to me."

The other cop turned to Mike and Julip in despair. Julip asked Mike if she could try, and he led her into the light.

"Ted, it's me. Did you get the license? Did you get our marriage license, darling?"

Ted glanced up at Julip as if she were a space alien, then he slowly recognized her and tried to reach into his pocket. The old man shrieked "Nothing doing!" so Julip leaned over and plucked the license from his suit-coat pocket, handing it to the old lady.

"Phony baloney," the old woman said, with less strain than before.

"We're supposed to be married tonight." Julip detached the sack of stone crab claws from Ted's grasp and handed them to the old lady. "This should be a fair trade for the flowers."

"Thanks," said the old lady, reaching into the sack. "These are big suckers."

"They cost me seventy bucks," Ted whined. "They're our wedding dinner."

"I want a hundred bucks for the flowers or I'm pressing charges on this crumb-bum," the old man hissed.

Julip reached inside the small watch pocket of her skirt, drew out one of the hundred-dollar bills Ted had given her to buy a new dress, and handed it to the old man, who was delighted. Feeling antic, he squirted Ted with the fake pistol. Ted fell backward, screaming, "I'm blinded!"

The old man cackled, "It's just a little ammonia and water to keep stray dogs from pissing on the flowers!" He retreated to his porch where his wife stood with the stone crab claws. Julip ignored Ted and leaned over to pet the Jack Russell terrier, who was a feisty little sweetheart.

*

Back at the house, they rinsed Ted's eyes — only one was a little pink — and sat him down to sign Julip's release form. "Whiskey," he muttered, still refusing to let go of the flowers tightly grasped in his right hand. At first he said he couldn't sign because the flowers were "locked eternally" in his writing hand and he would finally have to be buried with these "deliquescent" flowers. Julip was so nervous she studied the marriage license, her first; when I'm thirty-one he'll be fifty-seven, she thought idly. Charles became angry at Ted's coy refusal, then Arthur took over, keeping a water glass of whiskey just out of Ted's reach and guiding his left hand through a clumsy signature. Ted gulped at the whiskey, spilling half of it down his shirt, his eyes wobbling as he gazed lovingly across the table with the same bleary affection as her father.

"Now the little prick can't shoot his very own brother-in-law." He began to hiccup from the jolt of straight whiskey. "It's time to hit the sack, babycakes, my virgin bride." He lurched to his feet and Charles saved him from falling backward, guiding him over to the couch where he was instantly asleep, snoring mightily. Arthur had to put on a B. B. King tape to make dinner possible.

*

It was a fine goodbye dinner indeed, washed down with three magnums of Ruffino Barolo, though Julip sipped sparingly. Charles pried open a wooden box holding a bottle of Sire de Gouberville calvados and they all marveled at its autumnal flavors. Julip only sniffed it and imagined she was walking through an orchard after the first big frost, the windfall apples crunching under her feet. These guys sure have a lot of ways of getting there, she thought, remembering how her father stuck to the pints of Four Roses or Guckenheimer he stowed everywhere.

By tradition there would have been a few lines of wake-up cocaine and a tour of some bars but the maid's theft had negated that and neither Charles nor Arthur wanted to check around for any street stuff. Their regular man was a circumspect landscape architect who only dealt in daylight hours to avoid the last-minute riffraff. Then Arthur admitted it was probably his fault the coke was gone. A few days before, when the afternoon's fishing had been rained out and Ted and Charles were at the supermarket, he had tried to seduce the scruffy maid he had discovered sleeping stoned and in the nude on the pool's diving board, guarded by the dog she took everywhere. The dog was ordinarily amiable but not when it felt its mistress was endangered. Arthur was kept at a distance and the dog threatened him back into the house. He woke her by yelling and waving the bag of dope out the window, whereupon she came to him like a zombie, and he neatly shut out the dog after she entered the house. The upshot was that she must have seen where he stored the bag.

"You asshole," Charles said, smiling but drowsy. He put his hand on Julip's and suddenly his eyes brimmed with tears. She held a finger to her lips so he wouldn't say anything. Arthur was resting his chin on his arms, his eyes barely open but open enough to form tears, and then he was asleep.

Charles got up with difficulty and stumbled to his Barcalounger, covering his face with his hands in a lame attempt to be manly. She took an afghan from the couch, where

Ted continued his snoring, and covered Charles. Ted's face looked like her father's as he'd slept in the car that morning in blissful sedation against his terrors, real and imagined, it didn't matter which. She massaged Charles's neck, standing behind him so he needn't be embarrassed by his tears.

"I'll still train your dogs," she said.

"That's it?" he murmured.

"That's it." She massaged his neck for a few more minutes until his head tilted forward in sleep, then she gathered up the paper for the judge and the marriage license, which she would keep as an absurd souvenir. Before leaving she glanced at each of them and for the briefest chilling moment they looked like petrified babies suspended in dreamless sleep. It certainly was a struggle to have fun, she thought, walking out into the night, a dank and rotting blossom, the low-tide scent sweeping lazily over the city.

*

Julip slept the sleep of the righteous and was at the Monroe County courthouse when it opened, dropping off her makeshift signed form at the judge's office, then on to the prosecutor down the hall. He was late for work and she sat there listening to the receptionist whistle poorly until he came in, looking like he had slept in his car and not alone. He poured himself a cup of coffee and offered her one, which she declined, showing her into his office.

"You have the look of someone leaving town in a hurry," he said.

"Yes sir. I've got work to do back home." She noted that he had the accent of some of her father's hunting friends from Mississippi.

"I talked to Hinckley up in Starke, also to the judge. I'm going to have to insist on at least a year's detainment for your brother at a mental facility — more, of course, if deemed necessary. The psychologist of record, Wiseman, seems to think his delusions were caused by the death of his father, abandonment by his mother, the defilement of his baby sister by some rich playboys."

"I'm actually a year older," Julip interjected.

"Where I come from in Greenville, Mississippi, you're still the baby sister."

"Yes sir. Did you use that word 'defilement' at the trial?"

"Yes. Probably. I always liked the word, don't you? I think I said that despite the fact that his sister had been defiled, the young man had no right to take the law into his own hands. Why?"

"I just wondered. I want to thank you." Julip got up, feeling a little lightheaded at the end of the road.

"If you're still around at noon, I'd like to take you to lunch," he said, showing her to the door.

Just for fun she gave him the open-faced "anything is possible" look Marcia had taught her. "Maybe next time I'm down here," she said.

*

By noon Julip was in a phone booth at the north end of Seven Mile Bridge, offering Mildred to spend a day working Jung if she wanted, since the next day was Saturday. Mildred accepted, inviting her to stay that night, even though Julip was going to arrive late, because it was full moon and she and her husband were going to be up late drinking Bordeaux and watching all the film versions of *A Midsummer Night's Dream.* After Julip hung up the phone she stared at the heavy southbound traffic heading from Miami down the Keys, glad she was going in the other direction. A girl in a red convertible was beeping aimlessly, stuck behind a line of slow-moving pickups trailering boats. She looked closer, startled to see that it was Marcia, no doubt heading south to help her out with the Boys. She was certainly welcome. Despite the heat Julip shivered, waiting until Marcia's car was well out on the bridge before she walked to her own car and headed north, eager to get back to the dogs.

The Seven-Ounce Man

I

BACK HOME

IT WAS THE DARKEST and coldest summer of the century in the Upper Peninsula, or so everyone said. When in groups people spoke in muffled dirge noises; alone, their soul speech was a runt-of-the-litter whimper. If you were awake the night of the summer solstice, perhaps driving home from a tavern, you saw snowflakes. You wanted them to be a hatch of summer bugs but they were definitely snowflakes. Then the night of the Glorious Fourth, when multicolored pyrotechnic bombs burst in the air over Escanaba's harbor, folks huddled in their heated cars or sat on blankets in their snowmobile suits. By dawn every tomato plant in town lay supine under a crust of hoarfrost. The sturdier peas survived but the pods were already atrophied by the frigid dankness of June.

It was to be a summer without the pleasures of sweet corn, tans, beach parties, and most disastrously, tourism. Bridge crossings over the "mighty Mackinac" dropped to an all-time low along with beer sales. A trickle of diehard, dour downstaters with shiny vehicles arrived — RVs towing compact cars that in turn towed boats — but few of them other than the campers, known locally as bologna eaters, unlike the most welcome kind of tourists who stayed in motels and ate in restaurants. Even the bears suffered and became scrawny from the failure of the wild berry crop, invading the outskirts of town for garbage cans and toothsome household pets.

*

Since Brown Dog was not given to lolling on beaches he did not mind the weather which stayed right around a daytime high of forty-nine degrees, actually his favorite temperature among all the possibilities. He liked the symmetry involved in the idea that his favorite driving speed and temperature were the same. His grandpa had always said that nobody ever got killed driving below fifty so Brown Dog kept it at forty-nine, kissing the inside limit of fatality. The real problem was that he no longer had his own vehicle, what with Rose totaling the old Dodge van against a birch tree on her way home from her job cleaning the Indian casino. He visited the junkyard as if it were a grave site, fondly patting the undamaged parts, caressing the metallic wounds, a lump forming in his throat as he said goodbye to his beloved vehicle.

Where Brown Dog hurt the most, though, was in the double pocket of love and money. The truth was that he was out of both, the pockets utterly empty, and there didn't seem to be a philosophical or theological palliative for the condition. The presence of one somewhat consoles the absence of the other, and when one possesses neither, the soul is left sucking a very bad egg indeed — say, one that got nudged into a corner of straw in the hen house and was discovered far too many months later. What's more, he was dealing with a bum knee from a logging accident, and the five percent of the net profits from the Wild Wild Midwest Show had not "eventuated," as they say these days.

*

The October before, he had rediscovered his childhood sweetheart, Rose, though it must be said that Rose had never offered a single gesture of affection in their youth, and she wasn't overly forthcoming in the present. To think of her as a sweetheart at all would be called a far reach, in sailing terms. She was born mean, captious, sullen, with occasional small dirty windows of charm. The pail of pig slop she had dumped on Brown Dog's head when he was the neighbor boy might have been a harbinger for a sensible man, but as a sentimentalist he was always trying to get at the heart of something that frequently didn't have a heart. For instance, the afternoon Brown Dog had showed up after twenty-five years and taken off with Rose's ten-year-old son, Red, and seven-year-old retarded (fetal alcohol syndrome) daughter, Berry, for the first taxi ride for any of them, all the way up to Marquette to retrieve Brown Dog's van, he had returned to discover that Rose had drunk ten of the twelve beers he had dropped off, plus eaten most of the two chickens. There was a leg apiece for Berry and Red, and two wings for Brown Dog. Rose grandly split the remaining two beers with him, which made the score eleven to one. Her mother, Doris, only said, affably enough, that Rose was a pig.

Still, it was a homecoming, and when he stepped outside to quell his anger (and hunger) in the cold air he was amazed that Fate had brought him back, with her peculiar circuitry, to the small farm where his grandfather had raised him. It was a pretty good feeling that after the real threat of prison he had arrived back here even though the home was no longer his. But well behind his boyhood love for Rose and its resurgence at the not very tender age of forty-two, back in some primitive dovecote, there was the worry that he might not be invited to stay. The Son of Man might not have a place to lay his head, he remembered from the Bible, and this was not allayed by the nine hundred bucks in his pocket. He was one of the few poor people in creation who actually knew that money didn't buy happiness, this knowledge due to the fact that he always squandered money at touch, which left the dullish feeling of a head cold.

The front door opened behind him and he braced himself against the rotting porch railing without turning around. He hoped it was Rose asking him to stay, almost prayed though he had no verbs in his possession that might get a prayer going. He felt the retarded Berry clutching his leg, whispering insistently something that sounded like "whooper." He turned to see Rose standing somewhat groggily at the door.

"Ma says I should ask you to stay. There's no room out of the way except under the kitchen table. I need the couch for TV."

"Thank you. May as well." He looked down at Berry who continued her whispered incantation. "What does she want? What's 'whooper'?"

"Her and Red want Whoppers. Make yourself useful."

*

At the Burger King they ate Whoppers, largish burgers loaded with condiments, and Brown Dog tried to make some plans. There was a specific peaceful feeling of being here with the kids like a real father, and the mood lent itself to thinking about his future. The authorities had allowed him a single day to return to Grand Marais and pick up his belongings, but he doubted it was worth the three-hour drive to gather a winter coat, boots, and an old single-shot .22 rifle. He'd call Frank at the Dunes Saloon and have him hold the stuff.

It surely was time to take stock, as Grandpa would say. Brown Dog shuddered at his two brushes with prison, the first as a salvage diver when he found the dead Indian down in fifty feet of water for fifty years, perfectly preserved in the icy waters of Lake Superior, then stealing the ice truck in an attempt to transport the body to Chicago, followed by the arson of the anthropologist's tent and camping equipment — all to protect the secret Indian graveyard from certain excavation, the only Hopewell site in the northern Midwest. His so-called girlfriend, Shelley, was right on the money as Eve in the original Garden tempting him, or so he thought, barely noting the commotion that had begun to gather around him at the Burger King. His beloved Shelley, whose pinkish body he had tried to memorize that morning at first light before the meeting with the detective, lawyer, graduate student, and Shelley herself, where he diffidently marked the graveyard site on the map, was given a thousand dollars, and once again was forgiven for his mayhem.

His mouth was full of now tepid Whopper when he realized that the yelling was directed at him. A short man in a uniform was shouting, "Get her out of here," his prominent Adam's apple bobbing. Brown Dog then noted that Berry was jumping from table to table. Red had given up in embarrassment and was standing outside, looking in the window with the strange grin young boys affect when the nervous shit hits the fan.

"She's not right in the head," Brown Dog said, standing and making a shattering whistle at Berry, then closing in and missing the grab. Many diners were standing as she leapt the tables, making the cries and voices of birds and animals. When Brown Dog caught her she clutched his body like a frightened cat. He barely heard the shrieked insults of the restaurant employee: "You Indians catch all our fish, shoot all our deer, get drunk, and can't mind your own children, you welfare bastards." That sort of thing. But then the voice trailed off into a gurgle. Brown Dog turned to see a gawky, rawboned younger woman in a black turtleneck sweater shaking the man by the throat.

"Shut up, you racist pig, you piece of filth," she hissed.

*

Back at Rose's, he brought in his second-best war-surplus sleeping bag (the best was back in the cabin near Grand Marais) and arranged it under the table where Rose's mother, Doris, had pointed out a place. Both mother and daughter were watching a tiny TV with a cloudy picture. During a commercial Rose turned to him with a winning smile that fluttered his heart.

"Could I trouble you to get me a six-pack?" she asked with an imitation pout.

He crawled out from under the table wearing what he assumed was a sexy smile, though by then Rose's attention was fixed again on the television. He stood near the couch squinting at the wretched set. It required a lot of imagination to detect the outlines of floating images.

"Looks like you could use a new TV. Want me to pick one up with the beer?"

It was a real big-shot line, but not one he would regret since he had always proved himself an anti-magnet for money. Their reaction was slow but the brown chins of Rose and old Doris turned upward to him as he rocked confidently on his heels, the kind of physical gesture brought to success by the late actor Steve McQueen.

"How come you're talking new TV? You don't got a pot to piss in," Rose said, turning back to the visual mire of the screen. Doris, however, continued to look at him, her face as crinkled as a shucked pecan, her eyes shining out from the dim cave of her age. He wondered for a millisecond how such a lovely old woman could breed a screaming bitch like Rose, but this observation was mitigated by the worm turning in his trousers at the sight of Rose's big breasts rising within the confines of her blue sweater. There was still the fine warm smell of fried chicken in the room, one of his favorite odors along with a freshly caught trout, lilacs, the fermenting berries in a grouse's crop, the dense sourness of a bear's den, not to speak of a vagina within a few days of a shower.

And so it was that he flashed his remaining nine C-notes from the payoff from Shelley and they were off to Wally's Discount Palace at nine in the evening of his very first day with Rose. The purchases included a color TV with remote, a sewing machine for Doris, Taiwanese-made bikes for Red and Berry, a down payment on a satellite dish (fifty dollars a month for three years), a wall clock in the shape of an angry leopard, an army cot and a big roll of duct tape for Brown Dog himself. It had occurred to him the house was going to be too warm for a solid sleep and the barely heated pump shed would be a better idea. On the way home he swerved into a liquor store for a case of beer and a half gallon of the butterscotch-flavored schnapps Rose had requested. This shopping frenzy left him with only thirty-seven dollars but since the sum was in dollar bills it still felt like a lot of money.

*

It was well past midnight before he closed the romantic deal. The television set and sewing machine were unpacked from their commodious boxes and both worked perfectly. Rose began to watch and drink, and Doris to sew, laughing at the sweet and luxurious hum of the machine. Red took off into the darkness on his new bike but the toy was plainly impossible for Berry. Brown Dog wheeled her around until he was breathless, trotting down the gravel road until he reached the county blacktop, a big moon lighting their way but the night growing palpably colder. Berry just couldn't get the hang of the bike. He meant to work with her until she was a champion at the sport, no matter how unlikely the notion seemed. On the way back to the house they nearly hit a curious deer with Berry shrieking, clutching to his back, her teeth locked on his jacket collar.

Back at the house Doris patched up Red's scraped knee. Red was soon dozing from exhaustion and Doris whisked both grandchildren toward the bedroom, with Berry bidding Brown Dog good night in a jumble of Chippewa.

"She's too simple for school so she may as well know the old language," Doris said, glancing at her daughter on the sofa, sprawled before Jay Leno with a jam jar full of butterscotch schnapps. Doris winked at Brown Dog and he recalled that day she gave him his name while he stood in her yard in the cold rain waiting for a peek at his beloved Rose. He was only nine years old at the time, truly a young romantic. "Get on out of here, you brown dog," Doris said, and the name stuck though he wasn't, so far as he knew, one bit native.

With Doris and the kids gone he plopped himself down on the couch beside Rose, wishing he liked butterscotch schnapps so he could calm down his trembling.

"You're a good boy, B.D. What happened to your fancy girlfriend?"

"Shelley and me called it quits just this morning."

"Bullshit," Rose whispered drowsily. "She gave you some money and told you to hit the road. Nobody can bullshit me." She gestured to the bookcase overladen with mystery novels and crime magazines to explain her prescience, then lifted her blue sweater, revealing two very large brown tits, the captured heat rising to his face. He suckled one as her eyes closed to a commercial, his member setting up a wild twitching in his pants, then she drew it out while clicking the remote with her other hand. Arsenio Hall was talking to an actress who only ate fruit and cheese, so Rose went back to Leno. She flopped back and he had a difficult time pushing her tight skirt up to her waist, making the additional mistake as he mounted of not taking his trousers all the way off, allowing limited movement as the trousers constricted his ankles. He pumped away in unison to her burgeoning snores, his orgasm seemingly timed to when Leno changed to Letterman and her eyes popped open.

"You should know I love only Fred," she said, and then slept.

*

It rarely is, but it can be a blessed event when a dream dies. The bigger the dream, the bigger the vacuum when the dream slips off into the void. First love is always a somber though colorful thicket of images, and when Brown Dog pulled on his trousers and went outside the images tumbled and wavered through his mind: tracking Rose at twelve when she picked berries with her mother, looking so lithe and petulant in the patch of wild raspberries, wiping the August sweat from her eyes as she filled her bucket with the red fruit. He was sitting well up in a white pine to spy on them, and they stayed so long his need to pee became ungovernable and he hugged the pitchy trunk for courage, looking down at Rose and Doris as a bird might. At last his friend and Rose's brother, David Four Feet, came to help them home with the berries and he was able to pee out of the tree with shuddering relief.

This happened thirty years back but could have been only a moment ago, thought B.D. as he peed off the pump shed steps. The moon looked too big and in the wrong place and the wind had increased since the bike ride with Berry. One vast round cloud with a black bottom looked very much like an angry Mother Westwind in an illustration from a children's book barely on the edge of his memory. The big mother's face contorted into a howl and through her cloud mouth blasted the cold damp air that meant snow.

Now he felt his love sweat drying as if into a film of ice and the cold wind became so delicious he wanted to drink it. Far off across the fallow pasture dotted with ghostly clumps of dogwood he could hear a small group of coyotes yapping in chase. Three or four or five at most, he thought, taking the army cot from the van and setting it up in the pump shed, deftly patching the holes in the wood and the slat cracks with duct tape. As a mongrel anchorite he could not bear the heat of the house, or the way the TV seemed to attack you like a barking dog, or to sleep within the dank scent of heating oil. He had finally achieved his dream of making love to Rose and the feeling was much emptier than the pocket that had held all the money that morning. But then, just on the verge of opening the door, he had a sodden wave of homesickness for the deer-hunting cabin in Grand Marais, for Shelley's dainty undies, for his lost move up in the world and his plummet back to his original home. He could almost hear himself as a child pumping the morning water in this very shed as his grandfather cooked breakfast in the winter dark.

He dismissed his melancholy into the sound of the wind. He might be B.D. dragging along the earth but he actually was a lot lighter in the mind than nearly everyone else, save a few sages and master adepts sprung from the Far East. There was also the hot memory of the time he and David Four Feet had snuck up on the swimming hole up the creek and watched Rose and Ethyl, a plump pinkish girl with a cleft palate and David's main crush, swimming in the nude. Then the girls knelt on the bank drawing pictures in the sand with forefingers, their bottoms aimed at the boys, with Rose's bottom so trim and beautiful compared to Ethyl's big pink one. Now, just over thirty years later, he had fondled that bottom, albeit in a much larger state, and felt a sure and certain accomplishment though it was joined to the perennial problem all artists feel on finishing a work — what's next? Not to speak of the fact that he had nothing to show for his efforts except the lineaments of gratified desire.

*

Thinking Rose asleep he tiptoed into the living room, but there she was, big as life, cooing on the phone and watching David Letterman drop watermelons off a tall building, an activity B.D. instinctively recognized as worthwhile. Rose looked up, lifting her spare hand from her pubis, and made a shushing motion. "My pen is running out of ink, Fred, just know that I'm real hot to see you," she said to the phone and hung it up. She watched B.D. gather up his sleeping bag from under the table. "We could do it once more but it would have to be the last time." She held out her glass and he poured a few fingers of the schnapps. She smiled fetchingly and his legs hollowed. "I also got to send thirty bucks to Fred up in Amasa so he can get his carburetor fixed. Or else he can't come to see me. Can you spare it? If not, no pussy."

That left him with seven bucks after he counted out the stack of ones. And the thumping set-to that ensued gave him a back spasm, so he slept in the painful cold of the pump shed quite happy that love had died.

*

B.D. awoke temporarily famous but he was not to know it for an hour or so. Doris fixed him a breakfast of fried cornmeal mush with maple syrup which he shared with Berry wriggling on his lap. Though it was only late October the world was bright and beautiful with a full foot of fresh snow, and he had wakened to the grinding of the county snowplow on the section road, soon followed by the school bus to pick up Red. Rose was still on the couch, a green mound that snored, totally covered by an old army blanket. Doris showed him the empty refrigerator, a wordless cue that meant to get cracking, while he drew pictures of bears for Berry so she could fill in the outlines with her crayons.

"She saw her first bear in August when we were picking blackberries," Doris explained. "She run right toward it and the bear waited a second before it took off. She must have bear medicine. Rose told me she didn't eat no bear meat while she was pregnant but she might have done so when she was drunk." Doris looked off at the lump of her daughter noncommittally.

*

It was at the employment office that B.D. discovered the unpleasantness of fame. He stood there in his cold wet tennis shoes wishing his boots weren't back in Grand Marais but facing up to the fact that they were. There was nothing fresh up on the bulletin board except a crying need for snow shovelers — and him without even gloves, let alone his icy tennis shoes.

"I don't believe I recognize you. You'll have to register with us," a voice boomed out from behind the counter. It was a middle-aged man sucking on a dry pipe while he kibitzed with the secretaries. He beckoned B.D. back to his office with the amiable boredom of a mid-range civil servant. There was a plaque on the desk that said his name was Terrance Stuhl and framed diplomas on the wall from Michigan State University, four hundred miles distant, down in East Lansing.

"First things first." Terrance chuckled, pushing a long form across the desk for B.D. to fill out. B.D. had an aversion to such forms, in fact had never completed one, in part because he didn't know his father's name and had never seen his mother, so her name didn't mean much to him beyond giving him mental quavers. Besides this, he didn't have a Social Security number, which invariably closed the business of the day and he was sent packing off to the Social Security office to get one, which he never did. All through his youth his lumberjack grandfather had railed against Social Security as being communist inspired, and what's more, the government had no right to keep track of its citizens, a caveat that included the census and voting for any of the "mind controllers."

"I guess there's no point in this. I don't have a Social Security number," B.D. said, flushing at his hair roots. He ached to be in a swamp cutting cedar for fence posts. You didn't need a number for that.

Stuhl looked up from his morning *Detroit Free Press.* "You what? You don't have a Social Security number?"

"Nope. Never had a use for one."

"Then how do you pay your taxes?"

B.D. stonewalled, and then Stuhl threw back his head, laughing with his mouth wide open so that B.D. could see down his pink throat past the twittering gizmo known as the uvula. It was curiously the flip side of a porn magazine where you could see way up inside women. Stuhl wheezed as he picked up his fallen pipe and turned the *Free Press* and shoved it at B.D.

"So we have a felon with no Social Security number. You're out of my department, bub!" Stuhl continued to chortle as B.D. hastily read a large article in the Outstate News section featuring a big photo of Shelley with the rubric U.M. STUDENT DISCOVERS ANCIENT INDIAN BURIAL GROUND. The article went on to say that it was the northernmost Hopewell site and plans were being made, of course, to begin excavation the following summer. Off to the side there was a small photo of B.D. himself and a paragraph describing him as a "grave robber" who had attempted to sell the body of a dead Indian chief found at the bottom of Lake Superior, and that his further activities would be under surveillance by the State Police.

"Gretchen, Gretchen," Stuhl brayed into the intercom. "I've got a live one." He turned back to B.D. with a not unkindly look. "We're not involved in law enforcement here. I suspect you've never even filed for income tax, which could make you liable for twenty years in federal prison. Rest assured, your secret is safe with us. Our aim is to make you self-supporting, not to punish you."

B.D. sat there feeling, in a general sense, like he was leaking, his life's fluid draining away. When he stood he could not feel his feet. Twenty years in federal prison would just about take care of the whole thing, yet how could he make a run for daylight with only seven bucks in his pocket?

"I've got you an unemployable," Stuhl said, and B.D. turned to see the same young woman who had defended him and Berry at the Burger King, still dressed in a black turtleneck, all angles but with a fine set of breasts. Stuhl handed her the newspaper. "A little background." He chuckled.

Gretchen looked at Stuhl as if he were a dog turd and led

B.D. out into the hall. "I'm tied up until after lunch," she said. "Could you come back at two?"

"Count on me." B.D. was wary but at least he was talking to a woman.

"That asshole put you in a state of panic. You're not coming back, are you?"

"Nope." B.D. began to edge backward down the hall.

"How's your little girl doing?" She took his arm, restraining him.

"I bought her this bike but she can't get the hang of it," B.D. said lamely, desperate for escape.

"You just come back and I'll find you something. Do you understand?"

He mopped the frightened sweat off his brow with his coat sleeve, returning her direct glance just to get some courage back. She had the aura of a man but a lot nicer. He nodded then and rushed off, grabbing the pull tabs for snow-shoveling jobs as he left the lobby. You'll never starve if you're a good shovel man, he thought, out in the cold sunlight that glistened off the snow, the working folks leaning into the cold wind as they would for the ensuing six months or so until spring came in May. The wind rejuvenated him, made him a man to be reckoned with, somewhat the desperado what with his mug shining from the *Detroit Free Press,* a desperado falsely accused, but then he never put any stock in the offense of being misunderstood. As Grandpa used to say, it is not in the nature of people to understand each other. Just get to work on time, that was the main thing.

*

In the next four hours B.D. earned thirty dollars by shoveling five walks and two driveways. Rather than striking a deal before he started, he had depended on people's generosity, a specific mistake during the recent hard times. One old woman had given him only a buck for shoveling her walk, telling him he was probably going to spend it on liquor anyway. He didn't mind, assuming she was covering up for being broke herself. He ran out of work at about one o'clock when the wind clocked around to the south and Lake Michigan's waters raised the temperature to over freezing, and it occurred to everyone at once that the first big snowstorm of the year wasn't going to stick around. It was a disappointment to B.D. to see his employment begin to melt away. Before having lunch he went to a grocery store and bought pork chops, a pot roast, salt pork, potatoes, rutabaga, and pinto beans, plus a six-pack of orange soda for the kids. There was always the danger of stopping at a bar and getting carried away and he didn't want to face Doris without a sack of groceries.

He stopped at Shorty's, a crummy old diner he remembered from his youth as being famous for large portions, and ordered the hot pork sandwich at the counter. On Saturday afternoons his lumberjack grandpa and his cronies used to sit at a big table in the corner, drink coffee, and argue, allowing B.D. to walk down to the harbor if it was summer and watch rich folks fooling with their boats. It was unlikely that any of the local boaters were actually well heeled but to B.D. anyone who owned a boat must be rich. Boats, unfortunately, reminded him of diving for the dead Indian chief and he deftly cut a miniature trench in his mashed potatoes so that the gravy could sweep out over the fatty pork. He paused after his first taste, though ravenous, determining that it wasn't, in fact, pork gravy.

"Something wrong, dear?" asked the waitress, who was saucy and well built, if slender, though one of her legs was shorter than the other and there was a light hobble to her walk. She also spoke with a peculiar accent he couldn't trace, but then he had only been out of the Upper Peninsula twice.

"The gravy on the hot pork sandwich is not pork gravy," he said. An observation, not a complaint.

"Like it or lump it, dear. It's generic gravy and we use it on everything. It comes in thirty-gallon barrels straight out of Chicago. You're new here, so don't complain." She tapped her pencil and tried to stare him down. There was a grease stain about where her belly button would be and he lifted his eyes from the grease to her neck and lovely pale skin.

"Didn't say I didn't like it. Only said it wasn't pork. Besides, I was eating Saturday lunch in here when you still had pot rings on your ass." Quite suddenly the idea of any mark on her ass seemed desperately attractive.

"Should I call the manager?" She was smiling now in the curious way of women with not very straight teeth.

"What you should do is have a beer with me after you get out of work. Where'd you get that way of talking?"

"Louisiana. Near Bayou Teche. I come up here with my husband who's up at Sawyer Air Force Base."

She went off to service other customers and B.D. noted how trim her waist was in contrast to her firm but ample bottom, then he remembered his hunger and cold wet feet and shoveled the pork home, daubing up the gravy. Fuck, he thought, fondling the pepper shaker, I forgot to put pepper on it. He felt a hand on his shoulder and swiveled on the counter stool to face the breasts of the waitress. With a goofy edge he decided not to look up but to keep his eyes on the prize.

"What can I do for you? I hope it's something," he quipped.

"Nothing, you dickhead. Chief wants to see you." She gestured over at a very old man drinking coffee at a table in the corner, the same table at which his grandpa sat when he was hanging out with his cronies.

B.D. approached cautiously with a weather eye on the exit, but then this ancient creature couldn't very well be from the IRS. The man gestured at him to sit down and pulled a silver flask from his well-tailored, if rumpled, three-piece suit. B.D. swigged deeply and the whiskey hit the pork with a pleasant thump.

"This is not a good time to be wearing tennis shoes, you fucking numbskull. Doris called and said you were back in town. And I don't believe this for a moment." The old man pushed the morning *Free Press* toward B.D. "For Christ's sake, don't you recognize me?"

"Now I do. You're Delmore Short Bear, my grandpa's friend." Delmore was famous for being the only rich native anyone had heard of when B.D. was young. Delmore had worked in the auto factories of Detroit for years and bought a farm just north of the city because he couldn't stand cities. His farm was now part of the swank suburb of Bloomfield Hills and it was well known that Delmore had sold off for a pretty penny.

"Delmore Burns to the world at large. You can't have people knowing your medicine. Now Doris told me you spent all your money on them. I assume the anthropologist paid you off. You're a goddamn nitwit like your friend David."

B.D. stood abruptly and turned to go. He was used to taking criticism but the mention of Rose's brother and his boyhood friend caused a lump in his throat. David Four Feet had died in a fight in Jackson Prison, a fact that had been easier to accept before B.D. came back to home territory and saw reminders of David in every thicket, on every street.

"Guess I don't care to hear another rundown of me,"

B.D. said. "I help out a family, then wake up to see I'm known far and wide as a grave robber. If all you got is criticism, why don't you go fuck yourself. I don't need some mouthy old geezer with a fat wallet giving me a hard time." B.D.'s umbrage grew with his speech but had no apparent effect on Delmore.

"Twiddle-twaddle. None of us believe you're a grave robber. I owe it to your grandpa to keep an eye on you. How come you think the judge let you off so easy and gave your partner time when you stole the ice truck to sell the body in Chicago? It wasn't just that Republican cunt friend of yours and her rich father. You've always been up to nothing over at Grand Marais and I'm here to help you get good at it."

"Good at what?" B.D. slumped back to his chair.

"Good at nothing. It takes talent to be good at nothing. You were a master at it out in the boondocks but now you have to deal with Escanaba, a big city to you."

"I handled Marquette okay," B.D. said without conviction.

The waitress brought him a cup of coffee and a giant wedge of apple pie "to make up for the pork," she said. He watched her wobble to the end of the counter where she sat down with the *Free Press,* then glanced back at him. Word was getting around and he didn't give a shit. Beneath the odor of fried food, he detected the faint scent of lilac on her skin. His balls gave a pleasant twitch.

"You're pussy-struck is your main problem, among hundreds," said Delmore. "I want to warn you about Rose's boyfriend, Fred. He's a phony pulp cutter over in Amasa. He's mean and he's a lot bigger than you."

"How can you be a phony pulp cutter? There can't be a worse job other than pumping septic tanks." The pie wasn't much good but B.D. ate it so as not to offend her.

"He went to college and played football, I hear. Then he read a few books and is trying to go native. He likes to get in fights and thrown in jail in order to have genuine experiences. It's our times that cause people to act this way."

This notion transcended that of imminent danger to B.D. He liked the surprises offered by odd behavior himself, and he remembered waking early one morning a couple of summers before when he was supposed to help Frank, the owner of the Dunes Saloon, roof his house. Instead, he ate a can of beans and walked in a straight line for eighteen miles, over hill and dale, through gullies and creeks, skirting tamarack swamps, to a hummock he liked near the roots of the Two Hearted River. He carried a giant Hefty bag folded in his pocket for instant shelter, on the advice of old Claude, a Chippewa herbalist. At dark he drank a lot of cold spring water, climbed into the bag, and watched the first full moon in August out the hole near the drawstring, smoking an occasional cigarette to keep out mosquitoes. Before dawn he poked a hole and peed right out of the garbage bag.

"I like the way you think things over before you talk," said Delmore, watching B.D. think. "You're wondering why this guy Fred is after Rose if he went to college? Imagine Rose as an evil mudhole and men are pigs and can't help but wallow there. That's your basic answer. Women are a machine with a big panel of buttons like a drop forge. You can't ever hit the right combination of buttons without getting one of your limbs cut off. Meanwhile, stop by my place and get some boots and warm clothes."

Delmore got up and took both of their checks from the waitress, adding, "I'm not loaning you a penny so don't get any ideas. I just don't want you to get left sucking the mop." On the way out Delmore gave the waitress a five-spot as tip and pinched her butt. B.D. quickly followed to pick up on the good will.

"So your alias is Brown Dog?" she said, waving the paper at him.

"You might say that. What's yours?"

"Maybe it's Pink Pussy. Maybe it's Happily Married."

"Which is it today?" They were nearly nose to nose and the lilac scent now was working up through the sheen of cooking oil.

"I'm not sure. My husband, Travis, is way over in Somalia helping to feed black folks. It wouldn't be real patriotic to fuck you, would it?"

"Depends on how you look at it. I could just lay next to you. I wouldn't do nothing. In fact, we could leave our underpants on." B.D. was feeling like a smooth talker but it didn't seem to be registering with her. She looked off out the window, then made her way around the corner and poured herself a cup of coffee, paused with her back to him, then turned.

"If I go to bed with you, kiddo, I'm going to be in your face. Now get out of here. Check me tomorrow if you like. No promises." She limped into the kitchen without turning again.

He fairly pranced the first block toward his van. This was the promise of American life. You wake up wishing you were back in the cabin near Grand Marais. You have your ups and downs. You're down in the cold dumps of the employment office. You shovel snow after being slandered in the newspaper. You have a hot pork sandwich and love strikes you deep in the gizzard, besides which blessing your disappeared nine hundred dollars is just another burnt-out bulb. He nearly swooned with the thought of balancing the waitress on his nose when he was brought back to earth with a shrill cry.

"There you are! Where the fuck have you been? Hurry, goddammit." Gretchen grabbed him by the arm and dragged him up the street to the employment office. "You've been the victim of a media rip-off and you've got to stand up for yourself and your people." She batted at him with a rolled up *Free Press* for emphasis.

Parked before the office was a van from the local television station. Gretchen rapped at the window and out came the cameraman and the newsman, the latter chortling like Stuhl but with the dank, mellifluous baritone of his trade. B.D. got prickly heat when it occurred to him he was going to be on TV, but then summoned up the training he got from church, plus his aborted stay at the Moody Bible Institute in Chicago where he had enrolled in Preaching 101. The newsman did a flimflam intro including the notion that a local citizen had been accused of a "grave, possibly heinous crime," though in fact he had been convicted of nothing, due to an agreement between the "aggrieved parties."

B.D. closed his eyes and leaned against the van in the attitude of one lost in thought. He strained to come up with a Chippewa word to use other than "*wagutz*," a real nasty thing to call a female; all his other words in Anishinabe were names Claude taught him for birds, animals, and plants which would be hard to drag into this situation. The point would be to present oneself as the wronged party, coupling this with quiet moral superiority. He opened his eyes to the baffled mike approaching his face, and to the question, in a game-show timbre, "And what do you have to say for yourself?"

"Sure, I brought the body of one of our grandfathers up from about a hundred feet. I was a salvage diver making a living before all this happened. I wanted this chief to have a correct burial. We're land animals and don't want a watery grave. As far as the ancient burial mounds are concerned, I'm the only living person who knew their location and I was sworn to secrecy by a medicine man. I was tricked by these Ann Arbor anthropologists, including the famous *wagutz* Shelley Thurman, and then framed for burning one of their tents. I was facing thirty years in the slammer. Now the sacred ground is frozen, but by next late April and May these college folks will start digging up the graves of our relatives. I call upon all Ojibway peoples in the U.P., even Wisconsin and Minnesota, to defend this burial mound —"

"Do you advocate violence?" the newsman interrupted, a little embarrassed by B.D.'s quaking voice and the tears streaming down his cheeks.

"What would you do if you went to the cemetery on Memorial Day and discovered a bunch of folks with shovels digging up your grandpa who died in the war to keep this country free?" B.D. waved the newsman and camera away, realizing he was about to lapse into nonsense, though he couldn't resist finishing with a quote a woods hippie had taught him which he brayed into the mike: "Don't forget, stagnant water cannot contain the coils of the dragon."

*

An hour later, after dropping off the groceries with Doris, B.D. was making himself busy cleaning up a partially flooded church basement. The church janitor hadn't drained the outside faucet used to water the lawn, and the pipe had broken with the early storm and hard freeze. Gretchen had got him the job, demanding for him in advance fifty bucks cash on the barrelhead.

After the adrenaline of the media event their little interview hadn't gone well. He resented the notion of being unemployable and being chucked into the bin with others she termed "learning and physically disadvantaged" — what they used to call dummies and cripples. B.D. was in a third category of malcontents: crazies, outcasts, felons, the plain pissed-off residue of society. He felt typecast when all he had done was spend his life at odd jobs and at what Delmore Short Bear had described as "nothing." Gretchen wanted to pin him down about his background and "ethnicity," so he had acted remote and distraught over the TV experience in order to get out of there. When you got pinned down by questions from anyone, especially those in any branch of government, they were going to take advantage of you or try to keep track of you. Of course that was what they were in business for and it was all well and good for them, but there was no way he was going to be involved. Gretchen kept saying she needed to "share" his work experiences in order to help him, so he settled for one example, avoiding diving with scuba tanks to illegally pillage sunken ships in Lake Superior, a summer occupation that had gotten him into a lot of trouble.

"I get up at daylight and take a little stroll in the woods to see what's been happening there overnight. I make coffee and breakfast. I cut and split a cord of wood and sell it to a cottager for twenty-five bucks. I got plenty of orders from hanging out at the bar. Then I have a little lunch followed by a snooze to change my thought patterns."

"How's that? I mean, what you're saying about thought patterns." She was taking notes.

"The woods business can make you nervous. If you take a snooze, you can forget the stress of the guy acting like he's doing you a favor for paying for the wood he doesn't know how to cut himself. You lay back and think pleasant thoughts, say about birds and animals, like the time I saw a great horned owl blast a red-tailed hawk out of a tree just at daylight, or two deer fucking in late September, or a big raven funeral I watched."

"Birds have funerals? You're bullshitting." She was irked.

"Ravens do. I can't tell you about it for religious reasons. Anyway, after the snooze, I go do a little fishing or hunting depending on the season. Catch a few trout or pot a grouse and woodcock for dinner . . ."

"I personally feel hunting is shameful," she couldn't help but chime in.

"Tell it to someone who gives a shit. I'm answering a question you gave. After dinner I have another snooze, then read for an hour, then go to the bar for an hour or two. Maybe longer. That's it."

"What do you read?"

"*Popular Mechanics. Outdoor Life.* Girlie magazines. I also been reading this south-of-the-border novel called *One Hundred Years of Solitude.*" He hadn't actually gotten beyond the first fifty pages of this book given him by a tourist lady but he liked the title and the parts about the discovery of ice and magnetism.

"How extraordinary," she said, and it was then she got the call-in about the church basement. He noted the poster on the wall proclaiming "The Year of the Woman" and readily agreed. Despite his experience with Shelley, Rose, and dozens of others, women still beat the hell out of men to be around. You weren't always cutting and bruising yourself on their edges.

*

In fact, the church basement proved the point, a mudbath for the mind and body. Neither the pastor nor the janitor wanted to get wet, and watched standing on chairs as B.D. found the drain and reamed it out with a coat hanger, then worked laboriously with squeegee, mop, and pail. It was a good two hours' sweat, but then he had the two twenties and a ten already in his pocket, and kept his mind busy with thoughts of the waitress and Doris's promise that she would make pork chops, also pinto beans with salt pork and hot peppers, a condiment he had taken to when he had worked welding on a gas pipeline and met two Mexican laborers from Texas. The pastor was annoying with his spit-shined shoes, asking B.D. if he had "come to the Lord," to which B.D. responded that he was meek, and "the meek shall inherit the earth." This piqued the minister's interest but B.D. clammed up, preferring as he worked an involved sex fantasy about the waitress, all the more tasty because it was fabricated in a church. They were picking blackberries on a hot afternoon and she pulled down her jeans, leaning over a stump for a quickie. That sort of thing.

*

B.D. was wet and tired when he pulled into the dark yard, puzzled at the fairly new three-quarter-ton step-side pickup parked there. He scrambled back in the old van to sort through a pile of clothes, looking for something clean and praying that he would be allowed a hot shower or bath. His favorite flannel shirt had a crunchy BBQ stain on it which he sniffed for clues to the occasion. Doris tapped at the van window and he slipped open the side door. In popped Berry with a screech, another screech, and a *hoo hoo* in the manner of an owl in the half-collapsed barn out back. Doris held out a plate of chops and beans steaming in the cold air, the steam rising across the moon, and a warm can of beer.

"Fred's in there with Rose. They just finished the butterscotch schnapps. It wouldn't be safe for you. I'm real sorry."

B.D. gave Doris a pat. It was hard to think clearly what with Berry starting her bluejay renditions, so he ate his plate of food in a trice. Doris could fetch his sleeping bag from the shed but that might not be a good idea since it wasn't more than twenty degrees, a little cold for sleeping in the van. B.D. said, "The sucker's real big, I hear."

"Real big and mean. He ate a pork chop raw, covered with black pepper. He just don't care about man or beast." Doris shivered. B.D. sent her and Berry back to the house, starting the van and lighting their way with his deer-shining spotlight. Fred appeared at the front door, filling the frame, his eyes reflecting yellow like an animal caught in the headlights, raising his arm to shield his eyes. He brushed past Doris and Berry, knocking Berry over, and came down the steps.

"Hey, you motherfucker, shut off that light!" Fred bellowed.

B.D. backed the van in a half circle to prepare an escape route, keeping the spotlight in Fred's eyes. Fred roared and began trotting, then broke into a run, with B.D. keeping just barely ahead of him as he drove out the driveway onto the wrong side of the road. He was a man with a plan, sucking Fred toward disaster. Fred slowed and B.D. pretended to have problems shifting, spotting the mailbox just ahead. Sensing victory, Fred moved into a sprint, his hand on the locked door, when B.D. wiped him off against the mailbox perched on the cedar fence post. Not smart. But fun, he thought, shining the spot back at the huge man writhing in the snow-filled ditch.

*

The cheapest motel he could find was out on Route 2, next to the filled parking lot of a bowling alley. He stowed his van in back just in case Fred came out on the prowl. The room was only fourteen bucks but luxurious by his standards. He bought a pint at a party store next door and took a long hot bath, sipping the whiskey and trying to sing along with MTV. Out of the tub, he dried while watching go-go dancers jumping around in undies in a big cage while the singer kept snapping at the cage with a bullwhip. B.D. favored letting them out of the cage and being nice. He peeked out the window to make sure the bowling alley had a bar. Some did, some didn't.

*

Fortune struck true, a boon, a blessing, a gift probably not from heaven. It was ladies' league night at the bowling alley, and when he stood in the bar looking out at the lanes he picked out her trim figure on lane 7 in a gaggle of plumpies. He shuddered, easing out of the bar toward her like a crawling king snake. He reached her lane as she held a ball, stooped with her taut butt protruding, then skipped to the line and threw a strike which seemed to mean more than it actually did. She turned, shrieked with joy while her friends jumped and clapped and then she spotted him, rolled her eyes and danced in a circle, waving her hands in the air as if at a minstrel show. She came toward him, trying her best to minimize her limp.

"You possum dickhead! How did you-all find me?" she hissed, giggling.

"I just followed your lilac scent through the cold, dark night, Frieda." Her name was on the bowling shirt, which made it easy.

"I borrowed this shirt. The name's Marcelle. Maybe I'm ready. Maybe I'm not. What you got in mind?"

"I got a pint and a motel room next door. I want to root like a hog and turn you to butter. That's just for starters."

"That so? Sounds pretty good to me. What's your room number? I don't want these ladies knowing I'm fucking over Travis."

*

He paced the room, his breath and throat constricted as if on death row — or better, Saint Augustine in his monastic cell in a frenzy of religious doubt. He turned on the Weather Channel and watched the digital seconds tick away at the bottom of the screen. On his way back he had picked up another pint and he tried to sip sparingly on the first he had begun in the tub, knowing that whiskey was good for the noodle only in small doses. Then, just over the edge of despair, the knock came and she whisked in, immediately turning out the lights except for the bathroom. He almost said he liked to see what he was doing but remembered she might be shy. She took a slug from the proffered pint and went into the bathroom, closing the door all but an inch of yellow light. He decided not to peek, and flicked through the TV stations until he arrived at country music videos, somehow more appropriate than MTV, or so he thought. Back on the bed he slipped off his shoes to avoid the potential ankle trap, then leaned far out of bed, supporting himself awkwardly with his hands on the floor, feeling he deserved a peek. Times change. She was washing at the sink but the opening was too slim for more than a thin slice of the picture. Suddenly the door opened and out she came with her bottom half wrapped securely in a towel. Surprised, B.D.'s hands collapsed and he scrambled awkwardly back on the bed.

"Window peeker!" She turned, glancing at the TV, the light flickering off her breasts. "Garth Brooks sucks. Give me George Jones any day."

"I was just a door peeker." His voice had become very

small. With her clothes off there seemed to be a lot more to her. She moved to the side of the bed, right above his face. He glanced up and then away at the TV, then back, with Marcelle smiling down at him over her breasts.

"You might say I'm ready to get turned to butter." She laughed. "Cat got your tongue?"

"Nope."

She did a free fall over his head and he went down on her like the no-hands pie-eating contest at the county fair, an event he had won at age thirteen.

II

THE MIND OF THE MAKER

GAAGAAGFHIRMH! I found this on my notepad I kept for Shelley. It is the word the Chips use for raven. Claude told me so. Sounds like one if you say it right, not too loud from the throat's back end. The days they come and go as always. Delmore is hard on my case and loaned me this cabin which is only fourteen by fourteen he and his son built the summer of 1950, the year I was born. Delmore hasn't seen or heard of his son since 1952. He's got me logging my days and thinking to pay my rent. It's not like Shelley, who was always looking for the secret poison in my mind. I also have to cut Delmore's firewood which comes to two cords a week for that big drafty farmhouse. You don't have to be a scientist to know I am not getting a deal because I also shovel his drive and do repairs, like I had to dig up the main pipe to his drain field with a pickax because the ground was frozen and the pipe broke by a tree root. If you count up the worth of everything, I am paying about four hundred dollars a month for this midget cabin with an outhouse. I also have to haul my water about a quarter of a mile from

Delmore's on a toboggan, and there's no electricity so I use oil lamps. Read this and weep, Delmore, you old fuck. You're taking me to the cleaners but I've been there before.

*

Delmore said this morning at Shorty's when we ate breakfast that he can't help but get the best of any deal he ever gets involved with. It's part of his training in the Saramouni Brotherhood he went through when he was in the auto factories in Detroit. Their main saying was there is no God but reality, and if you look for him elsewhere you're out of luck. Something like that. It was up on the wall of this cabin but I took it down and threw it in the stove because I don't have to live every day with someone else's bullshit. Just remember, Delmore, you don't own me, you just got me rented for a short time. Here is the so-called clear thought for the day you asked me to come up with. A horse that shits fast don't shit long. I take this to mean you have to conserve your energies. I also advise you I'm moving over to Duluth when I get three hundred bucks saved. You could say this town is getting too small for me after one whole week. I can't get my breath if Fred is breathing down my neck, also Travis is bound to get home from Africa. I said to Marcelle, how come Travis will know about me? She says they exchange stories of their sex wrongs to energize their marriage. They like to go into rages, then feel peaceful afterwards. She also told me Travis is a black belt which didn't have too much effect. These weenies were always getting out of the service saying they were black belts, and the same pulp cutters as before would kick their ass. I hate to get hit myself as it digs a hole you don't quite get out of for a couple of weeks.

*

Tragedy struck Sunday morning. I've been bowled over for a couple of days so I couldn't work at the odd jobs Gretchen digs up for me. First of all, I loaned my van to Rose. Actually she took it out of Delmore's driveway but she left a note. Fred hasn't been around since he ran into the mailbox because he went down to Flint where his dad is sick. The van's not there when Delmore and me go off to Sunday morning breakfast. We stop at Doris's and the van isn't there and neither is Rose. We take Berry to breakfast with us because she likes both Delmore and me. She and Delmore say Chippewa words to each other.

It wasn't but about seven A.M. with few customers that got out of Mass, too early for the Protestants, and Shelley's photo was on the cover of the Detroit Sunday magazine which is part of the newspaper. She was dressed up to climb Mount Everest and was called "The New Woman" for her famous discovery of the anthropological site. I was only mentioned once as the grave robber that she sent packing. This in itself didn't ruin my biscuits with sausage gravy partly because Marcelle sat down and put her hand under the table and gave my pecker a little squeeze. Berry also poured some imitation maple syrup on Shelley's picture which was justice indeed.

Then in comes the State Police detective who warns me that my TV interview could be thought to be "inciting to riot" which is a laugh. He called Delmore "sir" and that shows just how much pull Delmore's got. Delmore then tells the detective that I am under his care and direction. This seems to please the detective who leaves but then is followed by the local sheriff's deputy in about ten short minutes. This cop wants to arrest me for leaving the scene of an accident. Delmore invites the cop to sit down and have breakfast and explains that Rose borrowed the "vehicle in question" to drive to her new job cleaning up over at the

Indian casino in Hannahville so that I am innocent of all possible charges. The deputy calls Delmore "Mr. Burns" and "sir." I already got a lump in my throat about my van because the deputy said it was totaled. It all made sense to him because he had arrested Rose later on over in a bar in Bark River for drunk and disorderly.

*

I guess I broke down when I saw the van out behind the garage that had the towing service. Delmore stayed inside because it was real cold. It tore me apart because it seemed to be the last of Grandpa because I bought the vehicle over ten years ago when he died and I sold the house to a realtor who sold it to Doris after her house burned down. I got fifteen grand and went west in my first and only new van and ended up spending the leftover money in the Bozeman hospital after a fight with three cowboys this girl got started. Now the roof was stove in and the frame buckled. Berry was upset when I started to cry so I quit and she helped me gather up the spare stuff like the shovel and chain, kindling, candles, a couple cans of beans and a pint of whiskey, all in case I got caught in a storm. On the way home Delmore said it was a cruel lesson but I was going to learn it by doing a lot of walking. I didn't answer. I just walked down the trail to the cabin saying to myself fuck the world that takes my last possession from me.

*

It's only early November but it snowed three days, strange indeed as Escanaba is thought to be the Banana Belt of the U.P. Just seventy miles up the road, Marquette on Lake Superior gets twice as much snow, and over in Houghton they often get more than three hundred inches. That's thirty feet but it settles a lot or there wouldn't be any Houghton.

I spent three days and three nights down in a mind hole. I am forty-two with no vehicle and about fifteen bucks in my pocket. If Fred showed up I'd just plain shoot him but my .22 and my single-shot 16-gauge are both over in Grand Marais along with my boots. I remember some of my Bible training from Chicago about Jonah in the belly of the whale this long but I don't get how he breathed. It's supposed to stand for something else but I don't know what. I can't say I feel sorry for myself, I just don't believe in the world for the time being. I didn't even eat the first day, if you don't count breakfast when I got the bad news.

*

The second morning, right at daylight, I was watching it snow and a grouse ran into the window jamb. I hurried outside and there was a great horned owl in a tree and that is what scared the grouse who broke her neck. I studied this wonderful bird for a while and found aspen leaves and a few dried wintergreen berries in the crop. The bird felt real warm but dead. I peeled, cooked, and mashed a few potatoes. The bird's bad luck was my good. I plucked, gutted, split, then roasted her over the potatoes in an iron skillet in the oven, basting her with butter and pepper. It takes a while to get the hang of a wood-burning stove and oven but I'd used one for a whole winter before. I must say it was a meal fit for a king.

Come to think of it, the main good thing out here snowbound in this cabin is that nothing is happening. Think of smoking that one in your pipe, Delmore. I've got this personal feeling things are not supposed to be happening to people all of the time. At least I'm not designed for it. There should be more open spaces between events. That's my clear thought for today.

*

The third day of keeping away from the world, the snow stopped and the wind eased up which is the pattern of a three-day blow out of the NW. I read in this old-timey bird book stored here along with Zane Grey and Horatio Alger (what a name) exactly how to build a raven feeder so that's what I did. You build a four-by-four platform about twelve feet up a tree and try to keep it supplied with roadkills. Didn't have a ladder so I built it in a white pine with good climbing limbs, made a large space, then cut off the limbs on the way down. The question is how am I to pick up roadkills without a vehicle? Now that I've calmed down I got the notion this problem will be solved by fate. Meanwhile, I'll hoof it, maybe get an old sled for roadkills. Not a bad idea.

*

This is the fourth dawn and I didn't even have a drink yesterday, an act which was made easier because I didn't have any booze left. I'd say it's time to stop the grief about my stone-dead vehicle. Goodbye, old pard. November tenth and it's already twenty degrees instead of the ten below me and the creatures have been dealing with these past few days. My homesickness for Grand Marais is gone because I'm in the same kind of cabin. Woke up in the middle of the night with this idea I should dig a huge hole and bury the van like a dead friend. Now this morning it is a dumb idea, besides being a lot of unpaid work. Got to get out for groceries as I'm down to the last of my pot of pinto beans. Sad to say I dumped a whole can of chopped jalapeños in them so they're damn near too hot to eat, also uncomfortable the next day in the outhouse though a handful of snow cools the butt, something they can't do south of the border. Bet Gretchen wonders what happened to me, also Marcelle though Delmore will tell her I'm out sulking in the woods. She was almost too hot to handle but this morning now that my tears have dried I'm about ready for another run at it. It was the least sleep I can remember. The Bible says a woman's womb is a horse leech that cries out *I want*. I'll buy that fact. In her defense it's a fact that Travis has been gone two months. The short leg is just like the other one only shorter. She says she was born with it just like I was born not to cooperate with the world. All I can say is my tongue was raw so my morning coffee stung like hell and my pecker was plain out of commission for a few days. Take that, Delmore. I saw you pinch her ass, you cheese-brained old fuck. Just wanted you to know I delivered the goods you can't anymore. I won't always be around to cut free wood. I just looked at your 1952 Sears & Roebuck catalogue and those girdle ad pictures are looking pretty good though they don't show the women's chests and legs.

*

Doris and Berry showed up at noon with a loaded toboggan. This threw me off when I saw them out the window because they're a section away, a full mile of woods, not even thinking of the swamp and creek. Then I saw their trail and figured they came down from Delmore's. Right away Berry shinnied up the tree to my raven feeder and when I came out of the cabin Doris was trying to get her down. I had gave away my pound of popcorn kernels to a flock of yellow pine grosbeaks, so couldn't make popcorn to my regret. The grosbeaks were making their odd calls in the trees and Berry was talking back at them. Then she jumped off the platform a full twelve feet into a big snowbank, and we ran over sure that she was hurt but she was burrowing around under the snow.

We unloaded the toboggan which was good and bad.

Doris had brought along her late husband's rifle because she wanted me to shoot her a deer. I tried to say the season didn't open for almost another week and I was a little close to town for violating but she just said again, "Shoot me a deer." Something smelled good and it turned out to be a small kettle of stew she'd made out of a bear neck someone had given her. She put this on the stove while I looked at the other stuff which turned out to be warm clothes from Delmore which were not exactly modern. I had seen stuff like it in army-navy surplus stores when I was a kid and wanted it then so I wanted it now. There was one of those coverall-type flight suits lined with sheep's wool, a lined pilot's cap, and a pair of good boots. Right away I knew you could sleep in a snowbank and stay hot as a sauna rock. I put the suit on and it was a bit short and the boots a little tight but I ran out and burrowed like a vole or gopher with Berry. You could wriggle along the ground blind as a bat, then pop up in a new place.

Back in the cabin I was in for a surprise. I was eating the bear neck stew (with onions and rutabaga) and Doris hands me this letter from Delmore and then three other letters to me that he already opened. I sat there trying to think of when I got some mail. There was one letter from Shelley the year before, then once a year from the state of Michigan with my license plate sticker. I fill out the top form. That's it. And this mail comes to the Dunes Saloon. So if you only get the one piece of mail a year and you know what it is, it's hard to handle the four pieces. So I didn't. I put them aside.

*

Just before dark I shot Doris a little spikehorn buck, gutting it and saving heart and liver. I shot it on her side of the creek so I wouldn't have to drag it through the water. Delmore, you're a sure-thing old asshole but I can't tell you how toasty that outfit is. I put a rope around the spikehorn's neck and got it through the snows to Doris's which was a bit hard as the snow was melting during the day, then a crust froze as the sun was going down. I can't tell you how thrilled Doris was. She fried up the heart and liver pronto, also a pan of potatoes and onions. Rose sat there like a dog turd on the couch with nary a word of apology for my van. She was watching TV as usual so Doris brought her a plate of food. Red and Berry ate so fast I could tell they didn't have meat for a while. When I got ready to go Doris told me to make sure I took some meat and I said no, I'm going back to work tomorrow. During a commercial then Rose told me Fred would likely kill me when he came back from Flint. I said, "Sounds fair to me," showing no fear. Then she said that the crippled waitress stopped by. She had already been to Delmore's looking for me. I left feeling good about being in demand. First a deer for Doris and her family and now Marcelle for whatever. Sad to say I could not track Marcelle down on foot so I headed home.

*

Flushed a group of roosting wild turkeys on the way home in the dark which scared the living shit out of me. These birds weren't here when I was young but the state game folks brought them back. I'm going to eat one to get even for my fright which was closer to home than the idea of big Fred trying to kill me, not to speak of Travis in a far-off land who will have the same idea no doubt. It was a fine walk making my way back by the moon and stars if you don't count the turkeys.

Back at the cabin I stoked the fire and laid out the letters in a row, saying eenie-meenie-miney-mo to choose the first one, which came to Delmore's, so I changed the rules and went from left to right. The first one was from this reporter from the *Marquette Mining Journal* who needed to talk to me about the violation of the burial ground, and whether me and "my people" intended to use force to defend it. Yes and no, I thought, getting into the mood. The next one came from another reporter. This one for the *Detroit News*, the other Detroit newspaper you didn't see so much in the U.P. This asshole was on the muscle a bit, suggesting that during all the years he had covered native politics in Michigan he had not been aware of me as a spokesman, and on viewing the TV tape he had wondered if I might represent a group "advocating a more radical approach." The reporter added that none of the local Anishinabe leaders seemed aware that I was politically active or had any idea if I was native or not since I wasn't on the tribal rolls, though Tom Deerleg Koonz said that my uncle Delmore Short Bear was on the rolls.

"These fucks got everything wrong!" I yelled out to the cabin's silence. Koonz had hit me over the head with a two-by-four in the seventh grade when there had been the promise of a fair fight, a battle over the honor of Rose because Koonz had been spreading it around the school that he had screwed Rose. Rose was an early starter in the fucking sweepstakes. Koonz is an asshole spreading confusion. I might look him up with my own two-by-four.

The third letter pulled at my heartstrings. It was from Marten Smith who was really Lone Marten (named after a real tough weasel), David Four Feet and Rose's little brother. Doris told me he was out in California and that's where the letter came from, in a place called Westwood. Had a nice ring to it. Marten thanked me for standing up for the People, and a Red Brother had sent him the TV tape. Help was on the way. I wasn't sure what help he was talking about. Then he said he was coming home before spring and had an investor for a business that would help the cause. I'm confused but it would be good to see Marten who was always a crazy bastard. He stole a little sailboat from the marina once and got way out in Lake Michigan but couldn't get back because he didn't know how to turn it around. Some commercial fisherman from Naubinway picked him up way down by Hog Island.

Delmore's letter was short and not too sweet:

> Maybe by now you have learned not to loan your vehicle. There's an old Studebaker pickup in the barn. If you can start it, you can borrow it. Meanwhile, I am not your enemy. I'll be needing some wood in a few days and I need you to take down a maple that is endangering my aerials. I opened your mail by mistake so went ahead and read it. See what trouble your big mouth is getting you into? I hope so. The media is a cruel mistress. Be here by seven A.M. if you want a ride to town. Doris called to say you got her a deer. I could have used a piece if you had thought of your benefactor. To show you I am not a bad old guy, go to the southwest corner of the cabin. The last board is loose. There is a bottle of whiskey. You can have two short drinks. There is also a shotgun and shells. I would like some grouse to eat. Marcelle showed up looking for you. She ran around naked in my living room. Ha ha.
>
> Yours, Delmore

The whiskey and the promise of the Studebaker made up for something. I had my two drinks then went to sleep. Woke up in the middle of the night with a boner thinking about Marcelle which got lost in a whirl feeling I was getting in over my head what with Marten and the reporters. I tried to think of the advice the frozen chief in the ice truck gave me but what I could remember is about reading a book about nature. I lit the oil lamp and chose between *Riders of the Purple Sage* and one by Ernest T. Seton called *Two Little Savages* about two little white kids trying to be old-timey Indians. It was real interesting but put me to sleep. Here's my clear thought for cabin rent, Delmore, you slave-driving limp-dicked old nut case. You never regret the ones you do, you always regret the ones you don't. I got that from a nature book.

*

My strength is about gone after a day of ups and downs. It seems I am unfit for the life of the city, however small. First of all Delmore gives me a ride to town and some more free advice so I turn up the radio. Things are not going well overseas. Then we have breakfast and Marcelle is all over me like a decal. She whispers you can't get a woman way up there in the air and drop her. I said that somehow I'd take care of the problem that day, and I was back in the woods in mourning for my vehicle.

"You chose that old piece of shit over me," she said real loud. I couldn't help but remember after our night of love she wasn't too impressed with the van. Still, it was like someone making fun of a recently dead friend so I walked out of the diner without finishing the last few bites.

Gretchen was glad to see me at the employment office. She and her roommate decided they wanted their bedroom and living room painted. She asked if I could paint and I said yes because I've painted a lot of cabins though nothing on the inside. She took me over to her house which wasn't much on the outside but real nice indoors. She showed me where she had got started but was too busy to finish. Afterwards I remembered that she said something about her roommate Karen being upstairs doing painting but artist-type painting and we wouldn't disturb each other.

But I got carried away and forgot this little item. What

happened was that Gretchen left and I did some looking around which was natural. It is important to know where you are at any given moment. Since I was to start in the living room I looked in the kitchen first, seeing that there were a lot more cookbooks than most people have regular books. I noticed a half-full bottle of jug wine and took a sip, then a couple of gulps what with not having a drink in four days, almost breaking the record from when I had Asian flu twenty years ago. I didn't open the refrigerator because I just ate breakfast an hour ago.

The real problem started when I went into the bedroom which I shouldn't have done because the door was closed, though not locked. The room for sure was dolled up like a love nest with art-type posters of naked women hugging each other so my red head started thumping a bit. I was about to leave when I began to wonder what kind of undies Gretchen wore. I guessed probably plain white cotton ones but when I opened a dresser drawer they were pretty fancy. I couldn't help but take a few sniffs and there was the telltale smell of lilac that sets me off. Also under the undies there was a Polaroid photo of Gretchen and another girl buck naked on a tropical beach. I couldn't help but wonder who the lucky guy was who took the picture. By now I was breathing pretty hard and had to wedge my pecker under my belt. I called information then got Marcelle at the diner and asked if she could take a fifteen-minute break and get on over here. She could, and she was at the door in a few minutes. It was like setting off five sticks of dynamite under a stump. We just exploded, doing it like dogs with her waitress skirt up to her waist and her breasts hanging out. We made about three revolutions of the living room floor just getting traction with Marcelle real noisy, yodeling and yelling.

I don't know how I forgot that Gretchen's roommate

was upstairs doing her art, but after about ten minutes — you lose track of time — Gretchen came running up the steps and in the door without knocking. Of course it was her house but we didn't get any warning. We were just finishing and Marcelle didn't notice anything like she was unconscious and Gretchen started screaming, "How dare you! How dare you how dare you you pig you pig I'm calling the police!" The roommate Karen was looking in from the kitchen and also was yelling and screaming. Marcelle was up and out of there in a split second leaving me to face the music. Once again I made the old trousers-around-the-ankle mistake. When will I learn, I thought, falling the first time I tried to get up. I covered my face in shame, also because I didn't want to look Gretchen in the eyes. It stayed quiet though I could hear her breathing. "I guess I was lonely," I said, and that set her off again. "Get out of here before I call the police," she said. "You're fired and don't come to the office again." I walked to the door trying to think of something right on the money to say. "I don't think love is against the law," I said.

*

My heart was heavy as I began the long walk back to Delmore's. It lightened up a bit when I noticed the wind had clocked around to the southeast and the snow was slushy, also I stopped into a bar setting a limit of two shooters with beer chasers because it wasn't noon yet. I can't say I was proud of myself but I sure as hell didn't shoot the President. Sure I made a mistake, but a mistake is not exactly a crime.

So I hoofed it back to Delmore's and the sun was out and glistening off the snow. When I got there a tow truck was just leaving and the old Studebaker pickup was out of the barn and running. There was another car behind Delmore's and a big man in a sport coat. Delmore was giving the man a drink out of his flask so I knew he could be from the IRS. His name was Mr. Beaver or something like that, and he was from the *Detroit News.*

Delmore took me to the side. "This guy is fine but don't get sucked in by the media," he said with a chicken cackle.

"As I said on the phone, the tribal leaders up here, including those in Sault Ste. Marie, seem to know who you are but don't know what organization you represent, if any." Mr. Beaver eyed me like that State Police detective but I wore my poker face.

"Our operation is top secret," I said, thinking there could be a group so secret that no one even knew if they belonged to it.

"Can you give me any indication what you intend to do come spring about the anthropological site?"

"Just write down that it's a lot more likely to be hot lead than bows and arrows. I'm sorry but I can't say any more. The brotherhood might kill me."

"Can you clarify 'brotherhood' for me?"

"Nope." I made a sign like my throat was being cut and then went over and took a good look at the Studebaker. The side windows were broke out but the windshield was fine except for a crust of swallow and pigeon shit from sitting in the barn for forty years. It was real thick on the roof and frozen hard. I had the clear choice of hammer and chisel or letting Mother Nature clean it off with wind and rain. I got in and took her for a spin, waving goodbye at Delmore and the reporter.

*

Shot two grouse out of a tree for Delmore. There were four but I left two for seed. If you start at the bottom you can get them all. I'm only a fair wing shot which is the better way to hunt but it was almost dark and I had to work in a hurry. Delmore invited me to dinner and I must say the old coot knows his business at the stove. He boiled diced-up salt pork to get some of the salt out because he's got blood pressure, then he browned up onions and carrots, browned the grouse I plucked, then put it all in the dutch oven for forty-five minutes. All the stuff on the bottom ensures a good gravy, and the short cooking time keeps the bird juicy. He fried pieces of cornmeal mush and served the birds on top. He poured some red wine which, like Gretchen's, wasn't sweet enough to have much punch. Once me and David Four Feet stole a case of Mogen David from behind the supermarket when the workers took a coffee break from unloading a semi. We got about three bottles apiece down our gullets that day before it backed up on us. Since that day so long ago I haven't been partial to red wine though I will drink it if there's nothing else at hand.

I told Delmore the terrible story of Gretchen catching me with Marcelle and the geezer laughed so hard he slid off the couch. I said it probably was funny if you weren't there and maybe it would be funny later on but I lost my job. He said I got a forty or two you can cut the pulp off. I said what makes you think I can cut pulp and he named three outfits I worked out of in Munising, Newberry, and Grand Marais. I said will wonders never cease, you're a fucking spy on top of a slave driver. He said I just kept track of you, we're second cousins but I knew he was lying there because Grandpa never said Delmore was his cousin, only an old-time friend. I said if you're Grandpa's cousin then tell me about my mom and dad I didn't get to know. He looked at me a full minute and took me off to see his radio room.

In his radio room which had RADIO ROOM on the door I understood why he had all the aerials and wanted me to cut the maple tree with dead branches down. The room had a whole wall of equipment and Delmore is what you call a ham operator. It's hard not to think of hams smoked off a pig when you hear "ham operator." That's just the human mind at work and there's no connection. Delmore said name a country and I said Canada but he said that's too easy name another. How about the lost country of Atlantis, and he said fuck you B.D., we'll contact old Mexico. Sure enough in a few minutes he was talking to a guy named Ricky about this and that including politics and the guy's family. He sent me to get the whiskey bottle and he contacted a lot of countries. Delmore's got this theory, not ready for the man on the street, that the world hasn't fit together since the Korean War. With these ham radios he can tell you where the shit has hit the fan anywhere at anytime within minutes, that way he is never caught off guard about anything. I didn't say so but I like surprises though I am not exactly up to date on the fate of the world.

Then I got a bit of surprise when Delmore took me into his Indian room though it didn't say that on the door. It was full of snake skins and shells of different kinds of turtles, some of them real big snapper and mud turtle shells. Over in the corner there was a full hooded bear skin, a war club, and a bunch of rattles hanging from a hook. Then Delmore says that the bear medicine he got as a boy up by Ontonagon was too hard to maintain unless you could give it full time. It was too much medicine for him when he went south to work in Detroit but on his farm north of town he had lots of dreams about serpents and turtles so he turned to them and they had stood by him. Then he asks about what animal I dream about and I said I dream about animals every night of my life because I've lived full time around them. I also dream a lot about dogs which seems reasonable given my nickname. He said he'd have to think that over and gives my face a little scratch with a snapping turtle claw for good luck. You're a true mongrel, B.D., which isn't all that bad.

*

There's not a lot you can say about cutting pulp all winter long except that it's easier than in the summer when the woods can be chock full of blackflies, mosquitoes, ticks, deerflies, and horseflies. I'm partial to the cold and live in the right place for it, and would rather freeze to death than boil any day. Grandpa told me I had been left in a hot cabin in August when I was a baby and that accounted for my love of cold weather and cold water. He said in another day I would have looked like a miniature mummy, the way Egyptians buried their dead like they were making venison or beef jerky, not that the dead minded that much.

Anyway I didn't write my memoirs for three months because pulp cutting didn't give me any memories. Everything was used up, simple as that. You cut the tree, trim the branches, cut the logs to the proper length, then every few days when you have a load a custom skidder comes in to haul the logs out to the nearest two-track where a log truck with its own hydraulic lifter can load up. There's a saying that there aren't any old pulp cutters. You wear out before that, or a falling tree bucks back and catches you, or a "widow maker," which is a loose branch or a tree that gets caught up on another, falls on you and you are so much crushed meat. What saves the job is that you're outdoors, and if you're troubled in mind you are too wore out at the end of the day to give a shit, period.

Delmore is only giving me fifty bucks a week plus room and board, which means the cabin plus the groceries he picks up, plus a free breezy use of the Studebaker without any windows but the shitty windshield. He says all that's worth about eight hundred a month in value so the fifty bucks cash per week makes me overpaid. You're not likely to argue if you don't have a choice, let alone a Social Security number. We should all be grateful for work if we don't push it too far.

Also, a few days after he showed up Mr. Beaver's article was in the paper speculating that I represented some secret "Red Power" group from Wisconsin or further west. He also said I was a well-known U.P. drifter with several scrapes with the law, and come from our "outcast subculture," the "forgotten outsiders" from the lowest ten percent of our wage earners. It was no wonder that I was outraged when my religion was going to be violated by anthropologists and archaeologists and that I and my organization might consider violence. He also added that the university people were within the law, and the State Police said I was being closely watched.

Delmore said the article should teach me to keep my mouth shut and it was easy for them to find a reason to put me in jail, far from whiskey, pussy, and a decent meal. I admit I got scared though I was interested in seeing myself described in print in better terms than in the court papers in Munising. There is supposed to be free speech in this country but you say a few things and they come down on you like a ton of shit. To be frank I was afraid to go to town and Delmore encouraged my fear because he liked my company for dinner. He said my spirit and body would die in prison and I would come out a shrunken man.

Every night after dinner and Delmore's lecture about life I'd head down to my cabin with whatever was left of my whiskey ration (a pint of Guckenheimer every three days) and stoke up the banked fire. One thing about a well-built log cabin is that once you get the walls warm it's not too hard to maintain fifty degrees in winter. I can't say your body will cook in that temperature but it will maintain life.

Sad to say Marcelle only came out twice, the second time after a deep snow, and she had trouble walking with her one short leg so I pulled her on the toboggan and being from Louisiana she couldn't stand the coolness of the cabin. Also, Travis was being sent home from Africa with a case of amebas in his intestines, all of which left me out of luck except for an occasional poke with Vera from the country bar, the Buckhorn Tavern, two miles down the road from Delmore's. I only go there on Saturday nights out of my police fear but it's hard to imagine them hanging out there. Sometimes Delmore comes along and he'll point out some old backwoods, scab-faced stew bum and say he might be working undercover for the police so I better behave.

Vera has been married three times and is not exactly a dieter but is full of affection which makes up for a lot. She said that before her family moved over to Felch she was in the third grade when I was in the sixth. I admit that I didn't remember her but she said that was a hundred fifty pounds ago and starts laughing. We sneak off to the storage room at the back of the bar for a quick one and it's comforting to see beer stacked in cases and rows of liquor stored on shelves, neat as a pin. The first time we did it she got to kicking and broke a few bottles. There was no way to save a single drop.

*

Late in January and I had a big nature day that filled my thoughts. First off there was just a bare hint of day when I got to the logging site. There were almost too many stars above and west and a trace of light in the east. There had been a small thaw the day before, then it went down to zero, so I could walk right on top of the snow. I carried my saw and a can of gas way back to the corner of the forty near the edge of a tamarack marsh. I stood still for a while thinking of where to start a fire to warm up my hands during the day when I heard a whooshing sound. I didn't have time to think before a snowy owl hit a rabbit on the edge of the swamp. There was a squeal from the rabbit then that's all folks. I had to stand there stock still for a half hour to make sure the big bird got his meal without me roaring him off. These owls come all the way down from the Arctic certain years when they run out of food up there, but it can be a long time between seeing one. Then around mid-morning I looked over about a hundred yards to where I had been clearing out smaller trees to fell a big one the day before and there were three deer feeding on the slender popple tops. When I shut off the chain saw they'd get edgy, but when I cranked up again they'd go right back to feeding. Some people know a chain saw is a dinner bell. Hunger must be a lot stronger than fear.

Delmore had filled a wide thermos of chili and I shook a bunch of hot sauce in it. I have to keep the hot sauce in my pocket or it will freeze up. I was feeling good so I took a stroll across the county road from the forty. I wanted a snooze but it was no fun waking up cold and stiff on the pickup seat so I headed into this real thick stand of cedar that even got thicker. It was grand being able to walk on top of the snow so I made a pretty big circle with an eye on the sun so I wouldn't get turned around. I came upon a small pond with a steep bank and a pile of deadfalls on the far side. I was about to pass it by when I noticed a small black hole in the snowbank by the tree roots and I smelled a musty smell in the cold air. I could have jumped for joy but I didn't want to make a racket. What happened is that I found my first bear den blowhole in my life. Grandpa showed me one when I was a kid and I did the same thing I had done years ago. I lay down and smelled the strong scent coming out of the hole which was only an inch wide, then I put an ear to it and listened to the slow stretched-out snores. I couldn't remember when I felt luckier. I would have to bring Delmore back here to help the bear medicine he gave up.

*

It was Thursday and when I told Delmore about the bear den he shook his head no and said it would be too much for his heart. He had killed a bear as a young man and that was its skin in the other room. His point was since he had abandoned his bear medicine this one might come out and get him. Then he wore another long face and said Marcelle told him that morning that Travis was looking for me and I shouldn't go to Vera's Buckhorn Tavern on Saturday. She was baiting me, for sure. Just when I get over the worry about the State Police spying on me even out in the woods I got this black-belt nut case on my tail. I told Delmore to tell Marcelle that this country was too small for both me and her husband. Delmore asked what movie I got that from and I said I thought it was one I saw with Randolph Scott when I was a kid.

*

Friday was a mean and blustery day in the woods and I damn near quit but there was no point in stewing in the cabin. I built an extra-big bonfire because it was darkish with low clouds whistling past out of the northwest. I tried singing while I worked but I don't know whole songs, only parts. "Yes, we have no bananas, we have no bananas today." And there was one my pardner in the diving salvage business, Bob, used to play on his pickup stereo called "Brown-Eyed Women and Red Grenadine" that was beautiful though I could only sing the title. I didn't know what grenadine was until I met Shelley and she bought it to pour in rum drinks. It is a kind of sweet syrup that wouldn't be good on pancakes. While I was singing "Row, row, row your boat, life is but a dream," it occurred to me why Travis, or Fred for that matter, wouldn't attack me in the woods. If you jumped a man running a chain saw you could get cut up pretty bad. I thought of this because once in the Soo, when Bob sold some ship's lanterns we got off an old wreck, we saw this movie called *The Texas Chainsaw Massacre.* I walked out halfway through and went to a bar. My idea of fun is not seeing people get sawed up. I also swore I'd never go to Texas. Delmore has been there and said they got a lot of cowboys but drove all the Indians out.

*

On Saturday morning I didn't work because I was fretting about my face-off with Travis that was coming up. I tried to read a book about nature with plenty of photos that Delmore gave me back at Christmas at my request. When I asked for it I was remembering that the dead chief in the ice truck told me to read a book about nature. Under a picture of a cottonwood tree it said the tree drinks two to three hundred gallons of water a day. This didn't seem possible but then I'd never seen one. Come spring I might just have the urge to head out west again like I did when my dead van was brand new. I'd check out cottonwood trees. Then there was a bang on the cabin door and I jumped for the rafters. It was Berry on her Bushwacker skis I got her for Christmas. They cost me more than a week's pay but I was thinking she might never get the hang of a bicycle, and these cross-country skis are short and wide, more like snowshoes so she can get around in the winter. What surprised me is that Berry only visits on Sundays. She comes in sounding like a flock of pissed-off bluejays and gives me a note from Doris. The upshot was that Fred was back in town from burying his dad in Flint and was on my trail. Doris heard Rose tell him she'd heard I was in the Buckhorn every Saturday night. Rose isn't allowed in the bar because she had a pretty mean duke-out with Vera last summer I was told.

Fine. Two on one, if that's fair. I made Berry hot chocolate in a soup bowl because she always wants seven marshmallows in it. We played one game of Chinese checkers though she doesn't know how and I sent her on her way so she could ski home before dark. Then I went up to dinner at Delmore's before the big showdown. Delmore knew about Travis but when I added Fred he was troubled indeed. He took me back in his pantry where he's got a big flour bin full of every light bulb he's ever used up. When I asked him why he said "Waste not, want not." From another drawer he took out a pair of old-time brass knuckles and gave them to me for extra help. They had a nice heft to them, especially on a haymaker. He also put a German Luger in his suit-coat pocket but he didn't have any shells for the pistol. He said he was willing to scare someone for me but wasn't going to jail on my account. He had made a good little venison roast plus the heart for dinner to give me strength. He made me eat the heart and I said deer aren't all that strong. "But they can run," he yelled, laughing his guts out, which picked up my spirits. It had been a long time since I'd had a fistfight but it wasn't likely to be the end of the world, just a real expensive way to pay for getting laid a few times.

Delmore and me got to the Buckhorn fairly early so we could get set up. We decided to sit at the bar and we played a few games of cribbage while we waited. There was extra size to the crowd which was usually twenty or thirty, the kind of drinkers who wore out their welcome in town. I guessed that some of them heard there was going to be excitement and showed up for it. I was glad to see Teddy, a great big mixed-blood I'd been to school with. His dad put him to work in the woods so he had to drop out in the eighth grade like a lot of my friends. Grandpa made me finish school so I'd have a diploma. I misplaced this diploma somewhere. Teddy waved to me and pointed at the ball bat he had leaned up against the fireplace on the far side of the bar. I had Vera take him a pitcher of beer as Teddy always drank straight from the pitcher. The ball bat made me feel a trace warmer in my very cold guts.

About eight o'clock in comes this tall, wiry guy dressed up like he was God's own commando. He was sort of dancing on the balls of his feet as his eyes swept the bar. He had to be Travis as Fred was a lot thicker when I saw him on Doris's porch and in the rear-view mirror of my van. It was then it came to me that these guys wouldn't exactly know what I looked like. Marcelle must have given him a general description because he sidles up and asks if my name happens to be B.D. I naturally say no, but B.D. is a friend of mine and is due any moment because we got a pool game coming up. I estimated Travis to be only about one-eighty but his arms were made up of cables. He orders a drink next to me and Delmore, looks around, and heads to the toilet.

Just at the moment Travis goes into the toilet (Bucks and Does at the Buckhorn) in comes Fred, half drunk with his eyes boiling red, his neck real thick like the football players on TV. To be frank I'd rather fight a bulldozer. The bar is silent except the jukebox which is playing George Jones's "He Stopped Loving Her Today." Again, he comes up to me and asks if I'm B.D. and Delmore interrupts and says what I was about to say, that B.D. is in the pisser. Fred starts jumping up and down to juice himself up, then heads toward the corner just as Travis comes out. Fred looks back at Delmore for a split second and Delmore nods yes, then they were engaged in mortal combat.

It was a real bar sweeper and enjoyed by all. Fred was

more powerful but Travis had the moves. Travis whacked and kicked him about thirty times and would have been the clear winner if he hadn't tripped on a chair. Fred came down with a knee on Travis's guts, then got him in a choke hold but Travis reached up and gouged Fred's eye and Fred whirled him around by the neck and threw him against the pinball machine which broke. That was enough for Vera who called the sheriff. I was surprised when Travis bounced up but he did. Teddy made his way up to the bar and said he thought I was the one supposed to fight and I said shut up. Then this old guy and other folks started screeching because Travis drew a knife, and Fred took out one of his own. I was sure glad I wasn't involved. They started circling through the tipped-over furniture and it was then that Delmore jumped off his barstool with a war whoop. Delmore always wears his old three-piece suit so he could be someone official. That and the fact he had drawn his German Luger got their attention.

"Fun is fun, boys, but now you are destroying public property. Throw down your knives or I'll blow you both to hell." They threw down their weapons so Delmore took it a little further. "Now lay face down. The law is on its way. Teddy, if they move you bash the skinny one while I shoot the other through the skull." Teddy bonked his ball bat on the floor near Travis's head.

So that was that for the meantime. The deputies came and took them away without protest. Everyone knows that the cops in the U.P. like to mix it up so there was no further trouble. Delmore who had only let me have two drinks to start bought a few rounds for the house. Vera said the pinball was on lease and nobody played it much, though I will miss the painting behind the glass, part nude woman and part robot. Next morning on Sunday we had pork chops and potatoes and coffee royals, a popular special-occasion morning drink in the U.P. (coffee, whiskey, sugar). Delmore liked to add a lesson to everything and said that spuds and pork had made America. He was still high with the last night's excitement and almost turned on the TV. He had pulled the plug during a thunderstorm years ago, then didn't watch again because Ronald Reagan said a lot of Indians were oil rich on their "preservations."

*

March came as it does every year and not a moment too soon. Except the weather didn't know spring was coming, and after that summer — March was as bad as December and January, and a lot worse than February. Delmore and me went over to the winter powwow at the junior college gym and next morning he took off on a bus for the Milwaukee airport with about thirty members of the senior citizens group to go on a jet plane for a week in sunny Las Vegas. He had a bunch of brochures about what they were going to do and see including the Hoover Dam, Wayne Newton, and a show with Sigfried & Roy who had trained albino tigers. To me, Sigfried & Roy looked as weird as a Christmas tree in June.

I enjoyed the powwow because I'd never been to one before, also I was tagging along with Delmore who was a pretty big deal among the local Chips. He got introduced to the whole crowd of about a thousand Indians, including some from over in Wisconsin and Minnesota. Then to my shock I also got introduced because I was a "wild" one who had been in the newspapers and on TV. A bunch of people clapped, mostly young men who then raised their fists so I did too thinking it must be some sort of sign. Until that moment I tended to brood about the newspaper saying I was an outcast and an outsider. When I had said something to Delmore about it he said not to worry because there were too many people inside which didn't exactly cover the situation. The best part of the evening was Berry in the crow and raven dance that all the little and younger girls took part in. There must have been fifty of them dancing around and around in a circle with the five drummers, beating faster and faster, and all the girls acting like crows and ravens, bobbing their heads, strutting, waddling, beating their wings. Berry was by far the best and Doris said it was probably because Berry didn't know she wasn't a crow or a raven which didn't take anything from it. There were also a bunch of white people of the better sort at the powwow, and in a room where they sold food I ran into Gretchen and Karen eating frybread. They just turned red as beets and walked away so I judged I wasn't forgiven.

We had to leave early on account of Delmore. What happened was that an old man of about a hundred years did his last bear dance of this life. He was completely caped in a bear head and hide and even his hands were hid by paws. He danced all alone real slow and every few steps he'd shake his war club at the gym ceiling. Delmore couldn't handle it so we left. He was shedding a lot of tears and it was lucky he was going to Vegas next day so he could get over it. I got a little edgy out in the parking lot because someone was following us. I slipped on the brass knuckles I had taken to carrying just in case Travis or Fred wanted another go-around. Under the parking lot light I could see it was a dark man in a dark suit wearing a ponytail. It turned out to be Marten, Rose's little brother, who I had seen earlier but didn't recognize with a bunch of huge braves from Wisconsin who showed up on Harleys. Marten whispers we can't be seen together because of State Police spies and he'd meet me tomorrow night at the Buckhorn and off he went. Delmore was already in the car and asked who it was. When I said Marten he said Marten was an agitator and whenever he came back to town he started trouble among decent law-abiding natives. Californians always did that. On the way home I argued how did he know about California if he'd never been there and Delmore used the old biblical saying "By their fruits ye shall know them."

*

While Delmore was in Vegas I was supposed to stay in the house but such was not to be. I was even going to plug in the TV but then tragedy struck. The wind had clocked around to the south and by mid-morning the deep snow was mushy and hard to move around in. I was trying to cut a big birch low to the ground so as to not leave too much stump. I wasn't paying too much attention because I was horny as a toad and was having sex thoughts about this Indian girl I met at the powwow who was so smart she went to the university up in Marquette. She was a third cousin of Delmore so she might have thought I was a bigger deal than I was. Delmore said she was "crane clan," whatever that meant, probably sandhill cranes. Anyway, in my mind we were out in the woods laying on sweet moss with her dress up when all of a sudden the birch fell, hit another tree, and bucked back. In a split second I came out of my pussy trance and threw myself backwards or the tree would have caught my head or chest and I'd be dead as a cleaned fish. Instead, the butt end of the tree caught my knee and blasted my kneecap up a few inches. It was a full minute before I felt anything. I just sat there looking at blood coming out of my torn pants, and then the pain hit and soon I was flopping around and yelling. Somehow I knew I had to crawl a quarter of a mile out to the road where Teddy had been trying to get the skidder started. I must have left quite a blood trail.

III

POINTS EAST AND WEST

To MOST, A HOSPITAL is a bright, shrill, utterly lonesome place — inhospitable, in fact. Visitors fail to make the slightest inroads on the notion that one wishes to be elsewhere, the nights full of slight but unaccountable noises, a factor of illness that penetrates even the vases of flowers, the professional smiles that you never quite forget are concealing skulls.

Brown Dog, however, was enjoying his stay after the initial post-operative discomfort natural to having a smashed kneecap put back in place and a few tendons reconnected. His only other time in the hospital, in Bozeman, Montana, had been far less pleasant for the simple reason of the subdural hematomas covering face and head. He was confident he could have handled two cowboys, but three were out of the question. Walking out of the bar for the fight, he had wrongly assumed there was a code of the West that guaranteed against gang rape. The good thing this time was that, unlike the head, you could distance yourself from your knee. It was simply there, the sharp edges of the pain dulled to a smooth roundness by drugs.

Before being wheeled into surgery he had made Teddy, who had accompanied him in the ambulance, promise to get the other half of a frozen roadkilled deer up onto the raven-feeding platform at the cabin. Teddy was strong enough to pitch the carcass up there and wouldn't need to use a ladder.

B.D. was mindful despite his inchoate pain that once you get the ravens coming in, you didn't want to disappoint them. He liked calling to them out the cabin window and often one or two would respond, though when he tried to slip quietly outside to get closer they'd fly away. On Berry's Sunday visits, however, there was the thrill of watching her gargle out her *gaagaafhirmhs,* her chortles from deep in her throat, caws, chucks, clucks, and whistles. The ravens would wheel around the yard in a state of frantic interest, resettle on the platform, and peer down at the small brown girl who spoke their language.

*

On the second day, when he was out of intensive care and ensconced in a ward with two very old, terminal men and a motorcyclist who had hit an ice patch without his helmet, B.D. enjoyed a train of visitors. Vera brought him a pint, which he slid under the mattress, and a real nice hamburger with plenty of onions wrapped in tinfoil, allowing him at his request the briefest glance of tit. Doris came with Berry but didn't stay long because Berry immediately took to imitating the groans of the motorcyclist. Doris brought him a cold venison steak between homemade bread and a packet of salt and pepper. She said Rose still couldn't figure out how he beat the shit out of Fred. Delmore had told Doris the real story which she thought wonderful. On the way out B.D. had Berry do her raven renditions and this brought a nurse on the run.

Being full from the snacks, B.D. was somewhat critical of the single pork chop, apple sauce, and salad brought for dinner by a nurse's aide named Elise. He complained that the pork was dead and affected tears which confused Elise, who stared at the chop in a new light. She was pretty cute though hefty, with just a trace of a downy mustache. He kept a hand at the edge of the bed in hopes she'd rub against it, which she did. "Look at my little tentpole," he said, pointing at the risen sheet around his pecker. She blushed and fled but he was confident of her return because he couldn't very well sleep with a tray above his chest.

During evening visiting hours Marcelle showed up but was slack-jawed and sullen. She wanted to know if she should alert Delmore out in Vegas to the accident, and B.D. said no, Delmore was getting old and should have a trouble-free vacation seeing Sigfried & Roy. Then Marcelle got all teary over the fact that B.D. had beat the tar out of Travis. It had never happened before and now Travis was pissed about their wayward life.

"You must have really got the drop on him," Marcelle said petulantly.

"You might say that," B.D. agreed, deciding not to correct her wrong impression. He tried to force her hand under the sheet but she was intent on whining about her marriage, so he grimaced in fake pain so she'd shut up. She made a halfhearted attempt but her hand was cold and her fingernails sharp. Finally Marcelle was put off and left when the old man in the next bed started vomiting. So much for love that can't overcome circumstances, B.D. thought. Even Elise made a rush job out of retrieving the dinner tray.

His last visitor of the evening took him by very real surprise. The nurse had just given him his bedtime Demerol and he was feeling the delicious tingling consequence when in walked Gretchen, a vision of loveliness in her habitual black turtleneck. He speculated on which of the dainty undies he had sorted through in her dresser she was wearing. The drug helped him see their pale, silly renditions of the rainbow. Unfortunately, Gretchen was in a business suit.

"Let's just forget your bad behavior, although I'd like an apology. Karen thought you'd like these fruit and bran muffins. I doubt you get enough fiber." She dropped a brown bag on the nightstand and took a pen and forms out of her shoulder bag.

"I apologize from the depths of my painful heart." His eyes became misty but when he reached for her hand she moved farther back from the bedside.

"Your employer, Delmore Burns, hadn't paid any workers' compensation insurance so we'll file through the state to make him liable. Let's start with your full name and Social Security number."

"Delmore's my relative. He'll take care of me. I can't be getting him in hot water." In his dope haze B.D. hadn't the strength to reenter the Social Security nightmare, with visions of the government carting him off to lifelong rest in prison.

"I need at least to know how much he's paying you so we can prorate a claim," she said. "We can do the rest tomorrow."

His look was so full of grief that a remnant trace of the mother arose in her. She leaned over and impulsively cuddled him, a breast brushing his face. When he told her he got fifty bucks a week, room and board, she flushed with anger and hugged him tightly. The situation was worse than the Chicanos she had worked with in Leelanau County.

B.D., with his face between Gretchen's breasts, drew in a new scent that reminded him of the Chicago student riots after he'd been booted from the Moody Bible Institute, having blown his tuition on a hooker. He would never know the scent was called patchouli. "It would be nice to know you when you're not working," he squeaked, nose to nipple, and she turned loose as if he were a hot potato.

"I have to be honest with you. Karen and me are twilight lovers if you know what I mean."

"I'm not sure I get you." There was the image of these

two nifty women walking at twilight, his favorite time of day.

"Lesbians. We love each other all the way." Gretchen was almost embarrassed but made yet another of dozens of leaps out of the closet with gusto. She rather liked B.D.'s naiveté and lack of presumption, the absence of bristling showmanship that repelled her in men.

"You don't say. Well, there's more than one way to skin a cat, that's for sure. Can't say I've ever met one that I knew of. If there's any way I can help out with you two, just let me know." His mind had quickly become a whirl of intrigue and pleasure, also he was flattered that this fine young woman had confided in him. She was a bit of an outsider just like himself.

"Thank you, but we can manage." She gave him a peck on the cheek, letting the alternative of being insulted pass by. He was such a goof, sort of like discovering a long-lost retarded brother.

When she left, B.D. struggled to remember the movie he and Bob, his partner in the salvage business, had seen in the booth at the porn shop over at the Soo. These two women who ran a flower shop were working each other over in the back while they filled the vases. One had the tattoo of a lizard on her ass. One of their customers was this jerk-off guy whom they tied up and beat senseless with dildos to get back at their mistreatment at the hands of men, or so they said. Gretchen and Karen were clearly a higher sort of people than these flower shop women and he hoped to become their friend.

*

Meanwhile, B.D.'s errant comments to the media had set in motion a troublesome set of decisions for the State Police detective, Harold "Bud" Schultz. He rather liked his temporary duty in the U.P., as his marriage back in East Lansing was in a state of travail — his wife had gone back to college and his two teenage sons scorned his profession. Schultz had quickly determined that B.D. was up to essentially nothing despite the media blarney, and that tailing the man resembled following around a stray dog. The prospective felon was being sponsored by a prominent native citizen, perhaps a blood relative, of impeccable reputation other than being a registered Democrat. B.D.'s rap sheet was dreary indeed, including a scrape in Montana, a number of drunk and disorderlies, suspected illegal selling of maritime salvage, the business of trying to sell a long-dead body from Lake Superior, the theft of an ice truck from Newberry, the arson of the anthropologist's tent near Grand Marais, all of which did not add up as a threat to public order. Still, Schultz liked the idea of spending his spring in the Upper Peninsula, far from domestic discord and the very real crime in southern Michigan.

The true impetus for the surveillance was that his superiors in the State Police and the governor's office did not want a replication of the civil discord in Wisconsin over native fishing rights which had a measurable impact on tourism. The upshot was that though it was relatively easy to determine that B.D. was a loose screw representing only himself, it was difficult to file such a simple-minded report in a political climate where conspiracy was the only satisfactory free lunch. B.D. appeared to be a happy-go-lucky pussy chaser, and the fact that he consorted with Gretchen Stewart, a feminist activist out of Ohio State, Marcelle Robicheaux who was from a family of Louisiana malcontents and small-time dope smugglers, and Vera Hall whose second husband was an auto thief from Duluth, added up to nothing whatsoever. Schultz's job therefore boiled down to the simplest imperatives: merely stop the nitwit from breaking the injunction to keep out of Alger County until the University of Michigan could do their gravedigging. In order to maintain the state's interest in the project and his own soft duty, Schultz would continue to plant intriguing items in the press. The sole, small mystery in B.D.'s file was that neither Social Security nor the IRS could come up with a trace of a record, nor the Selective Service for that matter. The only string on the man was his driver's license.

Schultz proceeded on his somnolent way, even reading Densmore and Vizenor on the Chippewa and their arcane customs, until the night of the powwow when a light bulb blew up and he spotted a true dissident, Lone Marten, a.k.a. Marten Smith, thought to be residing in Westwood, California, but from the local area. Schultz felt juiced indeed while he watched Marten talking to B.D. in the gymnasium parking lot, but the energy was somewhat dissipated when he got back to his quarters at the Best Western and did a sleepy phone check on Marten. As he reread his notes in the morning, it occurred to him that though he was an ex–American Indian Movement member, Marten was small time indeed, having shown expertise mostly in getting government grants from Interior, Health and Human Services, and the National Endowment for his dissident films on contemporary native life. Marten had also raised funds as the chairman of the Windigos, a supposed native radical organization, but the best intelligence had not turned up any other members. There was a dropped charge for manufacturing crystal methamphetamine, three motorcycle accidents, and the most miserable credit record Schultz had ever seen. In short, Marten was a chiseler, no doubt looking for a little excitement while he was home visiting his mother.

Or so Schultz thought out on the county road as he watched the ambulance carry B.D. away. He drove over to a pine grove down the road from Doris's house and glassed

Marten as he pissed against a maple tree, then tailed him as he drove his rent-a-car, gotten with a suspicious credit card at the Marquette airport, to a realtor's office. There Marten made a three-thousand-dollar cash down payment on an abandoned fake fort out on Route 2 that had once been the entrance to a shabby zoo for tourists, then a failed RV court, then a local flea market that expired when everyone was rid, finally, of their recirculated junk. Schultz found all this out when he opted to talk to the realtor instead of doing further surveillance of Marten. He picked up Marten's trail again that evening, when Marten appeared to be waiting for his co-conspirator B.D. at the Buckhorn, not knowing that B.D. was in the hospital. Just about everything led to nothing, Schultz thought, as he hit his Best Western sack with a two-week-old copy of *People.*

*

B.D. was more than a little annoyed the next morning when Elise was giving him a sponge bath and a new doctor interrupted. B.D. had almost got her to touch ole Mister Friendly when in walked this asshole sawbones and sent Elise away. Since B.D. was decidedly proletarian he lacked the bourgeoisie's reverence for members of the medical profession, thinking of them as body mechanics who were no more reliable than the grease monkeys at the local garage. The doctor merely stared at him from behind the austerity of white suit and surgical mask and B.D. looked away with growing anger. He thought of Elise as Fuzzy Wuzzy for her downy skin, and they had been talking about religion which he knew instinctively was the best sexual approach. When he was sprung from the hospital she'd go out with him if he'd go to church with her. Why not? he thought, as he guided the hand that held the sponge toward his pecker, truly a beautiful moment that had been destroyed by the doctor, who was flipping through his chart at the bed's end.

"Up to your old tricks again, Brown Dog," said the doctor. "You'd fuck a rock pile if you thought there was a snake in it."

"Kiss my ass, you dickhead butcher," B.D. barked, but then it dawned on him the doctor was none other than Marten. "Jesus, Marten, I didn't know you were a doctor."

"I'm not. I swiped this disguise down the hall. There's a detective following me and I need a little time to sort things out, man. How many people do you have behind you? If we're going to protect that burial site from the *wasichus,* we have to get organized."

When B.D. told him the grim news that he was working alone and at random, Marten admitted that he suspected as much, adding that his own group, the Windigos, was presently shorn of membership. "It's just the two of us to man the battle lines. In fact, today I bought an old fort as a cover for our operations. Actually I represent a group of investors — a fancy word for dope dealers, I suppose. My first love is film, but my integrity as an artist depends on my becoming *engagé* at times."

B.D. tried to buy time by offering Marten one of Karen's fruit and fiber muffins. He had taken a bite of one earlier and it reminded him of fruitcake pumped full of air. He didn't like fruitcake. Even gravy couldn't help fruitcake. Marten's comment about manning the battle lines brought to mind Delmore's Korean War theories. "The bottom dropped out and the top came off," Delmore liked to say. You could start as B.D. once had, with so simple an act of justice as pouring a cold beer down the neck of a truly mean-spirited woman, and end up in jail. The idea of standing with Marten and defending the ancient burial site against the college people, not to speak of the police, did not appeal to him.

"I'm going to have to think this over. They got an injunction until next October against my showing up in Alger County. Prison would make me a shrunken man."

"Go ahead and think this over," Marten said. "Just don't cop out on me. You got this thing started and I came from California to help out. I already invested in a fort."

At that moment B.D.'s actual doctor came in and Marten slipped out after advising a polio shot.

*

Five days later, against all advice, B.D. checked out of the hospital wearing an elaborate knee brace. He had been through a dark time what with the administration of fewer and fewer drugs and the brutal fact that Elise had been transferred to another wing of the hospital after having been caught toying with his weenie by her superior. He had written Elise an affectionate note and her reply had been discouraging: "You got me in dutch. My career is at stake and you're doing the devil's work. Don't be bothering me anymore." Somehow far worse was that all animals had fled his dreams and he realized the extent he had counted on them for good feeling to start the day. Now there were mostly people with big pink faces squeaking a strange language. With the bum knee and crutches he doubted he could even make it down the trail to the cabin. How was he supposed to live without ravens and other birds? That was the question. Also it was April Fool's Day, which meant trout season would start in three weeks — not that he was a great observer of seasons — and how was he supposed to wade creeks and beaver ponds in his current condition? This was not an occasion for self-pity, an emotion alien to him, but a question.

Delmore, fresh out of Vegas, was waiting in the car. An

orderly helped B.D. in and Delmore, without a greeting, waved a letter from Gretchen in his face. This cunt Gretchen Stewart was threatening Delmore with all sorts of financial mayhem over B.D.'s logging accident.

"I took you in as an orphan and now this," Delmore said, pulling up in front of the fanciest hotel in town, the House of Ludington, the same place Brown Dog had stayed with Shelley last October. In the dining room they were met by Delmore's lawyer, who patted B.D. on the back and said, "Just call me Fritz," so he did. B.D. was completely ignorant of Michigan's generous workers' compensation laws. He was plied with a half-dozen drinks and a T-bone steak which mixed wonderfully with the Percodan he had taken for knee pain. Before dessert he was asked to sign a paper releasing Delmore from all financial liability for his accident and injury for the consideration of fifty dollars a week for one year, plus the use of the cabin for that same period. To the consternation of Fritz and Delmore B.D. became cagey, almost captious, leaning back and staring at the paper as if it were a tout sheet. Finally he handed the paper to Delmore, ignoring Fritz.

"You forgot to put in the grub and two pints of V.O. It's time I move up to top-shelf whiskey. I also want one dancing girl a week and your bear skin for keeps. I need it and you don't. You agree to my terms or I'll sue for five thousand." He drew that laughable figure out of the hat because it seemed enormous at the moment. He had thrown in the dancing girl as a negotiating ploy to ensure the bear skin. Old Claude over in Grand Marais had told him that when your dreaming goes sour you should sleep outside naked, wrapped up in a bear skin.

"You drive a hard bargain, B.D.," Fritz said, holding up a hand to shush Delmore. He knew his client was getting the deal of a lifetime and wanted to close it forthwith. Such injuries most frequently result in a lifelong sinecure for the wounded.

*

B.D. slept off lunch on Delmore's sofa during which time Delmore burned Gretchen's letter with satisfaction, put the signed release in his strongbox, and checked B.D.'s coat for incidental information. There was a short note from Marten saying that "the plot had thickened" and to "burn" the note, which in fact contained no useful information other than that B.D. was needed back on board the revolutionary express.

The afternoon's *Mining Gazette* had printed an article and interview with Marten that would immediately have gotten him locked up in any other country in the world. Delmore suspected it was a case of reefer madness, as before Marten left for the outside world he and his cronies had filled the local forests with patches of low-grade marijuana, so that every time the sheriff and deputies uprooted a small patch they'd proclaim a million-dollar drug bust (street value). Delmore would have to speak to the detective to find out if there wasn't some way to ship this crazed urchin out of town without attracting the attention of the sharpsters from the ACLU. At least with Marten hogging the microphone, his idiot grandnephew might be saved from prison.

Vegas had done a real job on Delmore and he trusted the oncoming spring to eventuate a recovery. He had been semi-hot on a local rich widow until she insisted they sit through the Wayne Newton show three nights in a row. That nasalate dipshit had driven him hysterical with boredom. And the chintzy banality of Sigfried & Roy brought desperate tears, so he climbed over tables and chairs to get out of the room. What saved him from heading home was a dark lounge where a luscious black woman sang the old Mabel Mercer–type tunes he had loved in jazz clubs in Detroit in the late forties and fifties.

And now he had to give up his bear skin because Fritz had told him if B.D.'s case ever got into the hands of a good compensation lawyer, it would cost Delmore a minimum of a hundred grand. He went into the storage room and held the skin but not too close. The last time he wore it he had been dancing after a Mediwiwin ceremony up in Wisconsin when he was about B.D.'s age, thirty-five years before. For security he put on his turtle claw necklace and took the skin out before the fireplace where he examined it to the tune of B.D.'s slobbering snores. Goodbye my youth, thought Delmore, a somewhat pretentious emotion in that he was seventy-seven. His own son should have been wearing it, or his sister's son, who had been murdered in a scuffle on a fishing boat off Munising back in 1950, after he had knocked up B.D.'s grandpa Jake's worthless daughter, who had then run off with Delmore's own son to disappear forever. How much native blood anyone had never meant anything to Delmore — true Indians were those who observed the religion and the attitudes. Where it did matter significantly was in the area of fishing rights where Delmore figured a man ought to be one half by blood, and also when it came down to the pathetic benefits offered by the government. In the old days in the U.P. the bottom quarter of whatever background married whoever was available. He had even read how the Finns up in the northern areas of their country were actually a different kind of Indian. Delmore had never needed a free dime from anyone so a lot of the prolonged native nightmare meant nothing to him. He had also read enough to know that notions of genetic virtue had caused the world a lot of problems in its sorry human history.

Delmore laid the bear skin over B.D. on the couch so that the great toothed mouth was open near his face. He had shot the bear, a male of about three hundred and fifty pounds, up near the Fence River between Crystal Falls and Witch's Lake. It took him two full days to drag it out, and when he brought it home his mother and young wife and all the neighbors had quite a celebration, though without alcohol, as they were traditional.

B.D.'s eyes opened to the fierce countenance and he kissed the bear's nose — a good sign, thought Delmore, who had been hoping for a frantic wake-up call. He made B.D. take a hot bath, then put on some fresh clothes, including the old plaid hunting shirt Delmore had shot the bear in and saved. Any more ceremony would have been wasted, though he relented a bit and opened his medicine bundle. He took out a small leather bag containing the bear's gallstones. B.D. treated them as if they were diamonds before he pocketed the pouch.

B.D. was wondering again if he could make it to the cabin on crutches, so they went out on the porch to check the weather. It was the beginning of twilight, the air warm enough for the crutches to penetrate the snow, with the sky's cumulus billowing a promise of the first rain. Delmore wanted company for dinner and his post-Vegas depression but B.D. was eager for the cabin with its deep, non-hospital scent of pitch pine, the sound of a running creek rather than groans, pukes, moans, and nurse whispers.

There was no way for B.D. to carry the heavy skin, so Delmore wrapped it around him, tying the arm and leg thongs and fitting the hollowed head over B.D.'s own. He had become a standing bear on the porch, then a walking bear on crutches as he headed off down the trail toward the cabin. Delmore had wanted to give him a hug for the first time but then thought it would increase his own internal quakiness. After the rifle shot so long ago the bear had stood up, its forepaws on a deadfall log, and howled and roared at Delmore for taking its life. That was certainly too much medicine to deal with at his age.

*

At the cabin B.D. lit a lantern, then burned a green cedar bough over the kindling to remove the musty odor. He had fallen three times on the trail for lack of a flashlight, but by God he made it, throbbing knee and all. He pumped a quart of cold water, then frightened himself when he looked in the small mirror on the kitchen cupboard. He quickly shed the bear skin, listening to the hiss and crackle of the fire. It would take hours for the cabin to warm, so he got in his sleeping bag, drawing the bear skin over him so the head was on the pillow beside his own and the lantern light shone off the teeth.

Deep in the night he got up to stoke the fire and take a pain pill. The rain was deafening on the roof, and over that he could hear the roar of the rising creek down the bank. There was only one pleasure on earth to equal that of a hard rain on a cabin's tin roof, or so he thought as he peed out the door into the night. He suspected the tiny creek in the gully between the cabin and Delmore's place would be filling with water, so he was doubtless trapped on this island in the forest, far from his only problems on earth which included Marten and his own big mouth. He had known it was wrong to show Shelley the ancient graveyard in the first place, but then she was that rare college woman who could have taken first place in any skin show. It was definitely her wiles that led him astray, and though he could not specifically name the principle he had wronged by showing an anthropologist the burial mounds, he knew there was one.

*

At daybreak he noted that he was ill provisioned for his isolation. There were three cans of pork and beans and one of Spam. He didn't care for Spam unless it was fried hard in lard, and the closest lard, he thought, was around a pig's ass on the farm down the road from Doris's place. He heated a can of beans, reflecting that Mr. Van Camp was cheap with pork. At least there was flour and a single egg left. He could make a loaf of bread which would be a bit chewy as there was no yeast. Better to use the egg for cornbread. He glanced over at the bear skin and remembered the idea old Claude spoke of: going without food to purify your mind and body. It was called fasting and he thought he might give it a go-around after the beans. The minute in which you got thrilled with an idea passed into the next minute when you weren't. For instance, at the hospital Marcelle was a pea-brain dipshit and he didn't want to see her again, but with the first spoonful of beans halfway to his mouth he remembered the charming way she cocked her bare butt at him like a house cat.

By noon he had reached page one hundred of *One Hundred Years of Solitude* and marveled at how people bore up under the burden of all the things that happened to them. He liked a genuinely empty future, and his own smoke-blowing ideas for disrupting the excavation, plus Marten's solider plans, stood off on the horizon like an immense nugget of doom, definitely spoiling the view. He was staring into the cracks of the floor when last night's dream came to him. He was holding his childhood teddy bear to his chest. It was missing one leg and the fur was crinkly and singed from the time he put it in the oven to dry it out. The teddy bear started out cold and damp, then got warmer and warmer against his chest, then began to squirm and move of its own accord, wiggling and stretching, coming to life, then stood on its hind legs and looked around, whuffed as bears do, then curled up and went to sleep. What a relief, B.D. thought, to have my dreaming back, then he heard three rifle shots in succession and scrambled for his crutches.

It turned out to be Teddy and Delmore standing on the other side of where the gully was filled by the feeder creek, Delmore in a yellow Great Lakes Steel slicker and Teddy with a bag of groceries, his rifle leaning up against a tree. It was a good thing Teddy was there, because Delmore never could have pitched the cans of food across the water, especially a fair-sized tinned ham. When it came to the pint of whiskey B.D. leaned his crutches against a tree and caught the bottle, falling in the process, but then it would have been quite the kick in the balls if the whiskey had broken.

"Delmore, you cheap sonofabitch," B.D. yelled, noting it was Four Roses, not the agreed-upon top-shelf V.O.

"I forgot. I'm real old." Delmore laughed, flipping him the bird and turning back to the trail.

"You got any pussy over there?" Teddy yelled, his voice booming through the rain.

"Not so as you would notice," B.D. called, trying to figure out how he'd carry the stuff back to the cabin on crutches. It wasn't as if someone would steal it if he left it there until needed. He settled on taking the whiskey, a fatty piece of chuck steak, a loaf of bread, and a can of peas. Halfway back he dropped the peas and let them lay for the next trip. At that moment he remembered that the Chippewa name for bear was "*mkwa*" and kept repeating it over and over until he was yelling it out to the downpour by the time he reached the cabin. On the platform three ravens fed on the remains of the deer Teddy had tossed up there for them. They let B.D. pass unremarked.

*

A full week later he was out at the fort, unable to further avoid Marten, who had appeared the night before at the cabin, stoned almost senseless and making chicken sounds through the window. There was a temptation to shoot him but he ran off in the dark, hooting and clucking. When they were young if someone called you a chicken as Marten had, you either took the dare or fought on the spot.

Rather than barge right in, B.D. pulled his breezy Studebaker off the road a few hundred yards away and peered at the scene through an old spyglass he borrowed from Delmore. At the fort they were as busy as bees. The rickety structure was made of upright half logs that had become quite warped. A half-dozen motorcycles were parked outside and it occurred to B.D. that they must be owned by those tough Red Power types from Wisconsin he had seen Marten talking to at the powwow. There was a pretty good-looking woman in a tight Levi's outfit and B.D. zeroed in when she leaned over to pick something up. Now that he was out in public again he might as well track down Marcelle. He swerved the spyglass, seeing a low-flying hawk cross far down the road. He didn't pick up the hawk but back in the evergreens there was a man with binoculars watching the fort, then swiveling to look at B.D. himself, who lowered his spyglass. It was the detective who had come into the diner when Delmore had defended him the same morning after Rose totaled the van.

At the fort B.D. told Marten about the spy in the underbrush. Marten looked through the spyglass, then went into what he called his official office, coming out with a couple of cherry bombs and an M-80, which he lit one by one and launched with a slingshot toward the vicinity of the detective, who had disappeared. B.D. was introduced as the original hero to the Red Power guys, who were generally immense, with long black hair in braids and favoring tattoos. He was wondering what happened to the woman in Levi's he had spotted when Rose came around the back corner of the fort with her dreaded boyfriend, Fred. B.D. made for his Studebaker as fast as his crutches would carry him but Marten stopped him.

"It's time to put aside our petty bourgeois miseries for the sake of the cause," Marten said, drawing them altogether.

B.D. couldn't get over what Rose looked like. He recalled that three months ago at Christmas Delmore mentioned she was taking the cure but he hadn't paid attention. She must have lost thirty pounds of her bloat after she quit drinking. He was stunned.

"B.D., you started this fucking thing and it's time for you to stop hiding out," she said, giving him a hug.

"You don't look like you're supposed to. You're the other guy at the bar with that old man," Fred said, puzzled but amiable.

"A case of mistaken identity in the great north," B.D. said, glancing over to where two Red Power guys were hauling out the big sign Rose had been painting. The sign read WILD WILD MIDWEST SHOW and everyone but B.D. stared at it with solemn admiration. You had to be light on your feet to keep up with Marten.

"Give me a ride to town," Marten said, drawing him aside. "The shit-sucking Nazis came and got their rent-a-car."

*

They went to a used-car lot down Route 2 owned by the brother of the realtor who sold Marten the fort. B.D. stood nervous and well aside as Marten made a thousand-dollar down payment on a three-year-old black Lincoln Town Car with a phone that had been repossessed from one of the thousands of developers who tour the Midwest every summer looking for fresh land meat. The dealer was enthused as the car had been on the lot all fall and winter eating up interest. He decided to sell it to Marten, who his brother told him was a "live one," for only twice what he had paid at the wholesale auto auction. When they were drawing up the papers a local signature was also needed, or so the dealer told B.D., handing him a pen. B.D. noted that Marten had signed "Luke Olsen, Pres., Windigo Corp.," so he signed B. D. Robicheaux because he was thinking of Marcelle's fanny.

B.D. followed Marten downtown in the Studebaker to the army-navy store and when Marten got out of the Lincoln he gave the finger to the detective passing in his car. While Marten was in the store, B.D. wondered how much, if anything, his phony signature meant. "B. D. Robicheaux" had a certain substance to it. Marten came out with a hard-billed cap and put it on B.D.'s head while explaining the whole deal. Because his injury prevented him from doing hard work, B.D. would busy himself driving Marten around so Marten could keep his mind clear for the goal ahead. The proceeds of the fort would go into a kitty, but since B.D. had started the whole movement and couldn't live on air he would receive five percent of the net profits of the Wild Wild Midwest Show, the cover for the revolutionary activities which would start with a demonstration at the burial site when the anthropologists showed up. Marten had a spy at work down at the University of Michigan who would tip them off.

"I told you I got an injunction on me," B.D. said angrily.

"Injunctions are made to be broken. It is clearly unconstitutional to keep you out of Alger County for a purported unconvicted crime. Also it's time for lunch."

Lunch at the diner wasn't all that pleasant because Travis had punched Marcelle around and she had a few bruises on her face, neck, and arms. B.D. couldn't remember when he had been too angry to eat. He seethed as he stared down at the congealing fat of his liver and onions, finally demanding from Marcelle Travis's number at the supply depot up at Sawyer Air Base. They didn't want to put B.D. through, so he said he was Travis's brother and there was a tragedy in the family. B.D. smiled out at his diner audience as if on stage.

"Travis, B.D. here. In case you don't remember, I kicked your ass out at the Buckhorn. If you lay another hand on Marcelle I'm going to squeeze your fucking head clean off and cram it up your ass. You understand?"

Many of Marcelle's customers cheered and clapped. Marcelle reheated the liver and onions in the microwave and B.D. was able to sit up and take nourishment, his anger subsiding, though Marten was pushing to get to a camera shop.

"You got a prize coming and it's not a tamale," Marcelle said after French kissing him at the door, the taste of her snapping Dentyne merging with the liver and onions. Love was grand again.

*

A few days later the mystery of Marten's camera was received rather brutishly by Detective Schultz when he was suddenly called back far south to headquarters in East Lansing. The chief of all chiefs and an ACLU lawyer from Ann Arbor met Schultz with a large envelope of photos that Marten had taken of him in the act of spying on the Windigos, including a photo of Schultz asleep in bed with Rose at the Best Western. Schultz felt as if his bowels would empty while viewing the adverse evidence. His curiosity about the Chippewa had gotten the best of him and when he had met this handsome, albeit husky, Indian maiden at the casino she had been all over him like a washcloth. After fucking him into a rag pile she had obviously opened the door to the photographer. The real point the lawyer was making was that the State Police had been instructed years before by the legislature and governor to stop spying on political groups. The lawyer said he was keeping the photos for insurance against further noisome forays against the Windigos and walked out of the office after demanding and receiving Schultz's files on the case. The chief had a real aversion to the threatened rush of newspaper reporters and handed over the pathetic sheaf of notes. Schultz was sent off to do the prep work on a case of pill-popping osteopaths in Kalamazoo who purportedly were black-marketing the French abortion pill, or so tipped a pro-life group.

*

B.D.'s trout season opener was without the usual solitary grace. Marcelle had slept over at the cabin, which he couldn't very well blame her for because he insisted, partly to avoid the walk up the trail on crutches in the dark to take her home, and partly because she had been telling him her sexual history starting with when she "came out of the chute, kicking and bucking" at age thirteen. Southern girls weave a better tale than those in the North and B.D. lay there with a sore weenie listening to her dulcet-voiced confessional, quite sure that he had missed out on a lot of life but that couldn't be helped.

The upshot was that he didn't get up at dawn to fish, though he had taken the precaution of catching a half-dozen illegal brook trout for dinner the night before. Marcelle did a beautiful job frying the fish, evidently another Louisiana art, while describing a set-to with a couple of good old boys from the New Orleans Saints at a Breaux Bridge motel. Several times he put his hand on his head to see if his hair was standing straight up. He was rigging his fly tackle at the time, looking at the Wheatley box of terrestrials given to him by one of his cordwood clients, an old cottager from Birmingham, near Detroit, who was the best fisherman that B.D. had ever known. The man would look at the bugs in the air and the ones crawling around on the banks of the stream or beaver pond and then select the closest imitation from his fly box. B.D., who had always fished with worms or spinners, had been astounded at the man's skill and success, guiding him back to a number of top-secret beaver ponds. Once, at B.D.'s holy of holies, his more remote pond, the man had caught a four-pound brook trout on an ant imitation, an incalculable trophy, then broke down in tears and gave B.D. his six-foot Bill Summers midge rod as a present, an expensive item indeed.

So B.D. blew the opening morning by taking Marcelle to work in the Lincoln. On the way she called on the car phone to advise that she'd be a few minutes late — her feelings toward B.D. had warmed considerably since the advent of the fancy car. She pushed the electric seat back and put the heel of her good leg on the dashboard and scratched her lovely thigh with no more modesty than if she were serving a slice of banana-peach pie.

He was supposed to pick up Marten at Doris's house but figured he'd fish for a couple of hours first. Marten had been distressed by success of late. Not only had the gumshoe been withdrawn but the university had announced to the press that no excavation would begin until their right to do so had been established in court. Marten was pissed that his infighting skills had sent the excitement flying out a dirty legal window. He was reassured, though, when his Ann Arbor spy reported that Shelley and some other graduate students were still coming up to Grand Marais in May to survey the site, a technical exercise to establish the boundaries of the dig. To Marten that was blasphemy enough to plan some sort of assault, especially since he was running low on money, his troops from Wisconsin were getting surly and restless, and his latest arts fellowship required that he be back at UCLA in mid-June to head a colloquium: "Will Whitey Ever See Red?"

*

While B.D. was struggling to make it along the creek into the swamp to where a burbling spring emptied its contents into a stream, causing a deeper hole, Delmore was taping a note to the Lincoln's windshield: "B.D., take this auto back to the dealer. I know him and also know you didn't sign your right name. I won't tell if you return the auto. You should know that falsifying a credit application can get you three to five years. Your guardian angel, Delmore."

Delmore was splenetic over Marten, who reminded him of the low types who stuffed the confines of Vegas, full of glassy-eyed greed and rabid behavior. Delmore had tried to talk to Doris about the problem but she was mostly pleased that Marten wasn't violent like David Four Feet and had limited his criminal activities to credit cards, dope, and an infatuation with fireworks that had started early. Delmore even stopped by to see Gretchen, hoping she could figure out how to extricate B.D. from Marten's clutches. She began the encounter in a hyper-abusive state over Delmore and Fritz's con job in regard to B.D.'s accident, relenting enough to hear the old man out.

"He's just a big baby," Delmore said. "He acts so ordinary he can't see anything coming. If you don't help, he'll end up in the Big House." Delmore had a flash where he envisioned B.D. as James Cagney up on a tower, taunting the police, firing on them until he was riddled with bullets and his world burst into eternal flames. "In the old times he could have gotten along acting that way but nowadays the world is full of sharp edges."

Gretchen promised she'd look into the matter and Delmore left the employment office casting about mentally for reinforcements. Back home it occurred to him to call his third cousin Carol, since B.D.'s eyes had lighted up when he met her at the powwow. Her family were fire-breathing traditionalists and had always made Delmore feel uncomfortable, as they thought he had the makings of a spiritual leader and shouldn't have run off to Detroit to make money. While at college Carol also worked as a stringer for the native newspaper in Minnesota, and her mother had proudly sent Delmore some of Carol's articles, which were dry and analytical. The thinking of the sanest of the Anishinabe seemed to be you could only fight the white man for land and fishing and hunting rights with superior lawyers, since the entire white modus operandi was conducted in legalistic rather than moral terms.

He called Carol and she wasn't encouraging, saying she was aware of what Marten, B.D., and the other worthless nitwits were up to — all you had to do was read the newspapers — but she'd give it a try to honor Delmore. The only other thing Delmore could think of was to withhold the fifty-bucks-a-week payment but Fritz had warned against any loss of punctuality that might invalidate the agreement. Delmore held his turtle claw necklace to his chest, trying to remember the details of an old movie about an alcoholic woman called *Leave Her to Heaven.*

*

Moment by moment, B.D.'s days altered in mood from manic confidence to feeling like a dead fish, the contents of his life dissolving in the push-comes-to-shove slag heap that is the substance of nearly everyone's life, but a conflict with which he had little experience. He dreamt twice of the Munising judge's stern warning to stay out of Alger County, and in the dream the judge's face was scaly green and his tongue forked like a snake's.

After the night in the cabin he had tried to see Marcelle but the proprietor of the diner told him she had flown the coop back to her husband up at the air base. B.D. couldn't help but see a very pink, featherless chicken flying above the forest from Escanaba to Gwinn, soaring low over one of his fishing spots at the confluence of the West Branch and the Big Escanaba, a pink chicken with women's parts dipping her wings goodbye. Marcelle had been the best he ever had, saving perhaps Shelley, who wouldn't have been afraid of the dark at the cabin like Marcelle had been. According to Marcelle, way down where she lived cabins out in the swamps were threatened day and night by alligators longer than a car and moccasins bigger around than a man's arm. The fishing was supposedly good but given the other horrors it reaffirmed B.D.'s notion that he lived in the right place.

That afternoon Marten tracked him down at the cabin where B.D. had been rigging a rope and small pulley to hang his bear skin. While he was out fishing some mice had worked over a paw and he felt that in itself this was a dire omen. Marten was utterly pissed and lectured B.D. on his failure as a limo driver and revolutionary, saying that he was nothing but a pussy-crazed backwoods rooster. B.D. was inattentive to the dressing-down, lost in the thought that his beloved skin had been raped by rodents while he was fucking off elsewhere.

It was definitely time to pay attention to the things that mattered, though he couldn't pin them down with Marten prancing around and shouting. He took the cane that had replaced the crutches and jerked Marten's ankle, upending him, putting the foot of his good leg on Marten's neck, and explained Delmore's note about the car purchase. He released the foot pressure and Marten scrambled up, white-faced with rage.

"I'm fucking sick of your middle-class worries. Let's go. Everyone's waiting for rehearsals. But if you want to betray the people over a car, maybe you should stay here and trade your balls for another can of beans." Marten hurled a can of beans through a window which delayed their departure until B.D. made repairs with cardboard and duct tape.

*

Rehearsals turned out to be sort of fun because there was a case of cold beer and the day was warm and sunny. Marten played the director as the six Wisconsin braves rushed out of a pine thicket and mimicked a rifle attack on the fort, shooting B.D. and Fred, who stood in open windows, at which point B.D. and Fred would fall backward on cushions. When B.D.'s leg got better they would fall from a platform up on the top edge along with some other white boys they'd hire. Rose, in the part of a vicious squaw, would run into the fort and cut off everyone's ears and balls and reemerge with a full bloody platter, what Marten called "a real show stopper." B.D. wondered if this wasn't going too far for tourists and Marten said his integrity required "absolute historical verisimilitude," to which they all nodded in sage though uncomprehending assent.

The Wild Wild Midwest Show would be repeated every half hour between ten A.M. and six P.M., and the charge to the inevitable hordes of tourists would be five bucks a head.

B.D. quickly toted up that that would be sixteen plummets a day in addition to driving Marten around to keep his hands free for the phone. It would be a real busy summer, but then Marten assured him five percent of the net proceeds might well be an astronomical amount, certainly enough for a new custom van to replace the Studebaker.

They were all feeling effusive and glittery, a true show-biz high aided by the beer and joints Marten rolled, when up drove Carol to throw a wet blanket on the afternoon. She was calm and deliberate which made her points more effective, accusing them of political adventurism, histrionics, meddling, interfering in a process of grave legal consequences that tribal leaders and their white legal allies were already dealing with in negotiations with the university's archaeologists and anthropologists. Marten was too stoned to deal with her, and she insulted him in Anishinabe, then turned to the six Wisconsin warriors and began shrieking at them in the same language. Marten had forgotten most of the words he did know, and helplessly watched three of the men pack up their Harleys and the other three scatter to hide in the woods. Marten, in his dope haze, flapped his arms like a wounded crow, thinking that if all the native women in America joined the feminists, they could blow the country sky high. It would be a real party, he thought, relieved as Carol drove off.

B.D. generally avoided dope, as it made him cry at the beauty of nature or women, depending on where he was, then fall dead asleep, waking up an hour or so later with a passionate need for a cheeseburger. He was busy weeping over the afternoon light shining off Lake Michigan when Gretchen drove up, looked around with an angry maddened glare, especially at Marten, and drew B.D. aside.

"You're coming with me. I can't bear to see that dipshit lead you into prison."

"It's too late for that," B.D. said, carried away by waves of sentimentality, his throat filling with sobs. He couldn't seem to get off the upended pail he was sitting on. He wanted to stand and embrace Gretchen goodbye.

"It's not too late for anything, goddammit!" She stooped beside him and took a hand. "You can finish painting the rooms minus that slut."

"Nope. We move out at midnight tomorrow. I have nothing to look forward to. Our love was never meant to be." The tears were still streaming but he felt the approach of sleep. He buried his face in his hands, thinking that he'd likely fall off the bucket, but then, worse things had happened. She scratched his head as she had her girlhood dog so many years ago. He heard her walk away across the gravel and her car start. With tremendous effort he lifted his head but she was gone.

*

When they were fully conscious B.D. and Marten drove off to get topographical maps, then on a whim they picked up Berry and Red at Doris's and took them to the Burger King for cheeseburgers, though as a precaution B.D. settled on the outside carry-out window. Marten let Berry make bird and animal noises to the operator on the car phone, and at Red's request Marten dropped a lit string of Zebra fire-crackers out the window as they left the Burger King. B.D. had snooped in Marten's tote bag and it was full of wonders, including a couple of swiped license plates, all sorts of fireworks, dozens of credit cards, and various prescription bottles full of ominous-looking pills, a couple of slingshots, a makeup kit to disguise Marten in criminal situations.

That evening for their farewell dinner Delmore had made a batch of snapping turtle soup. B.D.'s spirits were diffused into melancholy by scratched Bach organ music on the old

Zenith phonograph that Delmore said he had bought back in 1956. Delmore paid him a week ahead on the allowance, which was somewhat startling but Delmore said he had had a dream that B.D. was going away and would miss most of the summer of beautiful clouds, Delmore's favorite natural objects.

"You mean jail?" B.D. was nervous.

"Worse than jail but not death. I sent you a plane ticket and you came home in a new haircut afflicted with insanity. You lost the last part of your ticket and I had to drive clear over to Minneapolis to pick you up. Then the dream ended."

B.D. pushed his luck on the solemn occasion and tried to get some information on his parents, but Delmore just held up his hands and said "Nope." They played a game of cribbage and B.D. had the specific feeling Delmore had cheated while he went to the bathroom. It was only a matter of thirty cents, and he supposed that to stay ahead in this life you had to work at it all the time. When they said goodbye Delmore gave him his first hug since he was a boy and had brought Delmore a mess of trout.

*

It was a warm night for May, with bright roundish clouds scudding across the moon, and the ravens croaked above him as he passed under their roosting tree. There was also the call of the whippoorwill from down by the creek, the mournful notes doom-ridden and settling beneath his breastbone. How could he leave this lovely place for a series of acts that might land him in prison? He stopped to think things over in the cabin clearing amid the friendly whine of mosquitoes. All of the ifs of his life descended on him: he could have been a preacher, a licensed welder, a captain or even a mate on an ore freighter, an important guy in a high skyscraper, a world-famous lover. Instead, he felt like the small print of a painting in Grandpa's living room called *Orphan in a Storm* where a tyke in a thin coat faced the wintry blasts alone, perhaps to die a frozen death. Grandpa would never tell him whether the kid died or not, though he did warn him against trying to fight the battles of others. He certainly wasn't an Indian, or not enough so that it mattered. It wasn't as if a noble and ghostly voice had told him to further defend the burial site he had betrayed. He had already gotten his ass in a sling trying to balance that score. But maybe not enough of a sling, and as he drew closer to the cabin he felt, at least for a moment, that he should die for this cause. It was a real difficult concept for him but there was no question that he had fallen in love and betrayed his honor. Shelley was a beautiful woman and she had dangled him on strings as if he were Howdy Doody, finagled his secret, paid him off, and sent him packing. "That bitch!" he screamed at the night.

In the cabin it occurred to him that he had done so much worrying he had been neglecting his drinking. He poured the last two ounces of a pint, then remembered that Delmore, the tightwad peckerhead, hadn't given him his new ration. A dim light bulb lit up when he recalled that the burial site couldn't be more than a mile from the Luce County line. If he parked on the main logging road south of Potter Creek, then walked up the trail across the makeshift bridge, he would only be a half mile from the site and maybe be able to get back to Luce County before being caught. Perhaps he could wear a disguise. He had always fantasized about having a giant ruffed grouse costume to scare snowmobilers. Maybe a giant beaver or woodchuck costume, but they were all out of the question. In the pale yellow light cast by the oil lamps he stared up at his hanging bear skin. Of course it was sacred, but then so was the burial site. He couldn't very well leave his most prized possession behind. He hadn't slept outside in it yet, as Claude had instructed, because the nights had been pretty cold. Also he had forgotten to. He lowered the skin with the clothesline and pulley and embraced it, his father bear. He filled a plastic milk bottle with cold water, grabbed his mosquito dope, and headed out near the raven platform, wrapping himself in the skin and staring at the moon as if she might tell him something. He had thrown a nice, fat roadkill raccoon up on the platform a few days before and he hoped he might wake up to ravens. There was the mildly troubling thought that bears can help you if you stay out in their world, but not in your own. Time will tell, as Grandpa used to say.

*

B.D. awoke at dawn from bear dreams to a very real bear, a full adult weighing over two hundred pounds, its neck craning toward the carrion on the raven platform while the ravens whirled and pitched, trying to drive the bear away. The air was thickish and dew-laden, and when B.D. growled at the bear it scooted off through the grass in a shower of mist, turning for an instant at the edge of the clearing to see the source of the noise rising upward from the grass.

The Muskol had worked fine on the mosquitoes save for a protruding ankle covered with welts. B.D. scratched, yawned, shivered, peed, figuring it had been the best night of sleep ever, peering out now and then at the drifting moon from beneath the bear's jaw. His mind was empty, clear as a ringing bell or spring water, and he did not say what ancient warriors had said on the eve of battle: Today is a good day to die. Such an awesome utterance would have distracted him from the course that was set, locked into, predestined by everything that had happened to him in the past two years.

*

Out in Doris's yard he played a version of Ring Around the Rosie with Berry while Marten ate his breakfast and packed. He and Berry twirled until they were dizzy, then Berry would shriek like an osprey and they would throw themselves on the ground. It made his knee hurt so they stopped and he showed her the incision scar which she traced gravely with a forefinger. The school bus arrived and Red came running out with his lunch bucket, yelling to B.D. to "kick ass."

Out at the fort they had their war council on a picnic table pilfered from a roadside park, moving the table inside after a few minutes because Marten's paranoia was growing by the moment. B.D.'s attention was distracted by a pail of fresh smelt the Wisconsin warriors had seined the night before, also by the two cases of beer and loaves of bread he had noted in Fred's truck. That morning he had been full of bears and ravens, and after his last cup of coffee at the cabin he decided to fast to prepare for battle. Now a couple of hours later he had changed his mind about fasting. Of all possible meals God had concocted, fresh fried smelt with salt, bread and butter, and a couple of cold beers were one of the best. It was like Jesus with the loaves and fishes for the multitude.

Marten stirred him by barking, "B.D., are you in a pussy trance? Pay attention. You know the fucking area and we don't."

Luckily one of the braves and big Fred could properly read a topographical map, so B.D. was able to trace their intended route from Escanaba east to Grand Marais, then south into the outback, on only thinly defined log roads. B.D. was startled to discover that one of the warriors had been a schoolteacher and another a master sergeant in the army. They never said much but even B.D. sensed that they had a purity of intent lacking in both him and Marten. Perhaps even Rose had it. Meanwhile, he and Marten would be coming up from the south, walking about a mile in the dark before they started their cherry bomb and M-80 barrage at first light. Rose would be in Fred's 4WD pickup and the braves would haze the camp on their motorcycles. Rose was going to leap out of the truck and throw red paint on the anthropologist campers, for whatever reason. Fred's noble mission was to subdue any aggression with his bare hands, for which he was eminently qualified. Fred told B.D. that ever since he was a baby he had liked to knock heads, and that was what made him a successful football scholar in the Big Ten until he had pummeled an assistant coach into a rag doll.

When the wind turned and fog came in off Lake Michigan, B.D. started a bonfire as a tip-off to start thinking about a smelt fry. The fucking hogs must have hit the Burger King before he showed up, he thought peevishly. When the coals were ready he raked a flat bed of them aside, set the dutch oven in place, and filled it half full with oil. Since the smelt were small there was no need to go through the onerous duty of cleaning them, to which no one but Fred objected. "Then clean your own, asshole white boy," Rose said. There was no flour to dust them in, but there was a lot worse things to be without, B.D. said, whipping the bottle of hot sauce out of his coat to applause.

They ate the whole pailful and drank most of the beer, sleeping it off until near sundown. There was a quarrel about omens when the sunset made the foggy lake look like it was on fire. Marten said sententiously, "We push off at midnight."

B.D. went back in the woods to gather firewood and the notion occurred to him that he could keep on going. But no, the cards were on the table, the dice and gauntlet had been thrown, the genie had been unleashed, the circus animals were ready to make war. Fred wanted to sing "We Shall Overcome" but no one could remember the words beyond "someday" and their voices trailed off to the crackling fire. Marten applied some war paint to the Wisconsin braves' faces, then went out front with Fred to change license plates on the Lincoln Town Car and Fred's pickup. Rose beat on the upended pail and sang what she knew of a war song in an eerie, quavery shriek. The braves danced around and around the fire with contorted and violent motions, a mime of war, but always keeping an intricate step to Rose's thumping. B.D. thought the braves sure beat hell out of anyone dancing on *American Bandstand,* a program he had watched with Frank back at the Dunes Saloon for the obvious reason of all the beautiful pussy, especially the black girls. The immense difference was that the dance of the three warriors scared the shit out of him, as did Rose's chanting. Fred and Marten came back and one of the braves grabbed B.D., forcing him to dance with his cane in hand, then they all were dancing right up until departure. Marten made everyone take a black beauty, a type of magnum speed, to ensure alertness. Fred, Rose, and the braves were sent up and over by Route 28 while Marten and B.D. would take Route 2 over to 77. In case either group got stopped by the police the others could carry out the mission.

*

B.D. had been bright enough to let the black beauty spansule slip under his tongue, then to spit it in the weeds before getting into the car. The world was going fast enough all by itself without cranking up your brain. One night his salvage partner, Bob, had chopped up some white crosses and hoovered them, leaving a line for B.D. to snort before going out to a bar. B.D. had drunk ten drinks instead of the usual three, danced alone for an hour in front of the jukebox to Janis Joplin, slept with his feet in the river to slow down the world, and caught a bad cold.

In the car Marten was rattling on as if he had way too many batteries, so B.D. listened closely to the undercurrent of the radio on a golden oldies station and it was like hearing all of your used-up emotions. Before Manistique he had a brainstorm, to which Marten agreed, and called Frank at the Dunes Saloon from the car phone. Marten's Ann Arbor spy had been right on the money. Frank had snuck up for a look-see in case B.D. called, but all Shelley and her friends were doing was pounding in stakes and measuring. Frank hadn't seen a single shovel but had noticed a couple of deputies from Munising on the closest log road, no doubt waiting for a possible appearance by B.D. Also, when Shelley and the other graduate students came in the bar they had a real big guy with them who wore a sport coat and didn't act at all smart like a college graduate does. In addition, the man drank boilermakers, and Frank supposed the guy was someone Shelley's father had sent along to look after her.

Marten was thrilled by the news but B.D.'s sole operable thought was how he was going to outrun the deputies if they showed up, what with a bum leg and a cane. The main thing going for the Windigos was the earliness of the assault and the weather, which was getting bad with the wind coming around from the northwest and rain turning to sleet, not an uncommon thing for May in an area that has seen sparse snowflakes on the Fourth of July. B.D. was not one to deny his emotions, and as they drew near Old Seney Road off Lavender Corners he remembered Grandpa's remarks about Italian soldiers turning to froth and jelly. If you added incipient diarrhea and strange needle pains shooting through the neck, B.D. thought, you'd be right on the money.

When he turned off onto the final log road he made a prayer to a god unknown. The rain and sleet were picking up and the wind was bending the treetops. Marten had flicked on the dome light and was sorting through his munitions, stuffing them in a parka pocket. B.D. mused that if Marten caught on fire there would be shreds of him all over the landscape. One blockbuster was too big for the slingshot and Marten announced that it could only be used in the manner of a grenade if the enemy drew too close or chose to pursue them, or in any way hindered their escape.

"Where we escaping to?" B.D. asked, peering into the dark for the narrow trail that ran to the north. The trail had once been used by off-road vehicles until he had laced it with carpet nails which had settled the noise problem. He had also weakened a small wood bridge over a culvert they used.

"Westwood. I got a colloquium." Marten now had his ordnance sorted, jacket zipped, and was beating out a dashboard tattoo to the fading song "Young Girl (Get Out of My Mind)."

B.D. decided to pretend he knew what a colloquium was. He certainly remembered that Westwood was in California, which was a definite violation of the dead chief's advice not to go south of Green Bay, Wisconsin. More troubling was the notion that trout season had just begun and he needed to check out certain streams north of Escanaba he hadn't fished since his youth. His favorite fly, along with the muddler, Adams, and wooly worm, was the bitch creek nymph, a name of ineluctable sonority.

"Where am I supposed to fish in California?"

"They got the whole ocean, you jerk-off."

B.D. had pulled up alongside the trail and Marten was itchy to get going. It was a scant half hour before first light.

"I don't think I could handle the ocean. It doesn't move like a creek. There aren't any eddies or undercut banks." Now he was feeling plaintive.

"There's a pond in a botanical garden that's chock full of orange carp." Marten jumped out of the car and turned on his flashlight, his back to the wind-driven rain.

B.D. got out shivering and remembered that for the five-hundredth time he had forgotten a warm coat just because the day had dawned bright and fair. The thin army-surplus fatigues were no good in this fucking weather, so there was no choice but to haul the bear skin out of the trunk. It sure as hell had kept a living bear warm, he thought, and now it's my turn. Marten fidgeted as he helped tie the bindings and then they were off into the moist and windy darkness, the small flashlight beam a puny comfort.

*

Day dawned, but not much of it. The clouds were nearly on the ground but the rain had stopped. B.D. was cozy in his wraparound bear skin while Marten jumped and flapped to keep warm, studying the windage for the slingshot. Through Delmore's spyglass B.D. dimly made out three tents, plus Shelley's Land Rover and a big black 4WD pickup down the hill about fifty yards. He also glassed the closest log road, about a half mile away at the end of a long gully, for the possible sight of a cop car. It seemed to be getting darker again and he looked up from the spyglass only to receive a big raindrop in his left eyeball. He flipped the bear head back over his own as Marten readied the first shot which would be an M-80. They knelt behind a huge white pine stump, B.D. flicked the Zippo, and Marten sent the first charge soaring toward the encampment, followed instantly with a succession of three cherry bombs. B.D. went back to the spyglass and saw a big man running down toward the pickup. Marten sent an M-80 in the man's direction and he hit the grass, rolling downhill and hiding behind a stump. The rain began in earnest again and B.D. put down the spyglass because the Zippo was too hot on his other hand. He took out a spare butane, then noticed Shelley sprinting toward them, following the coursing fuses as if they were tracers. She was about halfway to them, dressed attractively in bra and panties and screaming when she wheeled, hearing the three motorcycles and Fred's truck attacking the camp.

"B.D., you motherfucker!" she screamed, at a dead run again. Before B.D. could stop him, Marten sent a cherry bomb in her direction but it didn't slow her down. Marten grabbed the spyglass and studied the mayhem at the camp, still stooped behind the stump in case the big guy started shooting. It didn't look good for Fred. The big guy was clubbing him into the ground despite the fact that Rose was on his back, jerking at his hair. The motorcyclists were doing a fine job on the tents.

"B.D., you motherfucker!" Shelley screamed again. He was swept away, peeking over the stump, watching her nearly nude form running toward him in the rain. If only it were for love, he thought, jumping out at the last moment with a mighty howl. Her bare feet slipped from beneath her as she threw herself backward, her screams now in terror rather than anger. He was on her like a bear, crawling over her, growling and howling, giving her a very wet kiss.

"It's just me, your long-lost love," he whispered, before he felt Marten frantically pulling him off. She opened her eyes for a moment, then rolled sideways, covering her face with her hands. Marten was yelling something and when B.D. stood he could see the big black truck heading toward them, jouncing sky high on the rolling ground. B.D. trotted and hobbled back toward the culvert bridge, turning to see Shelley running off toward the camp and the pickup closing in on Marten, still kneeling behind the stump and lighting his blockbuster. He held the fuse just short of disaster, then pitched it onto the pickup's hood. The big man threw himself sideways, the bomb went off, and the driverless pickup crashed into the stump. Marten ran for it and when he reached B.D. they watched the big guy wandering back toward the encampment, still in his underpants.

*

A scant but speedy hour and a half later they had crossed the International Bridge at the Soo, and in a few hours they were in a town on the Superior coast with the unlikely name of Wawa. B.D. had wanted to stop for breakfast which had astonished Marten, who had said, "We're on the lam, asshole." Back in the woods near Hawk Junction they slept for a while at the hideout cabin of a friend of Marten's, a Canadian Mohawk on the run from the government, then they traded the Lincoln Town Car even-up for a muddy, brown Ford Taurus station wagon with bald tires and ninety-seven thousand miles on the odometer. The Mohawk fried up a panful of venison which B.D. relished even though it tasted of cedar branches. The rule of thumb was that you never poached a deer before July Fourth when their bitter winter feed was out of their system. While Marten attached one of his fresh license plates to the Taurus, B.D. leaned against the vehicle thinking about how lovely Shelley looked in the rain. The worm began to turn. He doubted that she would ever forgive him but he knew she wouldn't forget him. They headed west.

The Beige Dolorosa

I lay down with my head towards the north to show
myself the steering point in the morning.

JOHN CLARE

I

I CAN ALWAYS HEAR the sound of running water, even when it's not there. Maybe I'm hearing my own blood. This may suggest a number of things, including the etiology of Alzheimer's, but then the practice of medicine has become one of our more prominent national vulgarities. There's a creek down near the corral but I can't hear it from here, so I deduce the noise is my blood trickling around in my body, however it accomplishes that repetitive task. A standard fillip of both English and American literature is the notion of blood "coursing" through our veins, but that's a little dramatic, isn't it?

I don't actually know if I have Alzheimer's but it has become convenient for me to think so. When Bob —— (I must protect identities), the chairman of our African-American Studies Department of three members (counting Bob), dropped me off at a medical center in a nearby city I trotted right through the buildings and out the back door, which served as the emergency entrance and where the staff were busy trying to revive a worker who had apparently suffocated in a mudslide at a construction site, or so I overheard. It was a discouraging experience for an onlooker — and for the man himself, I might add, whose face looked curiously white in a small circle like a clown's, where the slimy mud that covered the rest of his body had been wiped off for the oxygen mask, a singular effect indeed.

For want of anything to do as a substitute for my medical tests I went to a matinee of a movie called *Thelma and Louise,* an invigorating tale of doom among the trashier elements of our society, albeit technically a comedy in the Aristotelian sense, as the heroines did not fall from a "high place." Perhaps death was a step up, but this little witticism did not ameliorate the tugs I felt in my heart, the urge to run willy-nilly into the screen and save them. I preferred neither of the heroines, but wanted both, though the older of the two reminded me painfully of my ex-wife Marilyn, who, I understand from our daughter, is in far-off Tuscany ministering to the needs of a young sculptor with the uncommon name of Luigi. At our parting a decade ago, after eighteen years of marriage, Marilyn said to my very face that she loved me but that I was of insufficient interest to last a lifetime.

*

But, oh God, how did I get here from there? I'm about to tell you, and I better hurry because I'm losing interest in myself. During my extended crisis it occurred to me that it must be my personality that makes life disappointing. It's essentially the same life that others have, but they don't find it disappointing. Besides, when you take away the livelihood a man has practiced for thirty years there is suddenly a hiatus wherein it is natural to try to figure out what's left; in short, how much of our being has depended on our occupation for its existence? This sort of thing has become a daily banality in the newspapers but I assure you it's quite different when you're sitting in the lap of the vacuum.

Just now I noticed the three cow dogs sitting outside the cabin window waiting for their morning biscuit. Their names are Diana, Cody, and Gert, but I don't know which is which. They can hear Verdugo's cattle truck when it turns off the main road over a half-dozen miles down the canyon. They set up a racket then, and do little spins like ice skaters, though Verdugo is not overly pleasant to them. They were rather nasty to me until I bought a large bag of dog biscuits at the feed store in town last Saturday. Already they have learned that they get one each morning and that the biscuits will be tossed out the window in lieu of my initial attempt to feed them by hand, during which I felt close to losing fingers. Verdugo tells me that these dogs are known as blue heelers (God knows why!) and are functional animals rather than pets. The landscape is so tortured and geologically rumpled here in southeastern Arizona that dogs must be used to round up the cattle so that they may be trucked their miserable way to auction and their eventual deaths. With a bow to ancient alchemy, both dogs and cattle may be considered *prima materia* — though also dogs and cattle.

*

Frankly, it's my fiftieth birthday. It will go uncelebrated by me, and others who may have noted the date are over fifteen hundred miles distant. Little did I know last May, when I saw *Thelma and Louise*, that I would be joining their ghosts in the southwestern landscape. In fact, I had never been west of that dank, alluvial glut the Mississippi, which, according to my environmentalist daughter, is so laden with filth it makes the dread Ganges look like Perrier.

My office mate Bob was a leveling influence during my prolonged trauma, the aftereffect being the virtual exile on this ranch owned by my daughter's in-laws, who, according to Verdugo, have not visited the property in five years. The day after my aborted trip for medical tests last May I told Bob (Howard University B.A., Harvard University M.A. and Ph.D., with a concentration in all things Elizabethan) about the movie and he was intrigued by the thematics. Neither of us could remember our last movie, short of the Disney farragoes I took my daughter to in her childhood. Before that it was Orson Welles's *Othello* which Bob hadn't cared for. There was also the unpleasant memory of *Who's Afraid of Virginia Woolf?* which Marilyn dragged me along to when we were in graduate school at University of Michigan. I stalked out of this mudbath after a mere half hour, not being able to countenance a parody of my profession. Now that I no longer have the profession I might well enjoy the movie, though sitting in a darkened theater having one's nerves peeled is not my idea of pleasure.

This ranch is said to be rather large, but then the word "acre" is an abstraction for most, and thousands of them side by side are quite beyond a flatlander's ken. The main house is bundled up in the master's absence as if an invisible sheet had been thrown over it. Between my small cabin and the sprawling main house is the neat-as-a-pin adobe of the foreman and his wife, the Verdugos. Out behind the barnyard are the corrals, tack shed, bunkhouse, and all manner of inscrutable ranching equipment sitting in the weeds as if waiting their metallic judgment day. They remind me of my youth when all unknown machinery was referred to as gizmos.

*

Lunchtime and once again I'm having sardines and tortillas. I really don't know how to cook, and here I am twenty miles from the nearest restaurant of any sort. There is an open Jeep available to me but I don't know how to handle a standard shift. When Mrs. Verdugo said I was welcome to take my meals with them — her husband's aged mother does most of the cooking for the family and two ranch hands — I told her I knew how to cook well. There doesn't seem to be reason behind my gratuitous fib. She seemed delighted at this news and said perhaps one day I might cook them a "gourmet dinner from back east." I readily agreed, compounding my lie.

Right now it has begun snowing in Arizona and I have packed only summery clothes out of ignorance. The ranch is at an altitude of over six thousand feet which has an effect on the weather for reasons that aren't clear to me. One grows accustomed to seeing pictures of mountains covered with snow and now I'm sitting here watching the process for the first time! Marilyn used to tease me over the way I ignored the weather, wearing the same things each season, and switching wardrobe according to dates rather than "reality," her favorite catchword.

I'm dragging something and I'm not sure whether it's my feet, mind, heart, or soul. Allow me to race through the frayed details while my memory is still relatively clear of disease. Until last summer I was a full professor at a college in southern Michigan which thinks of itself as "the Swarthmore of the Midwest." This notion is repeated by members of the Athletics Department and citizens of the small town that encloses the campus, who have no perception of the Swarthmore of the East, the original one, just as children are unaware of the true nature of the song lyrics they sing. When my daughter was young and taking part in a school pageant she skipped around the house singing

"Give My Regards to Broadway" without the vaguest idea what "Broadway" or "Herald Square" meant.

I stray. I taught English literature, a subject to which there is no longer a noticeable inclination. I was granted tenure because of my early success at age thirty, when a university press published a revised version of my doctoral dissertation, called *The Economics of Madness in English Poetry,* which considered in depth the lives of Christopher Smart and John Clare. In fact, my mother was an English war bride, from Helpton in Northamptonshire, and a distant descendant of Clare himself, plausibly a fearsome detail if you put much faith in genetics. The greater public loves insanity, starvation, and suicide in its poets and my book was widely reviewed not only in scholarly journals but the larger press, including a third-page rave in the *New York Times Book Review,* with a photograph where I appeared properly anguished and quizzical. Historically, of course, England treated her poets no better than it did the Irish during the potato famine. Neither Smart nor Clare need have been institutionalized had their collective admirers offered nominal support. This is a far cry from today, when thousands of M.F.A. poets circulate the nation's universities carrying expensive briefcases while it is the scholars who are scorned as non-creative. But more on that later.

I was a full professor by thirty-five, living near the outskirts of town in a fine house on three acres, a delayed dowry from my in-laws, who were not initially pleased with Marilyn's choice. There were employment offers from Princeton, Berkeley, and the University of Texas but I chose to stay put out of timidity — I did not have another book idea to keep pace in the upper reaches of the academic world and, as Marilyn elegantly stated, I was better off being a big frog in a small pond. It was also better not to move our daughter Deirdre (not my choice of name) away from the security of small-town life. Naturally I did not know at the time that Marilyn was already in love with our department chairman, whom I shall call Ballard, and who later became Dean of Science and Arts.

Life passed on rather sleepily for years. Each summer I was given a travel grant and spent two months of research in London and elsewhere in England. Marilyn and Deirdre would go up to Harbor Springs, a haven for plutocrats in northern Michigan, and spend the hot months at her parents' summer home. It was there that Marilyn would have her assignations with Ballard, who as a *faux* outdoorsman lived during the summer in a log cabin some fifty miles away. I know because I checked the map.

Ballard always thought his sentimentality about the natural world was heroic. Once earlier in my career I had gone with him and several other professors up to his cabin for a long weekend. Our wives gave us a dinner party the night before as if we were Lewis and Clark headed for *terra incognita.* We jammed into Ballard's huge Suburban, the de rigueur vehicle for this sort of nonsense, the back stuffed with food and gear. I was the only one not in possession of a flannel shirt. It was a cold, rainy weekend shot through with false heartiness and beery camaraderie. Because of my late father's alcoholism I limit myself strictly to six bottles of Watney ale on Saturdays. It is an unwobbling pivot and I watched the others get puking drunk, read dirty magazines, fumble their cards at poker, make forays out on a laughably small lake to fish, from which they'd return cold, sodden, and empty-handed. The only fish we ate was tuna.

Back to the nightmare that lasted a late spring, summer, early fall, and which led me to this place. Rather, I was led by my daughter, who is conveniently a psychiatric social worker in Chicago and married to a pediatrician. They are a hauntingly non-venal couple and work together in a clinic, in a ghetto that I find so frightening I have only visited them there once.

It all started on the first fine day in early April when I errantly went into my Milton class and said, "Good morning, you ladies are looking lovely today," to a group of a half-dozen senior girls who had shed the usual outer garments they habitually bought at used-clothing stores in a nearby city. I will not comment on the irony of rich girls aping the clothing of the poor. The upshot was they reported me to Dean Ballard and I was called in that afternoon to explain my sexist comment. Now, Marilyn was married to Ballard right after she divorced me, her visit to the lawyer coming the day after Deirdre's high school graduation. During the past ten years, Ballard and I have spoken only when necessary, although he has attempted to become chummy, especially right after Marilyn left *him* at the end of a scant four years of marriage. Since then the town has become too small for her and she can best be described as at large in the world of the arts. Marilyn has always explained away her bad behavior as being part of her "journey." I was not inclined to be sympathetic with Ballard, though his wife went daffy when he left her for Marilyn, and he is now stuck with three unruly teenagers caroming drunkenly around town dressed in hiking clothes.

The meeting was brief and melancholy with Ballard saying he was obligated to record the grievance because of college rules, making a slight reference to a problem in February when a student named Elizabeth filed a complaint over comments I had made in my course called English Poetics: From *Beowulf* to Auden. She had stormed out of class when I quoted Ezra Pound, who, though an admitted fool and anti-Semite, had some wise things to say about poetry. My sin here had become leavened by the fact that Elizabeth, a rich girl from Shaker Heights, had spent the school year pretending to be Jewish and observing Jewish holidays. The year before, she had become a Native American. Bob said the black students were cringing over the idea that they might be next on her schedule of adoptions. This, and the fact that she was the girlfriend of Reed, the arch troublemaker and editor of the student literary magazine *Openings*, made Ballard take the problem with a grain of salt. Reed had called me a twit to my face outside the student union after I had cast the deciding vote to withdraw department funding from his magazine over an anonymous short story he had published, "A Girl and Her Dog," with somewhat explicit line drawings. Everyone knew he had written the story himself.

All of this in itself would have passed if it hadn't been for the Earth Day assault charge. The students were staging a massive eco-circus on the commons for the weekend, with rock bands, costumery, modern dances, speakers and poets who were advocates of the American wilderness, recycling, and whatever. I tried to pass by unobtrusively in the shrubbery to fetch some forgotten books from my office but it was sprinkling and the bushes were wetting my trousers and the high bushes were hard to negotiate with my umbrella. On emerging, I was spotted by the student mime troupe, who had painted their faces green and were dressed up ostensibly as trees. They surrounded me and attempted to mime my continued path to my office. I'm a bit of a claustrophobe and when they got so close that I could smell their breath, I attempted to shield myself with the umbrella, the point of which supposedly struck one of the mimes, who collapsed screaming. Another mime summoned a nearby campus policewoman and I was duly charged. The charges were dropped the following week when the injured party went off to New York City to further her ancient art form.

*

I must interrupt, partly because my heart no longer aches — I did not expect the anger to pass so quickly with the change in surroundings — and in part because I am watching something interesting. Before daybreak I was awakened by a generalized roaring. As I leapt from bed I thought it might be a tornado but it turned out to be an immense cattle truck, far larger than the one Verdugo normally used. The lights were directed at my window and I had to duck out of the way, not wanting to look foolish in my pajamas. After the commotion settled I decided to make coffee and read rather than go back to bed, although it was only six A.M. It was slim pickings as the several trunks of books I had packed hadn't arrived in the week I had been here. There was only a stack of *Arizona Highways* plus a half-dozen books Deirdre had purchased for me on our visit to the Desert Museum, an unpleasant event ending in a quarrel. We had made a dawn flight for Tucson out of Chicago's O'Hare, picked up our luggage and a rental car, and it still wasn't lunchtime. We drove to this museum under Deirdre's insistence that it would introduce me to the area.

The upshot was that the place, including the drive there, gave me a terrible case of vertigo and Deirdre asked me if I had taken my pills that morning and I admitted that I hadn't. "Jesus, Dad, but you're an asshole," she said. I agreed, but that didn't diminish the absolutely terrifying foreignness of the flora and fauna that surrounded us. The so-called museum was alive. As my eyes tried to refocus from the sunlight, I stood in a dark hall until I discovered I was face to face with an immense rattlesnake. Out on the paths through gardens of cacti there were all manner of alien creatures in cages. Of course I had seen them in books but their density, their otherness, had never recorded on me. I made a hasty retreat to the bookstore off the lobby, with Deirdre no doubt wishing that someone else had fathered her.

*

I certainly can't control my mind. After his before-dawn arrival in the huge truck Verdugo had gone back inside his adobe, perhaps for breakfast, then reemerged at first light with his two young cowboys. I turned off my lamp in the cabin so as not to be seen watching them as they saddled up their horses and headed off into the cold mountains. I felt an odd tinge of envy — I had been on a pony only once as a child. My father had rather flippantly promised a horse when I reached twelve, but I knew this was unlikely because we lived in a suburb of Toledo. I busied myself sending away the form on his packets of pipe tobacco which promised a horse of high quality to the winner. Most of our spare money at the time went to my father's drinking habit. My twelfth birthday came and went with a used bicycle for my *Toledo Blade* paper route but no sign of a horse. At the nether end of my route, at the edge of town and country, I often stood back in the trees and watched a girl from our school ride a roan horse. My pathetic little heart thumped for both the horse and the girl with the long black hair.

*

Verdugo and the cowboys returned at about one P.M., driving at least a hundred cattle before them. I put on my Harris tweed sport coat and rushed outside to watch this maelstrom of beasts as they were channeled into the largest corral. They resembled wild animals compared to the well-groomed dairy cows of southern Michigan and Ohio. When

I walked out the gate of the stone fence that surrounded my cabin Verdugo and the cowboys, who were Mexican, began to shout at me incoherently. I cupped my ears but I couldn't understand them until I noted a stray cow coming around from the path to the adobe, crossing the yard at top speed with the dogs giving chase. The beast was headed toward me and I waved my arms to no avail. I jumped up on the stone wall, thanking whatever gods may be that I had played handball every Saturday morning with Bob — a dreary game indeed — or I might not have made the jump. It dawned on me as the beast roared past into the cabin yard that this was not a cow but a bull, its balloonish pink testicles flopping around as it swung back toward me, the dogs yipping at its heels. I turned to see Verdugo and the cowboys riding toward me with Verdugo yelling, "Close the back gate!" I jumped down and headed off at a dead run and barely beat the bull. He glared as I closed the gate, rattling it fearfully with his horns, then opened his great mouth a scant few feet from my face and bellowed mightily, covering me with spittle, his red eyes full of hate. I admit I shuddered.

"Thanks. Looks like you got yourself a yard pet," said Verdugo as he rode up. "That old baloney bull's a pain in the ass." He noted my confusion. "Too old to cover many cows. Too tough for good meat. They'll turn him into baloney, so he's a baloney bull."

Verdugo's crone of a mother brought out beer and I accepted one despite the fact it was Friday. My father had been dead thirty-eight years and the danger of my becoming an alcoholic could be thought receding. Verdugo and the Mexican cowboys were rehearsing the event in Spanish and one slapped me on the back. I admit I felt a twinge of pride for being of some use for the first time since my tormented school year passed into history (what history?) last June.

I was invited into the house for late lunch and saw no reason to refuse. Verdugo's wife was still off at the country school down the road where she taught grades kindergarten through six. In their kitchen I was pleased to solve the mystery of local fireplaces, as there was no grate in my own in the cabin. They tilt the logs upright against the back and do not use grates. I meant to light a fire myself when I returned after lunch. The adobe was smallish but neat as a pin and I wondered at the fact that Verdugo and his wife had no children.

We were fed large bowls of a peppery stew, a bit too hot to the tongue for my taste, full of hominy and pork, over which you sprinkled chopped onions and radishes and a variety of parsley called cilantro. Marilyn used to grow it in her herb garden and I always thought the flavor quite foreign — appropriate, as this location was infinitely more exotic to me than England or France. As I ate I tried to make sense of the rapid-fire Spanish being spoken, having learned both French and Italian, and thinking the verb structure of all Roman languages to be similar. I can't say I picked up a single word, and instead stared out the window at the tarp-covered swimming pool and burlap-wrapped rose bushes of the main house perhaps a hundred yards distant. At that very moment I had the peculiar sensation that my brain was melting. It wasn't just the pepper sauce that Verdugo had pushed my way but a sense that my thinking process, my brain itself, could no longer bear up under its discriminatory pressures. The radio was on a station in Mexico, a country only twenty miles south. The radio in my cabin could get only Mexican stations because of the mountains to the north. I had the sensation that my melting brain was making me as dumb as a child who doesn't quite believe in the world except for the one directly in front of him. At that instant I regretted that I had flushed all my medicines down the toilet.

Verdugo tapped my arm — my reverie apparently disturbed him and his cowboys, who stared at me intently. I looked into my empty bowl and the old woman filled it again, tweaking my earlobe with a laugh. I was saved from further embarrassment by the sudden appearance of Mrs. Verdugo coming home from school. She was breezy as she always seemed to be and this evidently was not a matter of putting on a good face. Then Verdugo asked me if I wanted to ride up with him to Tucson with the load of cattle and I found myself saying no, that I had work to do, when I would have given anything, God knows why, to ride in that immense truck.

"Oh, I thought they'd let you go," Verdugo said before he could catch himself.

"You're probably writing another book," Mrs. Verdugo chimed in, then rushed off, returning with my *Economics of Madness* book. "Deirdre gave this to me." She passed the book to the cowboys and they handled it gravely.

"Maybe your next trip," I said, now trying to save face for this woman who had tried so hard for me. Then I bolted from the house, tipping over my chair in the process.

*

I did not get up from my bed, where I lay face down like a distressed girl. I listened to them load the cattle truck and heard it roar off, feeling a specific remorse. My father drove a similar truck around Toledo and environs, carrying on a flatbed trailer a crane he operated, and I had ridden with him several times. Quite suddenly I remembered the bull in the yard — when I returned from lunch I had forgotten he was out there, and it occurred to me I might have been ambushed. I got up and looked out the back window. The gate was broken off its hinges and the bull grazed serenely in a small orchard some fifty yards away. I opened the window and gave him a loud hello, at which he snorted and shuffled farther down the creek bed, turning his big bottom toward me, I suspect to make me disappear.

The missed truck ride still gave me a twinge of regret. I thought of lying back down but was fearful that the meltdown that had begun in my brain might continue and that if I dozed off I might awake with a skull full of putty. I started a fire, pleased at how aromatic the wood was, found a cutting board in the kitchen to use for a writing table, and pulled the rocker up next to the fireplace to make notes — on, I might add, nothing in particular. I've been making literally cartons of notes since my book was published just short of twenty years ago. I daresay many of my notes are brilliant but I lack the ability to connect all of their disparities. The vaunted "negative capability" that Keats ascribed to Shakespeare is a curse to a scholar who is then liable to delay his conclusions to the grave. We catch ourselves frozen and stuttering in incertitude. As an instance, I agreed over a year ago to provide an introduction for a paperback edition of a selection of John Clare's poetry. So far I have come up with "Clare was Clare" on a three-by-five card. What has held me back is the recurrent image of Clare throwing himself into any available body of water, not for the purposes of suicide but because, as he said, it "felt better." This appears to be a noteworthy example of his insanity but then, at base, why shouldn't a person throw himself in the water if he wishes to?

*

I must get the rest of the soiled details out of the way. After my collision with the mime troupe was put to sleep I was able to regain my balance for a couple of weeks, until one Saturday, after our handball game, I was sitting in Bob's den with my six Watneys, letting them warm up, listening to Purcell's "Come Ye, Sons of Art," sung by Alfred Deller, the renowned countertenor. Bob's Saturday habit was a bottle of Sancerre — he had taught in France as a Fulbright exchange professor and was as much a Francophile as I was an Anglophile.

As Purcell ended and Bob changed the disc to Esther Lammandier, he made the announcement that a student of his had seen Dean Ballard smooching with Elizabeth (Reed's "squeeze," as Bob put it) in a Chicago jazz club. This was startling news indeed. I was amazed that Ballard was foolhardy enough to gamble his career, as our little college was in the forefront of the recent move to ban all such relations between students and professors and administrators. In fact, Dean Ballard chaired the original steering committee on the subject. Bob surprised me by saying he felt somewhat envious of Ballard. Occasionally Elizabeth will shed her used-clothing disguise and wear a miniskirt and a soft cotton T-shirt with no bra, which causes no little local confusion. I'm sure it's at Reed's instigation, as he preens around the campus with her, cupping her bottom and breasts with a satanic leer on his face. All the English faculty have remarked puzzledly on why our most brilliant student must be our nastiest.

The upshot of the news about Ballard's misbehavior was that I drank my six Watneys too fast and didn't eat much from the cheese board that Bob had set out. Privately I don't care for the fetid odor of goat cheese but I wanted to humor Bob, so I nibbled it. Anyway, on the five-block drive home I was fuzzy and inattentive and I nicked the rear end of a car at a stoplight. As it happened, the car was being driven by the basketball coach, several of whose students I had flunked, and he alerted the police from his car phone with relish. The two policemen gave me a Breathalyzer and I narrowly passed with a .08. Two more hundredths and I would have gone to the hoosegow. The policemen were repelled by the odor on their instrument left by the single bite of goat cheese I had taken, and jokingly asked if I had been dining on dog poop. I cautioned them against getting fresh, and drove on after exchanging insurance information with the coach, who appeared disappointed that I hadn't been put in chains.

This experience in itself would have been enough to send any man into disarray, but I had one more nightmare coming that evening. I took a long nap in my commodious apartment on the ground floor of an old Victorian house, and was awakened by the first big thunderstorm of spring. I thought I heard Mrs. Craig's cat mewing and scratching at the back door for the usual snack or perhaps to come in out of the storm. Mrs. Craig lives upstairs and cooks me dinner five nights a week for a fee, unimaginative slop but the deal is too convenient to break. I've bought her dozens of cookbooks but she has failed to take the hint. Even her meatloaf falls apart, leaving crevices similar to those in photographs of the human brain.

Anyway, I opened the back door to the warm blustery rain and called for the cat, who owned the ridiculous name of Tabby. No cat, so I stepped out on the back porch wearing only my underpants and continued to call. Suddenly an ill wind blew the door shut and I was locked out. I covered myself as well as possible, which was very little, climbed the back stairs to get a key from old Mrs. Craig, forgetting that she was in Indianapolis for a funeral — going to funerals being a habit she has developed into a sport.

No relative is too distant, no friendship to vague, for Mrs. Craig to indulge her mourning.

I banged loudly at Mrs. Craig's door, in haste to get out of the rain that had now become a deluge. A tall, lumpish woman appeared at the door, obviously not Mrs. Craig (I later found it was her niece from Benton Harbor), and before I could say "key" she began her bloody screaming and slammed the door under the ludicrous notion that I intended harm. Even if I had stepped up onto a footstool I could not have achieved parity with this hysterical Amazon.

I retreated to my parked car in the driveway below, for want of a better option. I noted by the car clock that I was missing my NPR program of Scottish and Irish folk ballads. Soon enough the police arrived and I allowed them to wander around in the rain awhile before I beeped the horn. One of them was so startled he actually drew his revolver, and I could see how in contemporary America even the most minimal event could lead to violent death. As luck would have it, the police were the same pair that had arrived after my minor accident. I was asked to clasp my hands and they drew me out of the car by the wrists, observing to each other that it was unlikely my underpants hid an effective weapon.

We stood within my open back door and I managed to talk myself out of an assortment of charges, including drunk and disorderly and indecent exposure. One of them returned upstairs and secured my key while the other allowed it had not been my day, to which I agreed. Then he said, and this should be duly noted, that both of the day's peccadillos would have to be reported to the college administration as was the recent custom. We have reached the point where American higher education is beginning to remind one of the articles one reads about Cuba, where everyone is intent upon spying on one another and reporting it to a committee.

*

I have always dreaded the short days of December leading up to the relief of the winter solstice, when we begin to gain minutes of light. It was only four in the afternoon but looking east it was easy to sense the darkness looming there. I pushed back farther from the heat of the fire, then heard a commotion outdoors and went to the window, picking up a pair of binoculars, on temporary loan from Deirdre in the unlikely presumption that I was going to become interested in the natural world. My quarrelsome point with Deirdre on this matter is that man is nature too, and the study of what man has written must be considered my study of the natural world, to which she answered, "You're full of shit." Young women swear these days.

Through the binoculars I could see Mrs. Verdugo yelling at the bull, who was grazing perhaps twenty feet from her back door. She went into the house and came right back out with a broom, ran over, and began swatting the bull in the ass and it quickly trundled off. I admired her bravery, yet I suppose it somewhat lessened the quality of my own. I was surprised that the dogs who were dozing out by the corral didn't come to her aid but decided they must respond only to Verdugo's orders and not his wife's. Then a black-haired girl on a spirited horse rode into view, stopped to chat with Mrs. Verdugo a moment, and continued on the trail toward the mountains to the south.

On seeing the winsome girl I had a ghastly shudder pass over my body, remembering in an instant the girl I saw at the far end of my paper route, whose name was Miriam, and whom I loved with the desperation one is capable of only once in a lifetime, a childhood version of *Wuthering Heights.* At the same time I made an absurd and obvious identification with myself and the baloney bull — not that I was fearsome, but that after fifty I had been considered somehow worthless and been put out to pasture. If ours was more directly a cannibal culture, by now I would be so much lunch meat.

*

At four-thirty Mrs. Verdugo showed up on my doorstep holding a warm jacket, and asked me to take a walk. I could see the sure hand of Deirdre in this.

"Did Deirdre call?" I asked.

"Why, yes, how did you know?" Mrs. Verdugo only pretended she was flustered and I had caught her off guard. The emotional subtlety of the female compared to the male is boggling. I began to concoct an acid witticism but Mrs. Verdugo was undeserving, so I put on the coat instead. I had been a shut-in for my entire first week in Arizona in hopes that the containing atmosphere of the cabin would settle my mind, but I was unsure of the outcome. Bob had told me during my darkest time last September that the accuracy of the mind weighing itself is questionable.

We began with the Jeep. Mrs. Verdugo unscrewed the bald shift knob and replaced it with one from the pickup that had rubrics to indicate the position of the gears. She patiently rehearsed the moves but I was somewhat inattentive, turning to look at the dogs who had jumped in back. Now that I had become a possible source of fun, their eyes warmed to me and their tails thumped.

Mrs. Verdugo headed the Jeep up the same trail the girl with black hair had taken and I felt a touch of fear over the idea we might see her, so much so that I didn't hear Mrs. Verdugo yelling over the roar of the Jeep and she had to repeat herself.

"Call me Lillian." She stopped the Jeep and came around to my side. "Now it's your turn."

"I'll try tomorrow," I said, refusing to budge.

My day had been full enough, especially when you consider I had spent nearly five months in my darkened apartment except for an occasional hearing. When the bad news finally came in early September, I did not emerge until Thanksgiving weekend when Deirdre dragged me into the open air. I can't say I was all that unhappy, and had been able to fake normalcy when Deirdre called during my frozen period. I'd chat about the problems I was having with the classes I wasn't actually teaching. Meanwhile, I'd only seen Bob and Mrs. Craig during the last three months. Deirdre always called at dinnertime, and my deception was at last unraveled when she called the English Department to reconfirm her invitation for me to come to Chicago for Thanksgiving. The department secretary, Mrs. Haines, who is a preposterous gossip, then told Deirdre the entire sickening story. Mrs. Haines has known Deirdre since she was a little girl and it was inevitable that I'd be found out. Bob was sworn to secrecy, which was easy enough for him because he has peculiar theories about mental problems. "When the wine is bitter, become the wine," he'd say, cribbing from Rilke.

"I'm a teacher too," Lillian said. "You can't drive a standard shift, so I'll teach you. Deirdre said you can't cook, so I'll give you lessons. It wouldn't look good if you starved to death when we're supposed to be looking after you."

I told her I was very good at moping and brooding. Agenbite of inwit. That sort of thing. She had parked the Jeep and we were walking up a narrower trail. Above the tops of the pine trees there were troublesome-looking rock formations, the kind one would imagine appearing in local ghost stories. The dogs were careening around bushes but then one stopped on the trail ahead to sniff something. I was dismayed to find that one of Deirdre's nature-buff types had taken a dump on our pathway.

"How appalling," I said. "There's a Sierra Clubber out there who deserves a horsewhipping."

"Nonsense. It's just a mountain lion." Lillian toed the dried scat and moved on.

It took a few minutes for me to digest what she was saying. I'm not normally frightened by wild animals, but then I do not recall coming into contact with any. Since it was such a new experience I had no idea how to deal with it. I peered upward at the reddish cliffs a few hundred yards away and speculated that the lion might be looking at us from that vantage point, just as the Indians did in the movies of my youth. My reverie was interrupted when Lillian trotted back, assuring me that mountain lions are relatively harmless, although one did "nail a jogger" up in Colorado a few years back. I became busy resolving to continue my life, as always, without jogging, when the girl on the horse came cantering toward us, passing by with a merry hello. I was relieved to see that she was lovely indeed but she did not resemble Miriam from long ago, whose tenth-grade photo I still carry in a secret compartment in my wallet.

*

The final downfall came through what Bob called my gullibility. On the Wednesday morning after my weekend police difficulties I was summoned to Dean Ballard's office for a meeting which began with scant mention of my brushes with the law. "I see you had yourself quite a Saturday," said Ballard. Rather than myself, the core problem was Elizabeth, who represented the fourth generation of her well-heeled family to attend the college. It should come as no surprise to anyone that the children of families who can fatten the endowment are catered to. The department's only classicist, a dear old Oxonian lady, had run out of patience with Elizabeth and had consented to have her position as advisor to Elizabeth's senior thesis transferred to me. This was a complicated matter of academic etiquette, as our department prides itself on the strictest of standards which also rids us of any riffraff that might be sent our way by the Athletics Department. This includes Bob, who is particularly ruthless with athletes.

Our classicist was well aware that I was the only member of the English faculty as demanding as she was, and this cagey ploy was an attempt to dump Elizabeth out of the frying pan into an inferno. It was all quite irritating, as I had had Elizabeth in two classes and she was a whiner who barely reached the mediocre in performance, other than her silly personality changes. Naturally I understood Ballard's position which, at base, entailed getting the girl graduated in three weeks, and she could only manage that by completing an acceptable thesis. The fact that I was tenured protected me from undue pressure, but then tenure isn't what it used to be.

It was at this point I was offered a pact with the devil. My problems with sexism, mimes, anti-Semitism (the Ezra Pound quote), my difficulties with the law, were, as Ballard called them, "ounces," but ounces eventually added up to pounds. Even these minor missteps would eventually come to the attention of the president and the board of trustees when they made their annual review of the faculty. Anyone with three possible demerits had a red tag on his dossier and the problems were discussed. Of course, Ballard would defend me against the absurdity of the demerits but if they continued to mount up, there was only so much he could do.

During all of this I had begun to study Ballard's feet, which he had propped up on the corner of the desk. His suit was decently tailored but his feet were adorned with large, thuggish hiking boots as if he intended to launch himself into the wilds of the village park at lunchtime. I wondered if he had worn these selfsame boots into the Chicago jazz club with the girl in question. Rather than smell the true pungency of the rat, I simply asked him with mock sophistication what kind of deal could be made. He wadded up a piece of paper and tossed it expertly into a distant wastebasket. The gesture was a bit Oriental for my taste, so he spelled it out by saying that if I saw Elizabeth through her thesis difficulties, it was at his discretion to expunge my record. He had no such powers but the wadded-up paper meant that he'd simply destroy the record in question.

I wanted to delay my decision but he insisted it be made instantly. I said, "Oh, very well." We shook hands and I left.

My grossest error was in not immediately sharing my dilemma with Bob, who would have offered cautionary advice. I hate to be a bother to anyone and also I was ashamed to be involved in a mess which, after the fact, turned out to be an unprovable triple blackmail engineered by Reed, with the more than tacit cooperation of Ballard, who was saving his own skin.

*

Once as a youngster I was blowing bubbles. This irked my mother, Florence, who thought the burst bubbles would stain the furniture and walls. But I could blow bubbles with impunity, as my father, Ike, had forbidden her to strike me because he had been roughed up badly as a child in Kentucky. The soap mixture was just right and the bubbles were grand indeed, floating around the living room catching a shaft of sunlight through the south window. I asked my mother why I could see my reflection in the bubble and she replied irritably that I could see myself because I was trapped within the bubble and always would be.

*

Elizabeth, you among others are evil, and I write this to be shut of absolutely everything I have experienced up until the day I finish — that is, if the disease does not thieve my lucidity. Before I forget, I had a fine supper of fried fish and salad with Lillian. Verdugo wasn't due back from Tucson until late and she took advantage of the situation to cook fish which Verdugo refuses to eat. She said he was born and raised down on the Sonoran coast of the Sea of Cortés, ate fish every day as a child, and now refuses to touch it, which seems reasonable. I stood next to Lillian at the stove to learn the process and she said I turned the fillets rather nicely. Before I left she admitted that she would call Deirdre in Chicago to tell her she had gotten me outdoors.

But Elizabeth. When Bob did find out I had chosen to help her, he thought I was stark ravers, though I didn't admit the whole deal. Elizabeth fairly waltzed into my office without a specific appointment, carrying a book bag of notes, the odd paragraph, and a stack of musings, as it were. Despite her dinginess she was a woman of the world and had traveled widely, however literarily naive. It seemed odd that her boyfriend, Reed, was a penniless sophomore, but then I had recently read that older women currently favored younger men. Deirdre liked to say that I was middle-aged by thirty, which would make me old indeed at the present date.

The true bone of contention with the classicist was that Elizabeth wanted to call her paper "Sexism in Yeats" instead of the more restrained "Women in the Poetry of William Butler Yeats" that had been strongly advised. The two of them never advanced much past this battle in eight months, and the base of the quarrel gave me ugly tremors. Of what purpose was it to attack Yeats using values that were unknown to his culture? I tried to lighten the mood by saying, "This is like attacking Jesus for not flossing," which passed through her head with the speed of a neutron. She was dour in a sweatshirt and jeans, the crumpled notes spread out on my desk with all the charm of parking tickets. But then I had already compromised myself, so I acceded to her title.

"I guess what I want to say is that Yeats's creepy values are repulsive to today's women," she said, offering a tentative smile.

It was at this point I began to develop a sense of suffocation, as if I were in a dentist's chair to get wisdom teeth pulled, the gas mask strapped to my face but nothing in the tank, nothing at all that could be drawn by the breath. The problem had nothing to do with feminism (I had lived with two brilliant and shrewd examples in my wife and daughter) but with simple stupidity, also the profoundest sense that I was betraying a code of values, a tradition. Of course, I teased myself cynically, how could I think I was defending a tradition of learning when no one was attacking it? The tradition had become utterly ignored and here I was in the middle of life's journey, suddenly lost, unable to catch my breath or remove the lump or whatever in my throat and beneath my breastbone.

Department regulations against smoking were strict and had been in effect for a year. I was the only smoker left after an old colleague, a Howells scholar (William Dean), retired with terminal emphysema. I was also the only department member who didn't own or know how to use a word processor. I only mention these two facts because it was impossible to work with Elizabeth in my office while I frantically chewed stick after stick of Dentyne, dashing down to the back entrance to smoke with a janitor with an unsightly goiter who would wink at me as we puffed in common anguish.

So Reed would drop Elizabeth off at my apartment every afternoon at three, then drive away in her car, the poet manqué in the new Mustang convertible. We'd plunge immediately into the project with Elizabeth at her expensive word processor, a laptop model called, of all things, the Word Book, which the lovely dunce could work with expertise. We dispensed with the more elaborate variorum edition of Yeats and worked out of M. L. Rosenthal's excellent *Selected Poems and Three Plays.*

Unfortunately Elizabeth had an attention span on the order of a politician's, so I ended up dictating much of the paper which, though it had to pass a committee of three, mostly only needed the advisor's unqualified approval. In the mad rush to finish the vile chore I lost some of my hesitancy about making connections, spinning metaphors, twiddling similes. One warm afternoon while waiting for Elizabeth on the porch I even waved at Reed when they arrived. The next day he stopped to chat, saying that it was time to "throw in the towel" on the matter of the department's non-funding of his febrile magazine, *Openings.* The nasty little Iago referred to Yeats as an "old, outworn enormity," as if I didn't know the phrase had been coined by that fabulous brat Rimbaud.

The day of doom was a hot one and my hands tremble in the remembrance. I had wondered idly why Reed had kept sending Elizabeth to her chores in the same dowdy outfits throughout the ten-day duration of our project — one of her blue work shirts still contained a slight tincture of kerosene, a memory of working folks in Toledo so long ago. Predictably (if I had thought it over), she arrived the last day in a deep V-neck T-shirt, short skirt, and sandals, dropped off this time by two sorority sisters who sped off in her car. Ever so slightly to her credit, she seemed nervous that day as the plot thickened to its grand finale. She sped blithely through my dictated conclusion, adding her own *bons mots* so that the paper could be identified as clearly her own. We had our last spat about "For Anne Gregory" and its incendiary last lines:

I heard an old religious man
But yesternight declare
That he had found a text to prove
That only God, my dear,
Could love you for yourself alone
And not your yellow hair.

"What if she got cancer and lost her hair because of chemo?" Elizabeth had asked, bending over my notes so that I could not help but note her bare pert breasts under the T-shirt, then flouncing off to change one of the cache of Deirdre's old phonograph records she had discovered.

"I'm confident that doctors hadn't discovered chemo at that time," I said, noting with discomfort that Elizabeth had sprawled on her stomach on the floor, her rear in the scant skirt seemingly aimed at me. It may not have been devious on her part but I sped back to the kitchen and washed my face with cold water. I tried to reassure myself that the girl was barking up the wrong tree. In the ten years since my divorce I had tried to make love twice but found myself ineffective and have abandoned the habit. There was one pleasant goodbye session with Marilyn the day our divorce became final and that was that.

I headed back to the desk, trying to pass Elizabeth in the hall. She was heading, I presume, for the bathroom. She blocked my way and embraced me and I nearly fainted with the odor of lilac on her neck. I allowed myself a single passionate kiss, a clutch and a fondle, staring out the window at a bird Marilyn referred to as a grackle in the flowering lilac bush, certainly an unattractive name for so striking a bird. Elizabeth hiked up her little skirt and fumbled at my fly.

Somewhat to my surprise I was indeed ready to deliver the goods. What stopped me? I don't know. I pushed her away and fled back to the living room, and there stood Elizabeth's two sorority sisters who chirped, as if on cue, "What have you done to her?" From back in the hall we could hear Elizabeth begin to screech and sob, and at that moment it didn't take any prescience on my part to realize my goose was cooked.

II

I WAS KEPT awake quite late by the howls and yipes of the dogs which seemed to be circling the property with great energy in the night. I meant to question Verdugo on the matter, as during the entirety of my first week here the animals hadn't made a peep after dark. Then, soon after first light I heard Mrs. Verdugo call out and ring the dinner bell near the back door, our agreed-upon signal for a phone call, of which I had had none to that point.

I correctly assumed it was Deirdre calling from Chicago. The smiling Verdugos left the kitchen to give me privacy except for Grandma, who had reappeared after a day's absence and who also had given no sign she understood English. Still, I sensed tension in the household. Verdugo had returned very late without the immense truck which I assumed he had rented. While I talked with Deirdre I noted out the window that their late-model Ford had a crumpled front fender and Verdugo's face had looked a bit bloated when he was bent over his steaming coffee. Miles beyond the car, the top of a mountain glistened with snow. Our own particular canyon didn't get any sun until mid-morning.

It was difficult to steer Deirdre away from the therapeutic chitchat that is part of her profession. She wanted to know my plans for the day and whether they contained any activity beyond brooding. I said I was in the middle of a full-fledged campaign to learn the standard shift, after which I was going to take the dogs for both a ride and a walk. This pleased her, as part of her innovative work in group therapy is taking a gaggle of woebegone patients on long walks under the assumption that physical exhaustion lightens the mental load. There were other questions flirting around the edge of my "anxiety attack" at the Desert Museum. I was dangerously close to asking her about the sensation of my brain melting the day before, but I didn't understand the experience well enough to describe it, and also I didn't want to alarm her in case the melting was a further symptom of some dire mental disease, such as Alzheimer's.

Part of my hesitancy with Deirdre was due to Marilyn's addiction to oodles of mental self-help books of every imaginable discipline, from self-hypnosis to cranial massage. Years ago she had returned from her est week notably the same person. Deirdre concluded our conversation by trying to get me to promise to come to Chicago for Christmas, and failing that, asked if I had been reading the nature books she had bought for me. Of course, I said, but then was stumped when she asked what birds I'd seen. Fumbling around, I came up with a grackle, which made her shriek with laughter as there are no grackles hereabouts. I said it looked like a grackle, only with a bluish head. This stumped the expert and we said goodbye. I did, in fact, see the bird staring at me on the way to the phone, perched on the barbecue machine.

The Verdugos were disappointed when I announced I didn't feel up to the Saturday shopping trip. I actually surprised myself when I said no, and asked them only to get me a variety of canned soups. I suspected they were upset because on that particular day their marriage needed a buffer zone and I was to be it. There was also the glum prospect of the pre-Christmas shopping gaiety some fifty miles away in Nogales, though I hadn't been there. To change the subject I asked Verdugo about the shrill barking of the dogs in the night and he said it was just the coyotes chasing dinner, which gave me a new regard for my immediate surroundings. It was doubtless time to take a look at Deirdre's nature books, not that I was entering totally strange country — beginning in his childhood John Clare had been a relentlessly curious amateur naturalist, a part of his work I tended to ignore.

"Are you sure you're fine?" Mrs. Verdugo had followed me out in the yard and took my arm. "You're looking a little peculiar."

I insisted I felt okay and rushed to my cabin as if it were a refuge. In fact, I felt interior tremors, perhaps a coordinate to the liquefying brain of the day before. At least Lillian used "peculiar" rather than such psychologisms as "depression" or "nervous breakdown," which are pathetic euphemisms for the profoundest of life processes.

Oddly, the cabin seemed to have shrunk in size, although I could only focus on parts of it at once. I put on my borrowed coat and recalled one of Deirdre's trick questions: "Imagine you are in an empty house and quickly open a closed door. What do you see?" Out flows the gray extrudate of our culture and my life within it which suffocates me. I was pleased with my current answer, and yet the cabin continued to visibly shrink. I escaped outside, and not a moment too soon, circling around to the far side where I discovered that by looking in a window, through the cabin, and out another window I could watch the Verdugos' adobe unobserved. My aim was to practice the standard shift without any interference.

I stood there like a statue for over an hour. It was at this point that I made the odd connection between the muddied corpse of the construction worker I had seen in the medical center last May and the death of my own father during my twelfth summer. The crane he had been operating had slid backward into a deep culvert full of water and he had been trapped there. I wasn't allowed to see the body but I'm confident that it was muddy indeed. My thoughts turned again to the desperate exploits of Thelma and Louise, and my childish urge to help them out. After the movie I had stood outside a Mexican restaurant for quite some time, quarreling with myself about whether I should go in. Instead, I ate a foul hamburger at the bus station. Unlike Thelma and Louise, Deirdre and Marilyn had never needed any help that I could remember.

Eventually the Verdugos left and I hurriedly made my way to the Jeep, finding the keys under the seat where I had seen Lillian secrete them. The two cowboys were gone, evidently for the weekend. The horses in the corral lined up to watch my Jeep practice as if I were the moment's entertainment, and the three dogs appeared from nowhere, jumping in the back. I turned on the ignition and the vehicle that had won World War II chugged to life.

My first efforts to back the Jeep away from the granary failed with a jerky stall when I was precipitous with the clutch. Finally this was accomplished, and I paused to restudy the indented rubrics on the shift knob, which seemed obvious enough, progressing from 1 to 3. I was on the verge of success, easing the vehicle out of the barnyard, when the grandma trotted out and handed me a paper bag and the Jeep stalled again. She tousled my hair with unwelcome familiarity, but then I thought, Why get upset at the etiquette of this old lady who had given me a sack lunch? I said "*gracias,*" gave her a winning smile, restarted the vehicle, and was off for the mountains, or wherever whichever road took me, with a tremor in my heart rather than a song.

*

Perhaps in the years to come I will regard that day as the signal day of my life, but for the present I am terribly frightened, if a little thankful. The first hour I drove tentatively, then noted the dogs barked when I slowed down. So I drove faster, for want of anything better to do than please dogs. It beat the hell out of pleasing students, or more particularly Marilyn in the last few years of our marriage. Unfaithful wives are great fault finders because it fuels their sense of self-justification, or so Bob told me. It is not the sort of observation I'm capable of making. This came after I confessed to Bob that I had caught Marilyn with her elbows neatly arranged on the washer and dryer, catching it from behind from a visiting California poet. Marilyn loved giving parties for visiting poets, finding companionship, I suppose, in their extravagant personalities. I usually went to bed early and it was only by happenstance that I discovered Marilyn, thinking I heard an odd racket at two A.M. I backed away stealthily and she never knew I was aware of this indiscretion, only the prolonged affair with Ballard which, it seems, was public knowledge throughout our academic community before I knew it. Her unfaithfulness was too fundamental for me to be much surprised at the actual series of events.

I drove past what appeared to be a prosperous ranch with immense cattle owning a peculiar hump on their backs, similar to photos one sees of cattle in India. I headed back up a road leading into the mountains, deciding that I wanted to see snow at close range. The dogs seemed to agree, preferring the smells of the forested slopes to the pastures of the lowlands. We went up and up for nearly an hour and I was thankful that I wore the warm coat, noticing for the first time that it smelled like horses and cows. The dogs would dash from one side of the compartment to the other, barking at the passing sights and odors.

Finally snow began to appear on the narrow roadside, and quickly enough it covered the forest floor. I pulled off into a smallish clearing to walk for a while. The images of Marilyn, Ballard, and the college arose again but my mind lacked the energy to maintain their presence. They simply disappeared and I wondered if that meant I utterly did not care anymore. I experimented with images of Deirdre and Bob — pleasant enough, but they also drifted away.

I walked a few hundred yards through stunted trees and heaps of boulders strewn around and covered with snow, confident that I could retrace my steps but turning around several times to make sure. The dogs scooted in circles with mad abandon and I reminded myself to learn their individual names. For some reason the landscape began to give me the severest tremors yet, though my vision was wide and clear, unlike in the cabin. When it occurred to me that my inner trembling might have nothing to do with the landscape, the earth abruptly vanished and I was at the edge of a cliff, or at least a steep slope. Before me was a valley so immense in eastern terms that I drew in my breath sharply.

For a moment I questioned that I was imagining what I saw. Far across the valley was a range of snow-capped mountains I judged to be in Mexico, as the sun was in that direction and I guessed it to be south. I could see no sign of human habitation and this, perhaps, began to make me feel vertiginous. I backed away in fear of being sucked into this beautiful void and made my way over to a big group of boulders surrounded by bushes that I later learned were called manzanitas. I sat down in a dry area under an overhanging rock and was diverted by the idea that the dogs were uncomfortable about the place. There was a slight urine scent and some tufts of hair and I guessed that an animal also used the rock for shelter.

It was at this point that everything let go. The insides of my brain and body quaked and shivered and I began to weep. This caused a total loss of equilibrium and I tipped sideways from my sitting position. For a few minutes I could not tell up from down and tears literally flowed. For the first time I understood how a body could be "racked" by sobs. In retrospect, I could not remember ever weeping before, although my eyes were vaguely moist at my father's funeral, at Deirdre's marriage ceremony, and at my mother Florence's burial seven years ago.

I flopped around weeping for just short of two hours and was tempted to throw away my watch. The dogs were alarmed except for one who tried to comfort me, albeit crudely, by nuzzling my neck and chest and lapping at my tears. I wept so long my feet and hands got cold. My urge to pitch my watch came from those long post-Elizabeth months when in the dungeon of my apartment I logged not sunlight or weather or my thoughts but the clock. There were dozens of pages of notations of what time it was, a habit that didn't seem alarming to me during that period, though one day when Bob visited he grimaced at my current work, the strings of inane numbers.

There's a natural hesitation on my part to use so large a word as suffering, but I suppose it was the main part of the experience, lying there blubbering and squirming in some animal's nest. It seemed that for half a year I had been trying to ignore what was directly in front of my nose and this had further blinded me: my reality had betrayed me, the reality to which I had devoted my life had disappeared. I no longer had control of the world I lived in or a single one of its inhabitants, and I myself was at large. A world that had welcomed me for three decades had shown me the door, and at fifty I owed that world nothing but my contempt, which in itself was too worthless to be indulged. The idea that I was not alone in this experience was just another worthless humanist gesture that would cripple me even more. This was not a barricade I could man with anyone else but the dogs that surrounded me, their faces cocked into question marks.

It was noon, but then who cared? I made a mental note to research time as disease. There are strange things afoot in the universe. Even the obvious fact that I had shown all the alertness of a supermarket mushroom during the long nightmare meant nothing. I was not about to recast my hopes as people make vain New Year's resolutions. I could not remember a single overnight miracle in the sheer tonnage of fiction and poetry I had spent my life reading. There was suddenly the idea that I had learned nothing from this life. The question was how, if I knew all the best examples of world literature, all the exquisitely drawn varieties of deceit and chicanery, love and death, could this have happened to me?

From my youth I had been a stupendous reader of good books, occasionally sinking a bit to the crime fiction my mother favored, though the best of that genre, Raymond Chandler for example, was very good indeed. Maybe I ultimately read for pleasure rather than learning because any Raymond Chandler hero could have seen my own mess looming in front of him. Maybe not. My profession, my livelihood, served to set my love of books to a rather Germanic marching tune. My profession and its fretwork of rules had given me the boot. Their reality had been a comfortable enough consensus right up to the time I had been excluded. I recalled the punch line of a long, stupid joke Bob told me about an adulterer being caught in a closet by an angry husband, and the adulterer saying, "Everybody's got to be somewheres." Bob spent a few of his student years in Paris, and to him this answer was an existential moment, the exact definition of which is lost in the fog of my graduate school years. Here I was, not in someone's closet but under a rock overhang, shaking now from cold rather than my torments.

*

Nearing the Jeep, I noticed a pale green Border Patrol vehicle parked in front of my own. A darkly Spanish-looking man in uniform was putting gas into the Jeep's tank from a can that looked brilliantly red against the wintry landscape. He turned with a smile at the approaching dogs but was surprised when he saw me.

"Those are J. M. Verdugo's dogs," he said.

"Phillip Caulkins is the name. I'm staying at the ranch." I offered my hand and he took it after finishing with the gas. He said J.M. was always running out of gas and Lillian, who was his cousin, would call him and he'd have to drop everything if J.M. was real late. He added that J.M. liked running out of gas and getting stuck, which seemed to me to be a curious vice.

"Indeed," I said.

"Indeed? I don't get you," the uniformed man said. "You mean, indeed he likes to run out of gas?" The radio in his vehicle crackled and he trotted up to it. I opened the sack the grandma gave me. I was famished and took a bite out of a bean and meat burrito which, though cold, was delicious. I tore off sloppy pieces to share with the dogs, unmindful of my endangered fingers.

The man returned from his patrol car. "Lillian's worried about you. It's four and you've been gone all day."

My watch, an old wind-up model I bought in London as a student, still read noon, which meant I might have set the world record for weeping for a man my age.

"Indeed. My watch stopped."

"Indeed, it must have." He laughed but not mockingly. "Real ballsy of you to wander around way back here all day. But you're Deirdre's father and she's a real fireball. You must be proud."

It was disarming to receive a double compliment when I could not remember a single, though after the fourth month in the apartment Bob said that I was really "sticking to my guns." My head was scarcely turned because I knew I was ballsy by default and wandered up here irrationally, though what did that matter? Deirdre had inherited my single-mindedness but that could be a mixed blessing, as I was beginning to learn.

"The name's Rod, short for Roderigo." He handed me a knit watch cap and I wondered if the message Lillian left included the information that I was daffy. "Follow me until the road forks, then you take the left and I'll take the right. Pleased to meet you. *Feliz Navidad.* Put on the hat or your skull will freeze up."

*

It was embarrassing to be welcomed as a prodigal son. Verdugo, Lillian, and Grandma rushed out in the yard all abuzz with my return. The sky was darkening and I felt a little like my father, who would return with icy clothes from a day's work in the winter. Verdugo fetched me a beer and I went off for a hot shower to thaw out, puzzled at the sight of someone at their window, or so I thought. There was something white on the face that quickly backed away, as if it were wearing a surgical mask.

I drank my beer in the steaming shower, a pleasant experience, then made the mistake of closely examining myself in the full-length mirror on the back of the bathroom door when I got out of the shower. The image was humiliating and tears came briefly. I looked shriveled, flaccid, ghastly in this, my first total peek since May. I had always walked to work, and that, plus handball on Saturday mornings, had kept me reasonably fit. Now it appeared as if I had just been sprung from a Korean POW camp. My God, could this be possible? Of course, there it was. Smaller than life and nearly ready for a coffin. It was difficult for me to understand how the mind could make the body forget itself. Maybe it was because the mind had forgotten nine tenths of the mind. There was a discouraging glimmer here.

The sun was setting down toward the mouth of the canyon with the treetops ready to burst into flame. Behind me my shadow was specific. My body tingled but no longer shook inside. I turned on the radio and, as I dressed, I listened to a Mexican song I judged to be about love and death. At least I thought I heard "*corazon*" and "*muerte.*" Maybe I'd pick up a Spanish grammar, presuming there was a bookstore within the hundred miles or so to Tucson. Then I noticed a small package on the desk with Deirdre's return address. Inside was a monocular with my name engraved on it and a short note saying that she knew I'd never be caught with binoculars around my neck and this would fit in a jacket pocket. In the waning light I caught my magnified *faux* grackle in the tree near the gate, staring back rather malevolently, I thought. Perhaps there was an ethical question in whether or not birds wished to be looked at. The dinner bell rang.

*

Mrs. Verdugo was wearing a floral print dress and was playing Mozart's *Jupiter* on the stereo, though certainly not the best rendition. But then Mozart is Mozart and clearly better than anything else man has made, including penicillin. I had neglected my listening the past six months and the music was nearly too powerful to endure. To calm myself down, I went to the stove where the grandma was cooking a chicken dish. She said "*mole*," which I presumed did not mean the underground rodent. The smell was as fragrant as the music, though the ingredients were undetectable, certainly a far cry from Mrs. Craig's habitual slop. Near the stove was an enormous mortar and pestle which Lillian had explained J.M. had found in the mountains and might very well be a thousand years old. I was busy doubting this item but saying nothing when J.M. appeared, fresh from a shower in a pearl-button cowboy shirt — a valid wardrobe, as he was a cowboy. I asked him what his initials stood for. He tightened a bit, almost a flinch, which emphasized his bodybuilder's physique. However, I suspect, unlike Ballard, he had never touched a barbell.

"James Monroe Verdugo. I'll tell you the story somewheres down the line." While he got out two cans of cold beer and a bottle of tequila with a horseshoe on the label, I reflected that he looked somewhat less Hispanic than Lillian, though his mother at the stove looked more so. Thus I deduced a pale-faced father.

"My little sister is here," Lillian said. "She's quite a problem."

I wondered how little her sister could be, as I guessed both Verdugos to be in their late thirties.

"A sister from hell," J.M. added. "Too bad we can't parachute her into Yugoslavia." He handed me a water glass half full of pale gold liquid. "To your health. You sure as hell look better than yesterday."

"She's no worse than your brother," Lillian said. "Her name's Magdalena. Not after the Bible but the town in Sonora."

We went to the window as the woman in question came galloping down the driveway on a chestnut horse. It was just before dark so Lillian turned on the yard lights, which made the horse spin and buck. Magdalena screamed and swore in Spanish but held her seat, looking furiously back at the house, a large white bandage glowing on her face.

"She was in a car wreck," Lillian said weakly.

"Her boyfriend beat the shit out of her," J.M. said. "When he went to sleep drunk she took a tire iron to him. She got off on self-defense — the judge is one of her gentleman friends. Last year she shot a guy way over in Phoenix. She's all the time defending herself." J.M. poured us another drink and gave Lillian a squeeze. She had tears in her eyes.

"Momma was too easy on her. She was the baby of the family."

Magdalena had unsaddled the horse and turned it out in the corral. On the way to the house she played roughly with the dogs, swinging the largest around by its collar, evidently a game they had devised, because the dog came back for more. She cut a trim though perhaps overmuscular figure in her jeans. When she came in the door she eyed me as coldly as the grackle, then took a deep gulp of the tequila directly from the bottle. She grabbed my proffered hand, studying it critically and apparently finding it flawed.

"The smart guy from the East. Welcome. Try to be careful," she said, dropping my hand and washing her own at the sink. She itched the bandage, which covered most of the left side of her face where her eye was also blackened. Her hair was frizzy and stuck out in a dark halo, like many of Bob's students and the renowned malcontent from our past, Angela Davis.

*

That night I had great difficulty sleeping, what with a piercing headache from the tequila and very probably from my prolonged weeping fit on the mountaintop. By midnight (I had gone to bed at ten) I had conceived a hatred for the radium-dial alarm clock. The clock makes us wait. The clock invented the difficult concept of waiting. We are always eager, willy-nilly, for the clock to get on with it.

I got up, dressed, made a stack of Deirdre's gift books, and opened a fresh packet of five-by-seven cards, my first since May. The small gesture has always excited me with the prospect of a new idea, a catchy phrase to amuse myself. I wrote, "The clock is the weapon with which we butcher our lives," and felt pleased with myself. From the age of twelve and my huge paper route, the largest in the Toledo area, my life has been strictly circumscribed by the clock. There is scarcely a profession more time-conscious than the academic — outside the obvious trains, planes, and buses — given the classes, appointments, committee meetings, faculty meetings, perhaps "meeting meetings" that are organized to stuff lacunae. Even our annual Modern Language Association convention meetings include schedule items such as "5:10–5:35, Getting to Know Each Other Cocktails."

Now I was perfectly aware that I'm not alone in this dire

strait but I don't care any longer about our collective dread. It's everyone for himself — or herself, of course. Dad used to say that all the world cares about is that you get to work on time. What that means to me at this point in my personal history is that it's time to reject the world. As much of my life as possible must be sloughed like a snake is said to slough its skin. Visions of anchorites, pillar saints, Buddhas, begin to dance in my head. Under our system each twenty-four-hour unit is subtracted from the end of our lives which further increases the vertigo. Never mind the incipient Alzheimer's; I have been deeply diseased by time. I have been buggered to near death by the clock.

Deep into the night I fumbled with this material somewhat in the manner of Madame Curie stirring her potions. I even drew several versions of a new calendar containing no less and no more than three to seven days a month. The fools of the world forced me to retain their months, but within these months my deft Montblanc pen opened up an immensity of space. To show myself the seriousness of my intent, I wrapped my watch around the cord of the Big Ben electric clock and dangled them both in the toilet, flushing it a dozen times with the first full laughter I could remember. The damnable watch still worked. I put it on the floor, stepped up on the toilet seat and jumped, smashing the watch to bits.

It occurred to me I was getting a little excitable, so I took the remnants of the two timepieces outside and peed on them to complete the scene appropriately. I reached back in the cabin and turned off the light, the better to see the stars. They were so dense they made the sky look flossy, almost a fog of stars which had drawn infinitely closer to me than ever before, as if my destruction of time had made me a friendlier object for their indeterminate powers. I drank the night air in gulps until I dizzied myself, watching the stars in their dance steps, the swirling that is noticeable to the attentive.

I recalled that I had seen a couple of sleeping bags in the cabin closet and quickly brought one back outside, stripped to my skin, and did a jig on the cold dew-damp grass. Despite not having slept outside during a lifetime, I adjusted immediately to the lack of ceiling, staring straight upward into the black holes that astronomers say are up in the heavens.

It was there, with my back tight to the earth, that I had yet another revelation that astounded me, and once again I didn't care if this peek into the unknown door was useful to anyone else. It began with my thinking, If only Bob could see me now, then moved on to his notion that our populace is fascinated to the point of sickness with gossip about entertainment, sports, and political figures because the very idea of personality itself is in question. The popularity of the concept of personality is merely a substitute for tradition and community. The simple-minded crave news of "personalities" and develop banal symptoms of the same, ignorant of the fact that true personality emerges out of character and work. According to Bob nearly all of what people think of as their personalities are absurdist idiosyncrasies at cross purposes with their lives and happiness. Ergo: I meant to get rid of my personality which insisted on maintaining a world that no longer existed. I did not want to live out my life in the strenuous effort to hold a ghost world together. It was plain as the stars that time herself moved in grand tidal sweeps rather than the tick-tocks we suffocate within, and that I must reshape myself to fully inhabit the earth rather than dawdle in the sump of my foibles.

Before I slept I wondered what time it was! This was

grease that would not easily wash off the hands but I'd give it a try. Meanwhile, there was something in the odor of the grass an inch from my nose that disturbed me. I sniffed it deeply and began to feel sexually aroused and this revived the idea that I might be losing my mind — not a fearful notion when the mind was of insufficient interest to be worth saving. Another sniff raised the image of Magdalena, who, sitting next to me at dinner, left a scent of antiseptic from her bandages mixed with lilac, the same scent as the accursed Elizabeth exuded in the hallway of my apartment. I wondered how I could be fully erect when both women clearly repelled me. Magdalena's features were overstrong, with densely olive skin, big teeth, a Roman nose, and pitch-black hair. I sensed a mannish cruelty in her eyes. J.M. implied she was a bit of a whore. A *puta*, he called her. When she laughed out loud at her own spoken memory of a nasty childhood joke she had played on Lillian, she grasped my arm so tightly I winced in pain. Her grip was as strong as a man's and it came out in conversation that before her totally wayward behavior she broke and trained horses for a living. She also chewed with her mouth partly open.

Magdalena drank a great deal and after dinner Lillian teased her into a parlor trick, perhaps hoping she'd fall down. J.M. put on a Mexican polka tape and Magdalena bounced around the room in a squatting position, kicking out one leg and then another in the manner of a Russian folk dancer. The sight was more grotesque than attractive. If this weren't enough, she began chewing several sticks of bubble gum at once while she did dishes with Lillian. I was pondering a graceful exit when she sat down on the couch in the too narrow opening between myself and the grandma, who laughed at everything she did. Magdalena put her face too close to mine and asked for help with her English grammar which was plainly atrocious, then blew a large bubble that touched my nose before I ducked backward. After that I bade everyone good night without giving her a reply.

*

At dawn I am greeted by the dogs, to whom my stone fence is no barrier. My head, like John Clare's, is pointed to the north and a warm breeze blows up my body and nose, redolent of pine and the trees J.M. said are black oak. My fraudulent grackle is doing its versions of howling. It's unthinkable a single bird makes that kind of noise. Wearing my underpants, I fetch the dog biscuits. The dogs don't think it's peculiar that I'm sleeping outside because they do it every night. This time I make them take their snacks gently, worming them out from my partially clenched fists.

The morning immediately presents its first pratfall. I can no longer do a single pushup, when a year ago I began the morning with an even dozen. It is the grim result of atrophication — at age fifty even a head cold is a *memento mori.* There is a brief vision of myself as a grown-up thalidomide baby trying to escape a house fire by the strength of its flippers. The fact that I had been offered a partial-disability pension also came to mind. I had accepted an early sabbatical at half pay with no substantial promises other than another hearing this coming spring. This is tantamount to dismissal. My full sabbatical, to come in two years, would have been a complete year in London, living in a small flat within two blocks of Hampstead Heath. When that professional consolation disappeared, along with my twenty thousand in cash savings to a bumbling lawyer, I totally lost heart. Our college offered none of the employee assurances of major universities where my shoddy treatment would have been met with protest, perhaps near riot. It was paternalistic to the *n*th degree, and with tenure it was assumed you were safe until you were buried in the Boot Hill overlooking the athletic field, of all places. This has become a society of so many raw issues that no one can be thought to behave well.

This bit of emotional recidivism put me in a funk but there was a quick boon in noticing I no longer had a watch at my wrist. I struggled to accomplish a single pushup.

"What are you doing? Screwing the ground?"

It was Magdalena on the chestnut horse, peering over the fence. I hadn't heard her approach because I had been listening to my worthless thoughts.

"I see you're also a voyeur," I snapped, though rather wanly. There was no way to cover myself with dignity.

"I think that means 'window peeker.' I'm not seeing you through no window."

"Any window," I corrected, lying on my stomach and feeling absurdly vulnerable.

"I'm not seeing you through *any* window," she screeched. "You look like a piece of roadkill."

"Thank you for finding me attractive," I said in desperation.

"Just wish I had me a camera. That's all."

"Just wish I had a camera," I corrected again.

She stepped off the horse directly onto the stone fence, then jumped down within inches of my face. She stooped and ran a strong hand down my bare spine so that I shivered. "You poor old dog. You're not dead yet."

I squeezed my eyes shut waiting for further insults, but then off she rode. If this was indeed a courtesan, a prostitute, a *puta*, the fabled heart of gold was not apparent. Even so, my mother lacked a heart of gold. With my father's insurance settlement she had bought a shabby restaurant and renamed it Florence's English Diner, quite the success before urban renewal demolished it the year before her death. She was charming and very British with her customers but an utter shrew with her employees.

My eyes moistened then at the memory of my rebellion. Miriam, my first love, had come into the diner for the first time and with a group of friends our age. I had been caught sorting a platter of silverware in a wet dishwasher's apron, the single most embarrassing moment in my life; thirty-five years later I still cringed. When I told Bob this story he quoted Dostoyevsky: "I maintain that to be too acutely conscious is to be diseased." Bob was never without an appropriate quote. He's on another Fulbright year, in Marseille, and I can imagine him at this moment taking a late afternoon stroll along the waterfront in his expensive trench coat, ever knowledgeable and alert for what life grudgingly offers.

I rose to my knees and a mile or so away I could see Magdalena and the horse making their way up the umbrous mountainside. At that instant I realized that there was no actual connection beyond my permission between my five senses and the world. This gave me a lightheaded sense of freedom that immediately lapsed into the troubled thought that this was the reason three billion people had three billion different versions of reality. Little consensus was possible, and less so every day. My personality, my consensus, had pretty much evolved from a job that had vanished. This was akin, in biblical terms, to worshiping graven images. It was apparent that people had to ritualize their existence or go insane.

It was only at this precise point there in the cabin yard that I realized the extent of the nervous collapse I had suffered. I might have pitched down a well of despondency but a noise I heard was not yodeling dogs, it was sirens coming up the long driveway to the ranch. I dressed hurriedly, watching the arrival of two squad cars and the pale green Border Patrol vehicle. With my monocular I could see Roderigo talking to J.M., and four policemen milling around the hired men's quarters, going in and out, checking the tack and equipment sheds. Then one of the policemen headed toward me, growing larger in my spyglass.

*

We have experienced the thrill of a modest dope raid. Verdugo's two cowboys had been caught at dawn trying to bring marijuana across the backcountry border with pack horses, and the police had hoped to find a cache of narcotics at the ranch itself. For some reason I was made irritable when the policemen who interviewed me did so with profound boredom, as if I were too senile to be effective or dangerous, but then it occurred to me Roderigo might have told them I was a visiting professor. I had the brief notion that I was a living cliché as the cop took a desultory peek in the closets.

When the policemen left I went in to have coffee with the Verdugos and Roderigo, who had tarried. From my own viewpoint it was quite a tonic to deal with an actual event. The minimal legal problem was that one of the cowboys was an illegal alien, making J.M. culpable for hiring him, though Roderigo was sure he could "heal" that matter.

Lillian was angered when the two men speculated on whether Magdalena was somehow involved. Had she ridden off this morning to meet the culprits in the mountains, unaware that they had already been arrested? She knew both of them well, but she had only been brought to the ranch because she'd had the "crap" beaten out of her. The connection began to seem slight to the two aspiring gumshoes, but then a far more dire problem arose. J.M. was short two hands and his roundup, less than a third done, was running late. He had gambled on "late grass" which hadn't eventuated and now the cattle were short on feed. J.M. said that my son-in-law's father, though he hadn't shown up in five years, was a real bear when it came to the accounts. I tried to imagine owning such a lovely place and not bothering to visit it. I had certainly read about such people years ago while flipping through Marilyn's fashion magazines.

"Perhaps I could be some use," I offered with a not very strong voice. J.M. merely stared at me in his angst, but then Lillian chimed in, saying that Magdalena could also earn her keep, adding that she was as good as any man, probably better. Thus it was that I became, with due regard to accurate semantics, not so much a cowboy or a cowhand, but a cow helper. Within days J.M. admitted gracefully that I was better than nothing.

*

It is three weeks later, somewhere in January, and has been raining for days (I torched the calendar on the small barbecue grill I bought myself for Christmas). One doesn't think of this sort of relentless, cold rain in southern Arizona. On two of the last three days Lillian hasn't been able to reach the country school. The creek bed that crosses the driveway which was dry when I arrived in December is now engorged with water. I stood at its edge this morning with the dogs, watching an entire cottonwood tree float by at an alarming pace, also a dead rattlesnake washed from its winter nest. Lillian has assured me that these vipers sleep the season through and aren't a matter of concern until late spring. The baloney bull stood across the rumply flood, bellowing at me as if he were lonesome.

My bones ache and my body is bruised. We trucked the last of the cattle to Tucson three days ago, barely making it across the creek. I have been paid five hundred dollars for the over three weeks of work and the amount, though absurdly small, has thrilled me to no end. I keep it in the Gideon Bible I swiped from the Tucson motel where I stayed at Christmas. It struck me as inappropriate to take part in the family's Christmas, so I fibbed and said I had been invited to spend the holiday with an old friend in Tucson. This white lie angered Deirdre when she called the Verdugos on Christmas Day and I was absent. The Gideon Bible had been my only reading material at the motel, and anyone who has read Christopher Smart's *Jubilate Agno* as often as I have knows this material can become tiresome. I did, however, find myself amazed when I discovered I had never gone to the trouble to disbelieve in the Resurrection of Christ. It certainly seemed more plausible than our space ventures or the Republican Party. When I drove back from warm Tucson in the open Jeep I had even prayed briefly during an ice and snow storm on the highway north of Sonoita.

I'd give myself a C-minus or less as a neophyte cow helper, or perhaps an Incomplete. The fact that I was better than nothing is meaningful to me. J.M. might have found extra help because he is well liked in the area, but his position is similar to a tenant farmer's, and they are not his cattle, so no one is interested in making the rich owner richer. I rode Mona, a mare of the ripe age of twenty-three years. She was one of Lillian's personal horses and had been retired for two years. According to Magdalena, who is quick to point out the negative, in horse terms Mona was older than I am, and that I was riding a grandmother. She was, however, willing to show me how to do a better job with the cattle.

Oddly, I thought, Mona understood and performed ninety percent of her job without the least human prodding, and worked excellently with the dogs in getting the correct cattle headed in the right direction down the mountain from the three different BLM (Bureau of Land Management) and Forest Service leases. It is commonly known, though I didn't know it, that ranchers receive rather economical leases of public lands for grazing, somewhat on the order of food stamps or other entitlements. Years ago one particularly unattractive writer friend of Marilyn's had brayed from the podium that he was the last member of the free-market economy and the rest of us were slobbering at the public trough.

Admittedly Mona wasn't the sort of dashing horse that J.M. or Magdalena rode. Her age and good sense made her a plodder. At the foot of small box canyons she'd sniff the air, then thread her way gracefully up through the trees and around the boulders, seeking out the stray hiding cow. As I said before, these cows were wild creatures and lacked the placidity of dairy breeds. Mona was not above giving them a good bite if they failed to move along.

If it was a coolish day I'd start a fire to accompany our lunch which was packed along in Mona's saddlebags. Once during the first week I had nearly forgotten the lunch, after which the grandma put it in the saddlebags herself when we got up an hour before daylight. Twice I saw our baloney bull, who proved capable of trotting up an incline that would be difficult for all but the most accomplished mountaineers. He was not alone in being obstreperous — some few of the cattle were deemed so obnoxious that they were left to run farther up the wintry heights of the range. In this situation J.M. admitted that it would have been different if he owned them himself. He grudgingly said to me that Magdalena was a sight to see on a horse. Her legs and bottom were so strong she sat on the saddle lightly, a technique she advised to me when I complained about my chafed and purple hinder. During difficult maneuvers she didn't sit on the saddle at all, but crouched on tensed legs as the horse whirled and pitched after cows, both horse and rider decidedly mammalian.

One bitterly cold day I built the lunch fire against a boulder to further reflect the heat. While we drank our coffee J.M. prodded me to tell my woeful tale and I rendered a shortened version. Both he and Magdalena demanded additional details to determine guilt between Reed and Ballard, and though Reed had obviously blackmailed Ballard over Elizabeth, J.M. and Magdalena held to the belief that Ballard, as "boss," was the biggest culprit. I did not bother telling them that Elizabeth's father was funding Reed's literary magazine for paving the way for his daughter's graduation — though I, of course, had written the necessary thesis. Ballard himself was destined to be the next president of the college.

"You should have cut his heart out," Magdalena said, so softly I asked her to repeat it. "I'll help you. We'll get him to Chicago" (she said *Cheecago*) "and I'll seduce him and make him drunk. You come out of the closet and stab him, then we throw him out a high window."

J.M. was less sanguineous but he readily agreed both Ballard and Reed deserved to die horribly. (I reflected briefly on what a gory mess colleges and universities would be with these two afoot!) He cautioned me to not poison my life on schemes of vengeance. He himself had always wanted to kill his own father for abandoning his mother, older brother, and sister down in San Carlos, just north of Guymas. His mother's first husband had died and she had lived with an American for a few months by the name of James Monroe, who left when she became pregnant.

"But wouldn't you care to meet him?" I couldn't help but ask.

"I went to Los Angeles when I was nineteen to look for him. He made my mother so unhappy I was going to kill him. I don't know if I would have done the deed but that was sure enough my intention."

*

Many of us shrink from life, thinking that this in itself might offer us some protection. That attitude of humble correctness hadn't done me any good in the months in my dark apartment. I had been right, and that had held my minimalist world together. One member of the board of trustees, a prominent attorney from Pittsburgh, had sensed something was amiss despite all the circumstantial evidence against me. It was he who insisted I be given the fillip of a half-pay sabbatical until the air cleared instead of outright dismissal under the aegis of "moral turpitude." We met only briefly while looking out a window of the administration building during a break in my hearing. "What a squalid little place," the attorney said. "You have a fine mind. Pick up a law degree and I'll give you a real job." That was that. Not a reassuring prospect but it was kind of him not to treat me like the degraded fool the others had.

An absurd consolation was that I got to make three trips to the Tucson cattle yards in the immense truck which was unalloyed fun. On the third and last trip both Magdalena and Lillian squeezed into the capacious truck cab with us, and after we unloaded the cattle we went to an Old West–type steak house for dinner, drinking, and dancing. Magdalena tried to get me to dance with her but I was far too shy. If there is anything worse than self-consciousness, I don't know what it is.

I started smoking again. I had quit up in the mountains one day after I fell off my horse when the cinch gave way and I dropped my cigarettes. For several days there seemed no point in starting again — until, that is, I watched Magdalena doing her dance floor fandangos with several cowboys including J.M., who was an accomplished dancer himself. I finally shuffled around in a dark corner with Lillian, at her strong insistence, recalling Marilyn's willful abandon when we had gone to dances as graduate students in Ann Arbor. It occurred to me then that I should have married someone like Lillian, but that's not how it happens, is it? We are selected by mates during a phase, and the phase frequently passes. We were getting dizzy from the smoke, rare meat, and margaritas, so Lillian took me outside. When you haven't noticed the stars all that much since childhood they give you vertigo. (Is there another word for this dizzy unease with reality?) What in God's name is happening up there? Lillian tried to teach me the Spanish names for the constellations but all I remembered in the morning was *Osa Mayor* (Great Bear) for what we called, unhandsomely, the Big Dipper. Lillian also warned me to be careful because she suspected her sister might be setting a trap for me. That item seemed so far-fetched it brought me to momentary consciousness which lapsed into thoughts of how primitive peoples could trace a bear in the stars.

*

Within a few days of our roundup I began to congeal — in stasis we begin to congeal at the bottom of our characters — and I entertained the idea of writing down my insights, then feared that would prevent more from coming. There was the fleeting memory of something William Blake said about kissing the bird of joy as it flies, but he's scarcely the man to go to for advice, any more than Clare or Smart.

Poor Magdalena has had an accident while training a neighbor's recalcitrant horse, a badly sprained wrist and a slight ankle break, so she has to be in a foot cast for a few weeks. Last evening at dinner she got drunk and was insulting to everyone. Again, only the grandma thought it was funny. Lillian told me that J.M.'s mother had lived out her life as a totally beaten down, impoverished Mexican woman, so Magdalena amazes her.

It has been raining hard again and I am flipping through Deirdre's nature books like a dullish boy looking at his first Latin primer. I can see the creek rising out the window. J.M. got angry and told Magdalena she could either behave or go back to her boyfriend in his Nogales hellhole. Lillian wept but reassured us that it was mostly because the kids at her school can't go out for recess on rainy days and she was enervated. Latinos are so emotional, or do little to conceal their emotions, like children. As I walked back to the cabin in the rainy dark, there was a moment's temptation to become an outwardly emotional person but I supposed the necessary gestures had to be learned early.

This morning just after Lillian left for school J.M. drove off with his mother so she could visit her cousin in Agua Prieta, a border town south of Douglas and to the east of here. I was leafing through Frank W. Gould's *Grasses of the Southwestern United States,* curious to see what the cattle ate, when I heard the dinner bell ringing. Through the monocular it was amusing to see Magdalena standing in her robe in the rain, jerking at the bell as if the house were on fire. I didn't want to leave the coziness of my cabin and the mesquite embers in the fireplace but thought it might be Deirdre on the phone.

When I got to the house Magdalena was sulking at the kitchen table, watching a game show in Spanish, the same kind as our own only a great deal more animated. You would think they were handing over Fort Knox rather than a set of luggage. I had been called in for the uncommon chore of taping a kitchen-wastebasket-sized garbage bag around Magdalena's foot so she could take a shower without getting her cast wet. I held the bag open and she stuck her foot in, with the red painted toenails visible out a hole in front of the cast. I used a roll of duct tape to secure the bag tightly to her calf. She went off to the shower, gesturing with her injured wrist as she would to a dog, telling me to wait so I could take the contraption off when she came back out.

I turned up the television volume to drown out her singing in the falling water, replete as it was with Latino sobs, shrieks, trills, and extended notes that faltered off into evident despondency. There was an after-buzz in my ears and a shortness of breath I decided not to admit to myself. I dithered around the living room and kitchen, on impulse taking a swig from the tequila bottle, certainly the first morning drink of my life. I sat on the sofa with the Bible to compose myself (and perhaps for protection!) but it was the grandma's Spanish edition. The game show turned to a soap opera with a fake beach scene including fake palm trees and a bogus ocean. There was an ample woman in a scanty bathing suit cooing at a skinny young man who twirled a volleyball expertly with his fingers until she grabbed it away to get his attention.

The shower and singing stopped. I thought I could hear her toweling herself, unless it was my imagination. She came out in a slighter robe than the terry cloth version she had gone in with. This robe was a ridiculous shade of purple emblazoned with big white, drooping flowers. I did not look at her eyes as she plopped down on the sofa, handing me a small pair of scissors. I slid off the couch and knelt before her, searching for the tape end.

"You don't look near as bad as when I caught you screwing the ground."

"Not 'near' but 'nearly,'" I corrected. When I began to pull on the tape attached to her bare skin she shrieked and jerked up her leg. It was plain as day that she had neglected to put on her underthings. It was as if the bone and cartilage had fled my body and I managed to get the garbage bag off only with great difficulty and trembling hands. She leaned over and put a strong hand behind my neck, pulling me down to her.

III

WHAT I WANT to know is if I don't find freedom in this life, when will I find it? That one's got me by the *cojones*, as J.M. is fond of saying. Until recently I never got more than a mere taste of the sensations that surround you when you are shorn of your obligations. In academic life you live within the strictures of the sonnet form, and even the meter of your heartbeat becomes iambic. Growing up in Toledo, I could hear a distant drop forge day and night, the immense iambic hammers crumpling metal to its design. I think my father said the forge was making car fenders, and by the millions.

It is late February and spring is here. The days are much longer for reasons I can't quite recall, and their middles encapsulate a period of warmth from about eleven to three. There's a tinge of green in the cottonwoods, and in the closest village, seventeen miles distant, the strange tribe of birdwatchers has arrived. After Lillian made me an elaborate map I drove way over to a bookstore in Tubac, north of Nogales, in the valley that stretches way up to Tucson. There the trees and fields are already green, the area being three thousand feet lower in elevation than our own in the mountains.

After Magdalena left a month ago, J.M. noted I had become a little low and set me to work repairing fences. It took a few simple lessons before I got the hang of it and would saddle up Mona at mid-morning, returning by mid-afternoon. "Half days for half pay," J.M. called it, but it was perfect for me what with working myself into a frenzy of notetaking from dawn until I caught lovely old Mona in the corral by proffering a carrot. J.M. was critical about the carrots, saying that one day I'd be out of carrots and also without a horse to ride. One of the dogs would accompany me and the other two would go with J.M., who was handling the fence in the highest locations.

Frankly, I have discovered nature. I'm quite aware that billions have discovered her before and no doubt millions have studied nature exhaustively. For my purposes, that is neither here nor there. We are not in this one together. My excommunication made me quite alone and I have to use what's at hand to keep my soul from evaporating. If there's nothing there worth saving, we'll have to build something new. Simple as that. My somewhat cretinoid gestures of destroying clocks and calendars were not all that ill advised. I only quit smoking out of irritation at the dependency. The spleen over maintaining my position as the last smoker in the English Department went away with the English Department.

So I'd put Deirdre's nature books in the saddlebags with my lunch, sort out my fencing tools, and I'm off into the hills, not altogether unlike a woodchopper in the twelfth century. Uniqueness is another illusion of personality. When I first began closely observing nature a month ago I found the experience a bit unbalancing, though the concepts weren't new. Notions such as "otherness" and the "thinginess" of reality are scarcely new to a literary scholar. What is new is the vividness of the experience. For instance, one afternoon I was stretched out under a silverleaf oak (*Quercus hypoleucoides,* the identification got from Francis Elmore's splendid *Shrub Trees of the Southwest Uplands*) when I noticed movement under a clump of trees on a grassy hillside a few hundred yards away. There was a virtual pack of wild animals romping and flouncing around, reminding me immediately of the otter at the Toledo Zoo that Deirdre as a child had favored watching when we visited Florence. Now I recalled from a children's book I read aloud to her, *Ollie the Otter* or something equally otiose, that otters lived in rivers of which there were none locally. I crawled over to Mona, who watched me quizzically, and stealthily got a guidebook out of the saddlebags. The beasts were called coatis (*Nasua narica*) and were larger, more elongated members of the raccoon family. Quite suddenly they disappeared without my noticing how they managed to do so, leaving me with a hollow excitement in my stomach. They were described as social animals, and perhaps they had dashed off to their coati house or cave. The kicker was that when I got back on Mona a large owl flew out of the tree, startling me witless and making identification unlikely. I wondered how long this sort of thing had been going on without my noticing it.

To be truthful, this is all recollected in tranquility, and that's putting it in its mildest terms. After my experience with Magdalena I went daft, the condition intensifying a great deal when her boyfriend swept her away a few days later. I didn't actually meet the boyfriend, only glassed him from the cabin window with my monocular. He wore a pigtail and was big as a house, his ample belly folding over his belt, though somewhat light on his feet. He tossed her suitcase in the back of a car I recognized as a Corvette, which was frequently driven by rich sorority girls.

Making love — a wretched euphemism — to Magdalena was a mistake. Not making love to Magdalena would also have been a mistake. I read a parable in the New Testament that when you sweep a figurative room clean you're supposed to fill it with good things or the demons will return. My cattle roundup had been a purge of sorts but the follow-up was akin to beating one's head against a boulder, although I couldn't imagine not doing it. Such is the perversity of human behavior. I don't for a moment think it's possible to both love and loathe a woman at the same time, but then what does it matter what I believe against the sheer weight of my feelings? After she left and when no one was around I went into the bathroom at the Verdugos', hoping for what, I don't know. A scent, a trace, a touch of her malign spirit. In a closet there was a Kleenex with a blotch of her bright pink lipstick which I tucked in my pocket and later burned.

All these sensations after our time on the couch recalled a singular childhood trauma. My father's labor union was having an annual August picnic at a park on Lake Erie. I was shy and walked far down the beach from the other kids, rolling my inner tube in front of me. I paddled far out in the lake, a stupid thing to do because I swam poorly. Out of nowhere a fog swept in and there I was adrift and unable to locate shore. Naturally I wept. After an hour or so of inconsolable dread I made out the strains of merry-go-round music from the amusement park near our picnic area. I reached shore and made my way back to my parents. The fog had lifted. No one had missed me.

A few days after Magdalena left I rechecked the Alzheimer's text tucked away in my briefcase and tried to study it, then abandoned the task in favor of my nature guides. Why on earth should I care if I have this disease? Dementia seemed childish compared to my torments about the present. My arms still feel her weight. She was lighter than I thought possible and even stronger than I had suspected. Her hair smelled densely of sunlight and green leaves. It is evening now, and perhaps this is "sundowning," the clinical term for the way Alzheimer's patients lose control at sunset.

My nature studies have intensified for a number of reasons, none of them rational, but I don't care one whit. First of all I have had a Technicolor dream that instructed me to walk the border of the forest and open land, and at the same time to rename the birds of North America. This will be a long project indeed as there are over seven hundred of them. I do not question this dream assignment. It's certainly more pleasant than when Ballard assigned me Contemporary Poetics 373 when he knew I loathed the subject. If I completed the bird project before death, I could publish a new guidebook. So many of the current names of birds are humiliating and vulgar. For instance, "brown thrasher" or "curve-billed thrasher" for these lovely, secretive birds is an abomination. The thrasher is now called the "beige dolorosa," which is reminiscent of a musical phrase in Mozart, one that makes your heart pulse with mystery, as does the bird.

I have concentrated on birds and flora for the time being. Mammals are difficult, and other than the coati, I have only seen deer, a single coyote, and a group of javelinas, diminutive hairy creatures of the pig family. I'm already fatigued with Linnaean taxonomy, as the impulse behind it, admirable in the life sciences, is the precise motive that made graduate English such a hoax in retrospect. Literary scholars can be, too often are, guilty of science envy, creating absurd schemata as if Shakespeare needed a sounder defense for being unanswerably Shakespeare. I suspect my own bird taxonomy, as I progress with this project over the years, will be a private one based on the spiritual consequences of the natural world.

I must add that nature has erased my occasional urge toward suicide, along with not wanting to bring Deirdre sorrow. I suspect it's because this new world is not asking me to hold it together like the other one. For the time being I am too much of a neophyte to take part in defending it against the inroads of human greed. There is also the idea that I'm a newborn babe with a soft spot on the top of my head. My natural enemies, like Magdalena, could still crush me.

*

The other event that intensified my nature studies was a nasty piece of punishment. The morning mail brought a registered letter from Ballard notifying me that my hearing on the possible reinstatement of my position had been put off until summer due to budgetary considerations. This mouthful of mush meant, as the letter later implied and I had overheard the year before as gossip, that the "Endowment" had made certain unwise investments and each department had to sacrifice a position or two. Ballard urged me to accept the half-pay disability pension, not stating the obvious fact that it came out of our group insurance fund rather than the budget itself. Of course this would be paramount to admitting a type of mental incompetence, based mostly on the red check on my dossier and two joint visits by the college doctor, whom I knew well, and a female psychiatrist, also a college employee, whom I didn't know, who was a dumpy little parody from the Baltics. I allowed her two brief interviews through my screen door which, as Deirdre and Bob had pointed out, was not the best possible idea.

At age sixty-two the disability pension would slide into my regular one, but a quick tote meant about twenty-three grand per annum, not a lot in our world. In fact, barely a secretary's or instructor's wage. Deirdre had always insisted that she was holding a nest egg for me. When my mother died seven years ago she had left me nothing, out of her basic ire over my divorce from Marilyn. The Presbyterians got the bulk of her estate that came from her house and the urban-renewal sale of the diner. Deirdre had received thirty thousand in the will, which she said was growing and was to be mine when I needed it. I had always become quarrelsome over the matter, refusing the idea, even after she told me her husband, David, gave her more than twice that every Christmas in stock from his inheritance. Perhaps it was time to stop being prideful. I could buy a little cabin at some point and become a secretary of nature. Ballard's letter, however, brought me to the realization that I wouldn't return to the college at gunpoint.

This was not the nasty event in itself but what caused it. I was at the very hindmost part of the property, a Forest Service lease scarcely fit for grazing, with a hoop of new wire to replace a section destroyed by a falling corkbark fir (*Abies lasiocarpa* var. *arizonica*). To remove the compromising aftertaste of Ballard's letter, I was meditating on Keats's notions of "the vale of soul-making" which I had never properly understood. I had been guilty like so many in controlling myself when there was nothing left to control. In short, I didn't have enough substance to perceive what Keats was up to. Now in the deep forest glade it occurred to me that if you kept your heart and mind utterly open and were still full of incomprehension, you were exercising the glories of your negative capability and thus were plumb in the vale of soul-making. It was clear as day and I tingled with pleasure.

Of course J.M. had admonished me over and over to pay complete attention during the dangerous chore of fence stretching. When you cranked the ratchet handle you wanted to draw it drum tight but well short of breaking. If you were careless, the wire might break and come whistling back and "tear an eye out," he had said for emphasis. At the exact instant my mind had lapsed from Keats to a brief vision of Magdalena's bottom, I heard the *ping* of the wire but had no time to react. The wire missed my eye but hit my cheek and shoulder like a hideous lash. I must have screeched because Mona snorted and the dog came running from her sport of digging up ground squirrels and eating them for lunch.

I stood there for moments listening to the panting of the dog and my own scattered breathing, looking down at where I traced my finger along the bloody line where the wire sliced my shirt. The line broadened with red but the slice didn't appear deep. My left cheek was another matter and I lifted my hand to catch the cascading blood. I had nothing to stanch the flow so I used my undershirt, pressing it to my cheek lightly, then with more firmness. The shirt quickly soaked itself red but I was still calm, thinking it unlikely I could bleed to death through my face. I sat down in the grass against a tree, feeling the numb ache similar to the aftermath of getting a wisdom tooth pulled. Of all the things to do, I fell asleep there in the warm sunlight, only waking when the shirt was dried and caked against my face, still clenched in my hand. The doctor later said the sleep was the aftermath of shock.

By the time I got back home it was late afternoon. J.M. hollered "Holy shit!" and off we drove to the emergency clinic at the hospital in Nogales an hour away. Lillian had wanted to get me a clean shirt from my cabin, which seemed inappropriate, while Grandma merely handed me the tequila bottle from which I took a deep gulp. The doctor, who was a pleasant old man, asked if it was from a knife fight or fencing, evidently familiar with both. He was also disturbed that I hadn't come in immediately, as the elapsed time made a "neat job" impossible. It was then that he said something I shall cherish forever: "If you weren't such a worthless old cowboy, I'd send you up to a plastic surgeon in Tucson." He also asked if I had any money and I said no, because I'd left my wallet in the cabin. I was going to say my insurance would pay, or I had a friend out in the waiting room, but he wrote "indigent" on the form the receptionist had given me and sent me packing, my forty-nine stitches for free. It pleased me to no end to be taken for a cowboy.

Sad to say, later I had an argument with J.M. in a Mexican café. We drank several beers while I ate two bowls of menudo, a tripe soup the grandma often made and which I found delicious. Along with the tripe, calves' feet are also put in the pot, an item that is readily available in Mexican butcher shops. All I did, idly enough, was ask J.M. if on the way home we could drive by where Magdalena lived with her boyfriend.

J.M. virtually exploded on the spot. The upshot was he knew I had slept with Magdalena because she had told Lillian. How could I do such a thing? He knew she had worked as a call girl in Phoenix and Tucson and now she was involved with drug people, of which there are thousands along the border. I was told I knew nothing, unlike himself, about the world of evil, and perhaps Magdalena had slept with the dope assassin whose modus operandi was to dash out of an alley and bury an ice pick in an unsuspecting skull. I was a gentleman and professor, an intelligent man — how could I bring shame on myself and family by screwing such a woman? If she showed up again at his home he would kick her out pronto, and if Lillian forbade it he would leave himself, adding for a punch line that Lillian had even loaned Magdalena a chunk of their savings. When J.M. finished, the dozen or so people in the café were silent but staring at us, neglecting their drinks and meals. Then an old man piped up, "Why don't you shoot the bitch," and everyone laughed.

*

The yellow warbler is now the Delphic warbler. The previous name was as absurd as "blackbird." We show our contempt for creatures by allowing the unimaginative elements of the scientific world to name them. It is perhaps a job for those countless M.F.A. poets crisscrossing the land, wheedling bullies carrying their Hermès briefcases. I decided on "Delphic warbler" because their song is bell-like but attenuated, bursting the notes so that the seams of the music cannot contain it, much like Sappho.

I am back to my fencing despite the accident a week ago. What a wake-up call! After dinner last night Lillian took off the bandage and we stood side by side in the bathroom looking in the mirror. She frowned. It wasn't pretty but neither am I, the pinkish ridge from the dissolving stitches leaving an irregular Maginot Line down my face. "Care sat on his faded cheek," I quoted Milton.

Of late my sleep has been disturbed by a spring Mona had discovered by scent. The weather had turned warm in early April and we had taken to leaving at dawn. Mona always stays in any grassy area where I drop the reins, so I was surprised when she trotted off. I hurriedly followed because there were some dark clouds sweeping up from the south. To tell the truth, I felt like I was being abandoned by the most reliable person in my life, though she was a horse. She traveled a scant two hundred yards over a hillock and up a narrow gully too thick with varied shrubbery for me to stop to identify.

I heard the trickling of water, then the gulps of Mona drinking. There was a miniature rock pool of cold, clear water and I let it settle before drinking myself. Unlike most of the local water it was untainted by the effluvia left by the gold and silver mining back at the turn of the century. I stood there a long time leaning against Mona, listening to the disturbed birds come alive again. There were too many of them and I didn't want to upset them by getting out my guidebook. There were literally dozens of species flitting around, including inconceivably colored hummingbirds feeding from the flowering bushes. Mona had discovered a bird gold mine and it made me giddy. It wasn't so much the immense weight of my dream project, the puniness of language in the face of this splendor, but that the birds made me feel that I understood nothing, nothing at all. It was partly the energy of their otherness, the sheer mystery of our existences together in that tiny arroyo. There was a shudder as if I were going to take leave of my senses. I took Mona's reins to lead her away. A warbler unknown to me, but likely a Lucy's warbler (see what I mean!), sat on the pommel of the saddle, staring at me. I stared back until she began to shimmer, her outlines beginning to blur. Horse, bird, rider: it became uncountable. The sky swelled black and blue, making me wet but joyful.

*

Mona pulled up lame so I've been walking with my tools and guidebooks in a daypack. She neighed mournfully this morning, wanting to go along, her injured foot lifted like a dog's paw. I broke off a chunk of Snickers bar which she gnawed with pleasure with her worn teeth. The poor old girl doesn't know that her life grows short. She makes me think of the part of *Leaves of Grass* about animals, of which I only remember one line: "They do not lie awake in the dark and weep for their sins." One Sunday we came home from church with Florence all teary about the poor and hungry in Toledo. My dad was having a morning beer and reading the newspaper. Apprised of the problem, he suggested that she and her fellow church members "get their dead asses" across town and feed these people. I have neglected Whitman since graduate school, thinking him painfully sentimental like Dickens and Dostoyevsky. Maybe I'll take another look.

I dawdled around the barnyard applying liniment to Mona's ankle (J.M. calls it a pastern), and then Lillian arrived with the mail and groceries which meant it was Saturday. There was a letter from Bob in far-off Marseille, quite apologetic as he had only been sending the stray postcard. When he left in late September I wanted to make him feel good, so I had said I was going to London. He was more than a little overexposed to my problems at that point what with his own lifelong mental difficulties. His father had been one of the most successful black lawyers in Chicago and Bob had been found brutally wanting in his love of literature. Bob wrote that he had corresponded with "that pile of offal" Ballard and suggested that I accept the disability pension. What's more, there was a part-time position available to teach two courses in American literature to French adults that was mine for the taking. Bob had decided against returning to America himself and hoped I might join him. I could live nicely there on my modest teaching pay plus my pension. He would even search out a handball court.

I was touched by this, however unlikely the idea. Perhaps I could teach the fall and early winter semester in order to be back here in plenty of time for the songbird migrations. I would also have to do a little research to check if the Marseille area had forests and walking room. My eyes teared when I thought Mona might not be there for my return. One of the cats that lived in the tack shed rubbed against my leg and I stooped to pet her. The dogs growled, jealous of my affection, but dared not approach as I had swatted them before for chasing the cat.

I looked over and Lillian was standing under the cottonwood tree near the back door, her arms folded in evident concern. Why is it, unless they are furious, must you ask women what is wrong? I walked over, praying that it was nothing to interfere with my upcoming hike, and was left sweating and stuttering in moments.

"What's wrong?" I naturally asked.

"My sister needs to see you, and J.M. won't allow her around."

"He seems to have ambivalent feelings toward her," I wattled.

"J.M. doesn't understand that when Mom died Magdalena was fifteen and she didn't get proper mothering."

"I don't know where she lives. How can I see her?"

"She's over at your cabin. She snuck up the creek. She was going to wait there all day and then I caught you still here. Don't tell J.M. or he'll go crazy. I wouldn't mind myself if she moved to Alaska, but I love her because she's my sister." Lillian had plainly reverted far from her education and normal composure. I shrugged and headed for the cabin like a gunslinger, though in truth I felt my bowels might let loose.

*

There she was, big as life and death, sitting at the table and inspecting the contents of my wallet as if that were what one did on a visit. Thank God she hadn't found my beloved Miriam's photo or I might have lost control. I noted that her foot cast was gone.

"You only have thirty-five dollars," she announced.

"I use the bank," I lied, noting she hadn't had the inclination to check the Gideon Bible where I had accumulated nearly two thousand dollars with my roundup plus my fencing pay (five dollars an hour). She was wearing a white sleeveless dress perhaps to denote her purity.

"I'm pregnant. I need fifteen hundred dollars to go up to the clinic in Tucson. The cops are after my boyfriend so he took off. Besides, it's your fault."

"You mean I'm the designated father?" I had the tremors and tried to be ironic to quell them.

"However you want to put it. The timing is right. Perhaps you want to make love to me right now?"

"No," I said, the most outrageous lie of my life. The mere sight of this depraved creature sent my depleted hormones spinning, but this was akin to being mugged.

"Just pay up and I'll always be ready for you." She smiled, not her best gesture, and held out her hand.

I went to my briefcase in the closet and got a Michigan check, filling it out at the table and writing along the top, "Not admitting paternity guilt," slightly proud of my caginess. She took the check, gazed at it, then tore it into confetti.

"The clinic in Tucson only takes cash." She remained cool, stirring the confetti around with a finger.

"Then why didn't you cash the check in Nogales? You're no more pregnant than I am."

"Come and see me when you are willing to bring cash." She wrote down her address and phone number, then kissed me, her tongue probing against my clenched teeth.

When she left I went to the window, quite astounded when she vaulted the fence. This unfortunately reminded me of an old movie I did like, *Dr. Jekyll and Mr. Hyde* with Spencer Tracy. It was also unnerving because within an academic atmosphere we grow to think that all people are essentially the same and that the spectrum of behavior, barring psychotics, is quite narrow. Magdalena revived the notion, usually only a scholarly footnote, that there might be demons afoot in the land.

I had the immediate sense to calm down by wondering

what Raymond Chandler might do in this situation. Rather than dabbling with one of his heroes, I wished to enter the mind of the master himself. Was I the putative father? Why did she have to have cash? What was wrong with the check, my "not guilty" notation or something else? Could it be that a check can be traced to both issuer and casher, but what difference did that make? I knew that Magdalena was not a rocket scientist, as the young say, but what did she have in mind above ordinary mischief? The surest way to solve the riddle was to leave it unsolved and completely ignore her. It was difficult to throw away her number and address so I neglected to do so. There's that time-frayed saw about there not being any fool like an old fool, but then I had taught young people for nearly thirty years and never felt they had a collective leg up on us. Besides, how old is fifty? A question not the less stupid for my asking it.

*

Deirdre stopped by for two days, making a detour on the way to San Francisco to meet her husband, who was at a medical meeting. It was definitely a rapprochement and I was pleased to see how delighted she was with my condition, although I wish she hadn't used the word "progress," a musty concept at best. She was only mildly upset by my scar, which is understandable considering the daily bullet wounds in her Chicago neighborhood.

But stop. Reality is so peculiar. The other day I checked an old packet of notes found in my briefcase and discovered that the year has fried a lot of fat out of my thought and language. With your only child, you tend to gloss things over; ergo, in truth, Deirdre was pleased I was no longer shaking and raving. The scar was small potatoes compared to the fact that I apparently wasn't deliquescing at the speed of the calendar. Her own problems seeped out. The charity clinic she and David worked for was undergoing political convulsions and they were thinking of moving on to a similar operation in Rapid City, South Dakota, a place that sounds exotic to me and probably isn't.

Deirdre determined that my grackle is actually a Mexican blue mockingbird blown north by the winter storms. Her bird book is admirably dog-eared and notated, but she had to use a Mexican bird guide to locate this creature. Oddly, my only mental pratfall of her short visit can be directly attributed to birds. She took me to a Nature Conservancy property along a creek bottom some twenty miles from here and the area was dense with birdwatchers. I felt claustrophobic despite the beauty of the riparian thickets, as if I were being sucked back into the black hole of the ordinary. Deirdre joked that if she called the Audubon Hot Line, my cabin would be stormed by hundreds of birders in their crazed lust to add the Mexican blue mockingbird to what is called their life list, a tawdry system they use for keeping count and competing with one another. I was so appalled that I stepped off the legal trail and hid for an hour in a thicket, letting Deirdre continue toting the day's numbers. By a wonderful stroke of luck I was visited in this thicket by my beloved beige dolorosa. I sat in utter stillness on a log as if I, too, belonged there. The bird came within an inch of my foot, peering up at me as if I might be a tree. I resolved then that there would be nothing expedient or useful in my own renaming of these creatures, certainly no paintings or photos attached to vulgarize or explain away their beauty and mystery. My work would not become more fodder for "the deceitful coils of an institution," as the poet said. Readers would simply have to imagine what bird went with which of my sonorous names.

The second and last night of Deirdre's visit we camped out by my secret spring that Mona had discovered. We arrived late on a sunny afternoon and at first a strong wind dampened the activity and I feared I had imagined it all. An hour or so before twilight the wind ceased entirely and the immediate area of the spring became dense with life. Deirdre became so excited she put her guidebook aside and clutched at her hair, her eyes unblinking in excitement. When the dark came it seemed to emerge out of the ground rather than coming from the sky, with undetectable slowness so that we turned with shock to the quarter moon.

There was a raw moment around the campfire when Deirdre brought up the subject — another euphemism — of Magdalena. I was glad the fire wasn't all that bright because I blushed horribly over the idea that she and Lillian had spoken of my little fling, though "fling" is a slight word for an experience from which you are lucky to emerge alive.

"I've met her a bunch of times, Dad. She's not a very nice person. But I don't suppose that's what you were looking for. I mean, she's not exactly a coed."

"I agree," I said with the utmost lameness. Young women these days feel free to comment about their fathers' sexual behavior. My throat constricted in the effort to say something *à point*. "It wasn't serious. I doubt I'll see her again." I was suddenly in the thick of regarding my entire use of language as suspect, both past and present. Recently it had lagged so far behind my perceptions that I realized I'd have to make a major project out of changing this language.

Deirdre was struggling for the words to put the matter to rest when we both heard an odd noise. It was a soft sound somewhere between a chirrup and a cluck and it came from all around and above us. We looked up at the firelight reflecting silver off the leaves of a black oak. We were being watched and spoken to by dozens of tiny elf owls. Each would have fit inappropriately in a vest pocket, their eyes as big as black marbles below small tufted ears. They studied us for a scant few minutes and then, their curiosity satisfied, they flitted away into the surrounding darkness. I was overcome with the sense of feeling at home, whether I deserved to or not. Why should I break my heart wondering?

*

Deirdre left at dawn in her rental car. I rode with her the half-dozen miles out to the main road and walked back, discomfited to learn that the two gray hawks that nested in a cottonwood at the side of the long driveway were among only fifty nesting pairs left in the United States. Walking steals away anger but this was a troublesome detail. When I caterwauled about the noxious creative types, Bob would laugh and remind me that too many good writers at one time would knock the world further off balance and flood the insane asylums. Bob's ability to find bedrock in absurdity always made me envious. For instance, if I think "six miles," I'm liable to ruin a part of my walk until I rid myself of the six-mile notion which is nearly as corrupt as the clock. That's partly what Dostoyevsky meant when he said that two plus two was the beginning of death.

I detoured at the creek bed, walking west until I picked up Magdalena's tracks from her visit, following them to where she scooted under a fence to her waiting vehicle. There was a remote urge to sniff the tracks as a dog might, and a lump arose in my throat. If my youthful prayers had been answered, by now I would have lived out a fifty-year-long harp solo with my beloved Miriam, which had certainly not been the case.

On the way back up the creek bed I came upon a roadrunner and followed this bird in an anthropomorphic trance. The bird would trot swiftly ahead fifty yards or so, then stop to regard its approaching enemy, me. When I became too close the bird repeated the process, stopping again, its head cocked in inane curiosity. To break the monotony of this paradigm of my life, I sat down on a boulder and checked the driver's license: I was indisputably fifty years of age. In the distance the roadrunner waited patiently for my next move, eventually drifting off into a catclaw thicket.

The boulder had a comfortably sculpted backrest and I couldn't think of a single reason to continue a life of movement. Perhaps I'd sit there until my expiration date, a novel impulse. Bob had divorced early and his only child, a boy now in his late twenties, lived in an ashram, a religious commune of some sort out in Oregon, from which he sent a letter once a month, beautifully written but full of hygienic pieties. Last year there had been a package, a piece of wood which had been carved in rather ornate calligraphy: "Life is a housefire of impermanence." Bob had found the sign amusing enough to put it up on our office wall. I didn't say so but I thought the message a tad banal, though since then life had certainly whirred right along.

Sitting there in my stone nest, I thought of the proscribed limits of my father's life: coming to manhood in the rigors of the Great Depression, four years of World War II, marriage, learning how to operate heavy equipment, then death. Compared to that, I could finally admit that my own life had been spent on silk cushions in jeweled chambers. The process of getting a Ph.D. had threatened mind and body, but once that soporific rite had been endured there had been marriage to a woman with an ample allowance, frequent trips to England and, as I climbed to the top of the academic ladder, a work schedule that only entailed three courses per semester to small numbers of students. The system was designed to give me time for research and writing but had instead made me somnolent and dreary, albeit totally safe in a world suppurating with tribalism and chaos.

Now I was left with a pension that ensured something less than genteel poverty. I mulled and moped for a few minutes, then realized what with free lodging and a sublet apartment back in Michigan, I had not even touched my half paycheck. I had, in fact, supported myself by rounding up cattle and mending fence. I gave Lillian forty dollars a week for my part of the groceries, which is all she would take, and through Deirdre, her husband's family had sent along the message that I was welcome to the humble cabin as long as I wished. Perhaps I should kiss the ground as they once did in Russian fiction, or offer up a prayer or two, but I wanted to spare God any additional tedium. He was no doubt busy managing His black holes, one of which was said to be the size of three hundred million suns. It was also inappropriate for me to ask Him to free me of my random and troublesome thoughts of Magdalena, which stirred my loins uncomfortably. During our lovemaking session on the couch the heel of her cast had dug a sore area in the small of my back as if I had been a horse and she had worn spurs. The discomfort of this abrasion had been a nagging wound of Eros herself but I was somewhat disappointed when it went away. I was an expert on the subject of my mind but was still infantile about my emotions.

I tried to distract myself from Magdalena by the pleasurable thought that my life might henceforth be rid of students. Year after year my informal surveys of new students in my classes revealed that few if any had read an appreciable book in the previous year. The worship of the ersatz and peripheral was the norm. They had been so overexposed to the visual image on television they were dull to good art or fine photography. I was less knowledgeable in the area of their music, but I could only recall three students in my career who had cared for Mozart.

All of this suddenly wafted away because I no longer

cared for that world and the hideous sense that I was in danger of becoming a premature geezer. The immediate, heretofore unconscious question was whether a toss in the hay with Magdalena was worth fifteen hundred dollars. I knew enough of the world at large to suspect this wasn't a record, although it might be in my reduced economic category. There was humor in the idea of how much physical work it had taken to save that amount of money. I had inadvertently redeemed my body only to have it presenting me with this problem. If only I knew a winsome middle-aged lady who loved nature and Mozart, but I didn't. It is an alarming item to think you are sexually dead for a decade only to discover that you aren't. I had always presumed I understood what Yeats meant when he wrote the line, "The uncontrollable mystery on the bestial floor," but had no real idea at the moment aside from the sensation of dread and arousal.

*

It was a manic rather than a dark night of the soul. I couldn't stop talking to myself and my mental language blurred into a passionate gibberish. I got out of bed a dozen times, fingering the slip of paper that contained her phone number and address until the paper became as soft as cloth. I was more in need of a witch doctor than a psychiatrist. The fact that there was no phone in the cabin saved me from bedding down a demon. The image of me racing through the night in an ancient Jeep that topped out at thirty miles an hour was comic. The sensible thing to do was to use the cash I had earned through the sweat of my brow as a down payment on a spiffy 4WD pickup, the kind all cowboys pine for.

My head was buzzing and I began to hear running water, or blood, within it for the first time in months. I nosed around in my briefcase and came up with the papers on which I had kept track of the time back in my apartment: neat lists of my clock readings with the exciting minutes at the junctures of A.M. and P.M., P.M. and A.M., recorded with a bit more flourish. The notes made me shiver in their naive attempt to ritualize reality into an acceptable form.

I took a sleeping bag out of the closet, turned out the lights, and settled down in the yard. Close attention to the stars, moon, sun, and earth is genuinely helpful when you want to stop talking to yourself. We all hope for a superior brand of madness but our wounds are considerably less interesting than our cures. While walking I thought the only viable reality to be the present step. I considered counting stars, unable to remember Lillian's constellation lesson, but then counting seemed a vulgar intrusion for both the stars and myself. I sent a few prayers starward, not mentioning Magdalena but offering thanks for the universe that was making me well, and the request that I not forget the earth during my inevitable mischief.

*

The day of reckoning dawned bright and clear, deafening with birds and the sunlight creeping slowly down the mountain walls, the air so sweet I drank it in sips. I dozed on, listening to Lillian leave for school, then watching through the gate at grass line as the dogs jumped into the bed of J.M.'s pickup and he took off for the hills. It was my D-day, though not so auspicious as my father's participation in the actual event.

For breakfast, at my request the grandma thawed a container of menudo and heated maize tortillas for me. I boldly dialed the phone and an irritable Magdalena answered. She had been up late and why was I calling at dawn — in reality eight A.M. I said that my love for her was so great I couldn't help myself. She said to give her a few more hours of sleep, then come over, but not to forget the money. Of course not, I said. As an afterthought she said to dress like a professor, not a cowboy, as I could go on an errand with her. When I hung up the phone the grandma laughed, having figured out I was up to no good with her favorite spectacle. Magdalena's dress request made me wary rather than disturbed. There's no substitute for consciousness.

On the way back to the cabin I heard one of the barn cats mewing. Lillian had said J.M. didn't care for cats but they kept them to control the mouse and scorpion population. I walked over to the tack shed only to discover that my favorite cat had been torn open and lay in the dust quite dead, while its companion mewed a funeral service. I suspected the dogs, and such was my anger it was lucky for them they weren't around. At least a coyote would have eaten the poor creature.

I took a shovel out of the shed and buried my friend in the soft earth of the corral with Mona watching attentively. Was this an omen that I was going to die? No, it meant the cat had died. My mind chattered a litany of stray lines from Christopher Smart's poem to his cat Jeoffrey: "For he is a mixture of gravity and waggery. For he counteracts the powers of darkness by his electrical skin & glaring eyes. For in his morning visions he loves the sun and the sun loves him. For he is of the tribe of Tiger." Poor old Smart, batty and impoverished, but he knew his cats.

*

What a day it was, my emergence, my foray into the great world of sin, crime, commerce, the indigestible hairball of civilization. I will cherish this day until I am cremated, as it is my vain wish to be ashes rather than a carcass. Appropriately enough, though the day was hot, I dressed in the slacks and tweed sport coat, a J. Press shirt and brogans, that I had worn the day of my arrival. In the mirror I looked like I was on the verge of lighting a briar pipe and saying the word "tautological." All the way to Nogales above the rickety roar of the Jeep I hummed Mozart, buzzing along the road's shoulder to allow faster traffic to pass, including one of those old VW buses once favored by hippies which always sounded like a magnified Singer sewing machine.

Magdalena's neighborhood was less than reassuring and I rechecked, in my jacket pocket, the heft of my Swiss army knife, a gift from Deirdre, small change indeed against the automatic rifles used by the criminal element these days. The tweezer attachment had been good for pulling cactus thorns and the leather punch ideal for making a shorter notch on my belt. In any event, it was not the sort of weapon you could whip out in a microsecond.

The house itself was a shabby little bungalow, with splotches of shattered stucco revealing the adobe bricks beneath, a peek into the house's personal history. The porch was partly enclosed with a trellis of flowering vine loud with bees, and several hummingbirds I didn't feel disposed toward identifying. I tapped the toe of the silly Church's brogan and at the last possible moment took five of the fifteen hundred-dollar bills and shoved them far down my sock until they tickled my instep — an attempt to make my tribute to Eros two hundred, rather than three hundred, hours of labor. When I stood straight Magdalena opened the door, looking a bit sour and blowzy in a lavender peignoir, and nodded me into the darkened house that was airless but cool. In the kitchen she asked me to make her coffee while she showered.

The coffee chore was just as well, as I was having difficulty catching my breath and touched my breast to check my heart's accelerated tom-tom, deliberating whether this was an appropriate place to drop dead. I dumped the percolator's old grounds in a wastebasket overflowing with fast-food cartons, put the coffee on, and took a Dos Equis beer from the nearly empty refrigerator that cried out for a black banana. I sat down on the living room couch and sorted through a pile of horse magazines, finding underneath with not a little shock my book, which she had obviously borrowed from Lillian. The first part of the title, *The Economics of Madness . . .*, gave me a sharp case of shudders as if I had peed outdoors on a cold winter night. I slid the book back under the nest of horse magazines where I thought it might be happier blind to its author's fripperies.

All too soon she swept out of the bathroom hall, the very starkest of nakeds, toweling her mammalian mane and glowering down at me sunken on the couch. She reminded me of that vast and robust Maillol sculpture I remembered in the garden at the Museum of Modern Art in New York. She sternly held out her hand on which I slapped the thousand dollars. She hastily counted it and looked at me as if I were vermin.

"I said fifteen hundred dollars. You're five short."

"Oh, my goodness. I thought you said a thousand." I stared at my knees, crestfallen.

"It's fifteen hundred dollars or nothing, you cheapskate."

"I guess we professors are reputed to be absent-minded." I was staring at a droplet of water in her belly button. This was as far as you could get from Milton's theocratic mania. I got up abruptly, took the money back, and headed for the kitchen and the door. "I'm sorry I bothered you," I said to a wall clock that looked back from the plastic flank of a smiling donkey. Magdalena was hot on my trail and grabbed the money.

"You can owe me but you don't get the full treatment."

"But if it only takes ten minutes, that would mean you'd

be earning six thousand dollars an hour. In a full workday you could make a fortune, or at least go to Hawaii." I don't know why I was being so captious. I plugged the maddening drop of water in her belly button with a forefinger.

"You're too much of a smartass for your own good," she said, coming into my arms. I accomplished the mission while halfway on the squeaky Formica-topped kitchen table. Afterward I reeled and slumped, unable to get my sea legs. She made off to dress and I laughed softly in time to the perking coffee, feeling quite stupid but alive.

*

Our errand, as she called it, brought me closer than I ever hoped to be again to absolute disaster, mortification, imprisonment. We drove the Jeep to a gas station with me in a state of post-coital desuetude fueled in addition by a mostly sleepless night. I craved the sort of naps I used to have on Hampstead Heath after drinking three pints of Watneys in a nearby tavern. The day had become hotter and it had not yet occurred to me to take off my tweed jacket.

At the gas station we parked beside a white Ford pickup and Magdalena ran inside to get the keys. It was thirty yards or so away but through the window I saw her talking to a man who looked suspiciously like the boyfriend I had seen in Verdugo's yard. He looked out the window and I averted my glance to the back of the pickup as if it were a newfound toy in the sandbox. There was an old car seat in the pickup box and I caught the slightest whiff of something that smelled like lawn clippings.

Magdalena finally came out and we were off in the pickup headed south, for her namesake town, which she said was only an hour away down in Sonora. When we crossed the border I perked up, mildly thrilled to add a new country to my life list even though I had lived close by for nearly half a year. It reminded me of Deirdre's childhood squeal when we crossed the Blue Water Bridge on a car trip to Toronto. This definitely bore no resemblance to Canada and the slums looked decidedly friendlier than those of Detroit. On the outskirts of the Sonoran side of Nogales was a welter of American-owned factories, built there, so J.M. told me, because they need only pay wages of five dollars a day. This seemed unlikely so I asked Magdalena, who had been chattering along about her sick mother.

"American companies are cheapskates just like you." She patted my knee, a rare gesture of affection. She either got right down to business or skipped the matter.

Now we were out in a lovely hilly countryside of immense rolling, female shapes leading up to distant mountains that I guessed were the back sides of those I could see on my fencing expeditions, or near the cliff on which I had done my purgative weeping, an experience that seemed a lifetime ago. I was surprised to find the road a superhighway like our interstates, and its smoothness made me drowse off, waking when she stopped to pick up two women and no less than five children whose car was disabled on the road's shoulder. She talked animatedly with the women in Spanish and out of politeness I clambered into the back of the pickup with the children so the two women could ride up front. The children were sweet but shy. I gave each of them a dollar bill and held the youngest on my lap as we sat on the old car seat watching the world continuously recede behind us. I dozed off again despite the money itching against my foot within the sock.

When we reached town Magdalena dropped off our passengers at a gas station and I waved my merry goodbyes to the children. I was surprised when she then let me off in front of a small cantina. I wasn't totally conscious yet but she told me to wait there until she picked up a load of statuary and visited her mother. I didn't mind what with feeling rested from my short snooze and being quite hungry. I sat at the bar, the only discordant note coming from a table of American college kids in the far corner. Two of the girls were shaking their pretty little bottoms in front of the jukebox to the delight of Mexican workingmen sitting at other tables.

"So you know Magdalena," the barman said. "You're a lucky man. She's a spitfire." He spoke clear English and had evidently watched the woman in question out the window. I nodded in assent, ordered a beer and bowl of menudo, the second of the day. It is thought by the Mexicans to be both a hangover tonic and a sexual restorative. As for myself, I ate it because I liked the dark pungency of the flavors, reminding me that I was no longer trapped within the discrete squalor of a midwestern academic town.

At the exact moment I was served the food I wondered how Magdalena could be visiting her mother when Lillian had said several times that their mother was dead. I tore off a piece of tortilla, then paused at the thought that there was a strange odor on my fingers from riding in the back of the truck. On the way to the toilet to wash my hands I passed the table of college students and one of the girls smiled at me. She was a real peach, as we used to say, but then I recognized the resinous odor as that of marijuana. I had smelled it frequently from the bushes outside the student union building at college over the years, and heard the muffled "wow"s and giggling. I had smoked it once as an undergraduate and found the sensations intolerable, as if my body had been reduced to the cartilage one finds in a turkey leg. Under its influence I also had eaten an entire bag of Oreos and had felt quite ill the following morning.

When I returned to my menudo there was an urge to hop the bus I saw passing out the window. It wouldn't really matter which direction the bus was going, but how could I travel in this country without knowing the language? It was time to abandon the bastard genre of making notes and learn Spanish. Lillian had said she would be glad to help but the best way was to enroll in a school down in Hermosillo that offered an intensive month-long course. I was intrigued by the city's gorgeous name, presenting as it did the possibility of intrigue and romance, though Veracruz might be better, as it abutted the Caribbean. There were definite opportunities for a man not fully atrophied and wizened in his own private bell jar.

Deep in my menudo, which wasn't as good as the grandmother's but savory enough, I tried to tell my own fortune in the swimming pieces of tripe and hominy but couldn't get past the idea that Magdalena was up to no good. It was impossible not to think of J.M.'s bellowed lecture in the café. The border was indeed rife with the mayhem of smuggling, the local weekly paper I read at Verdugo's including long lists of charges for amounts ranging from a few pounds of marijuana to a ton of heroin in a produce truck. In the northern Midwest and upper New York state, cigarettes in large quantities were being smuggled into Canada because they cost four bucks there.

It was well over an hour before Magdalena returned. I wasn't the least bit restive as the college students were jumping around to Mexican polkas and some young locals were teaching them the steps. It was frolicsome music and my toes tapped against the barstool. How was I to court a lady unless I learned to dance? I saw myself gliding across the burnished dance floor of a supper club with a woman who owned a tennis or birdwatcher's tan. We were doubtless doing the foxtrot.

When Magdalena arrived I had just ordered another beer so she had one herself. She went through a panoply of moods in the first minute, trying to select one to suit her devious purposes. I asked about her *faux* mother and her eyes moistened. She put an arm around me and cooed in my ear as if I were a film star, rubbing a hand up a thigh toward my groin. Over her shoulder I could see the college boys regarding me with envy, and in truth Magdalena made their girlfriends look like clones of Barbie dolls. The boys were not in the position to afford her, and neither was I.

All this preening and affection was directed to her announcement that I would have to drive the pickup back to Nogales by myself; her mother needed her that afternoon. I was to get her house key from the man at the gas station when I dropped off the truck. She would meet me early in the evening for dinner and "a night of love."

"For free?" I couldn't help but ask.

"Free, but you still owe me five hundred bucks." She gave my member a friendly tweak.

*

Outside the cantina I was amused to see that the back of the pickup was loaded with a dozen or so large statues of the Virgin, garishly painted — the kind you see in the Midwest, enshrined in porcelain bathtubs stood on their ends on the lawns of the devout. They are usually surrounded by small flower gardens and people of my ilk usually make fun of them which now seemed mean-minded.

Magdalena kissed me goodbye and as I drove off I beeped playfully at a college boy who was vomiting his freight of beer off the steps of the back door of the cantina. He lifted his hand in a wan salute. Soon enough he'll be bound, along with his friends, to the dreadful bourgeois treadmill, mere bungfodder for the dissolute economy.

It was past mid-afternoon and I had driven two thirds of the way back to Nogales, enjoying the scenery I had missed during my snooze, when my skin began to prickle and my stomach churn. It was not the fabled bowel ailment *turista* but the dawning of reality that had been obscured by the two beers and the upcoming putative night of love. It was almost as if the voice of Chandler himself were whispering from the grave, "Are those statues of the Virgin full of sour air or something else?" I was immediately awash with sweat. It was damnably possible that I was a sodden patsy in a criminal conspiracy, plugging down the road toward the border check with a load of heavy Virgins.

Within a mile or so I found a tiny dirt road leading off the highway and along a brushy, dry creek bed. I swerved on the shoulder to avoid a litter of broken glass and beer cans, a half-burned mattress. My heart was thumping audibly by the time I drove a quarter of a mile or so, pulling around behind a dense thicket so that I was well hidden from the highway. I got out and calmed myself into lucidity by studying the flora, which were quite different from the ranch's at this lower altitude. From my study of the guidebooks I recognized cholla, prickly pear, and ocotillo, the latter being one of the most strangely shaped of all life forms. The thicket was mostly palo verde, greasewood, and a larger shrub I didn't recognize. I took out my Swiss army knife to cut off a small branch for later identification, then the ticking of the engine heat brought me back to my senses. The Virgins looked silly en masse and deserved to be seen alone, however clumsily they were made and painted. I tried to bore into one well below her bottom with the leather punch and had no success until I drove it in with a rock, knocking a quarter-sized hole. The dark green marijuana was packed in there as tightly as baled alfalfa. From the prison sentences announced in the newspaper, the pickup load was more than enough to use up the rest of my life.

For unclear reasons it was simple enough to figure out

what to do. I took the same rock and the leather punch and flattened a tire with a mighty hiss, then walked away from the whole mess. I stood beside the highway for only a few minutes before a car with an Arizona license plate came to a halt and began to back up toward me, no doubt because of my reputable appearance. The car contained four very hung over and sunburned college boys who didn't welcome me into their vehicle until they determined I could contribute gas money. I gladly offered my last twenty dollars, other than the sock load which had continued to itch throughout the day. The boys were students at the University of Arizona and had just had a Mexican beach vacation they pronounced as "awesome," a doubtful word for anything they might have experienced.

I wasn't out of the woods yet. I had the boys drop me off a block past the gas station where the Jeep sat innocently in the late afternoon light. I needed to collect myself and construct a plan, though it seemed easy enough to make a calm approach, then sprint to the vehicle with the keys, which is just what I did. Sad to say, Magdalena's big thug came bouncing out of the station by the time I got the Jeep started and ground the gears into reverse. We had an inane conversation, the rationality of which was colored by my unalloyed fear. Where was the truck? I said I had had a flat tire. He said he would get a spare tire and drive me back to the truck so I could bring it back here. I said that would make me late for an important dinner engagement but I'd be glad to draw him a map, which I did, on a notepad on the seat that I normally reserved for my nature sightings. He kept insisting, of course, that I be the one to retrieve the truck, and I kept refusing. There was no point trying to speed off when I could be caught by a bicyclist. Finally I delivered a punch line by saying that if he didn't stop yammering and let me go I was going to discuss the matter with my friend Roderigo of the Border Patrol. He slumped a bit then, accepted the map, and shook his fist. I said if he couldn't be more polite I would go ahead and speak to Roderigo, and he said that wasn't necessary, he'd send someone else to fetch the truck. It was impossible for him to determine how much I knew and he stood there thinking his grave thoughts as I drove off into the twilight.

*

On the way home I stopped at a pull-off near Sonoita Creek where Deirdre had told me that a rare bird named the elegant trogon had often been seen. It was apparent to me that in my dream project certain birds had earned the right to retain the names they already had. Not many, but a few. The trogon was a fine name, and so was whimbrel and Hudsonian godwit.

I sat on a boulder next to the stream until just before dark, letting the dulcet and purling sound soothe me. Bob had told me that in India the peasants will tie a madman to a tree next to a river and the water would draw off his madness. He had neglected to tell me how long the process took. If I was still mad as a hatter, the condition had become far less irksome and I was no longer a danger to myself. One might never know perfect sanity, but then again it might resemble the elongated harp solo I had imagined with Miriam. If only Bob were here so I could recount the day's adventure, the tension of which had passed downstream with the creek's flow.

*

At the foot of Verdugo's driveway the Jeep ran out of gas, an event that J.M. was said to enjoy but didn't seem all that much fun to me. There was the consolation that I hadn't had my walk that day and the two-hour stroll up the driveway would ensure a good night's sleep. It was the warmest night of the year and I had a momentary thought about rattlesnakes, but that seemed insignificant compared to Magdalena and her compadre. I doubted if the fabled Bird-man of Alcatraz had seen all that many species through his barred window.

There was a small piece of moon to light my way, and my walking meditation was full of pleasant thoughts about my limits. A horse could walk, trot, lope, canter, gallop, and run. As children we had scooted around with our cap guns, slapping our own asses as if we were both horse and rider. Of course a horse couldn't read and I was very good at that. Counting was a matter that could be pretty much ignored. Far off along the creek bed I thought I heard a whippoorwill, sometimes called a goatsucker, from the nightjar family (Caprimulgidae). The future was acceptable rather than promising. It was certainly my choice.

p4 "panoply" - "esso" - "torturous"

X = awk

17 - "to 99 out of 100 men..."

238 - self-consciousness

246 - title ("berge Dolorosa") reference

249 - sleep the aftermath of shock

250 - Great AZ Mex cafe scene (captures regional character)

196 - "baloney bull"

202 - American higher ed as totalitarian System

248 - Keats' "the vale of Soul-making"